The Great Agony
and Pure Laughter
of the Gods

RISTO'S JOURNEY

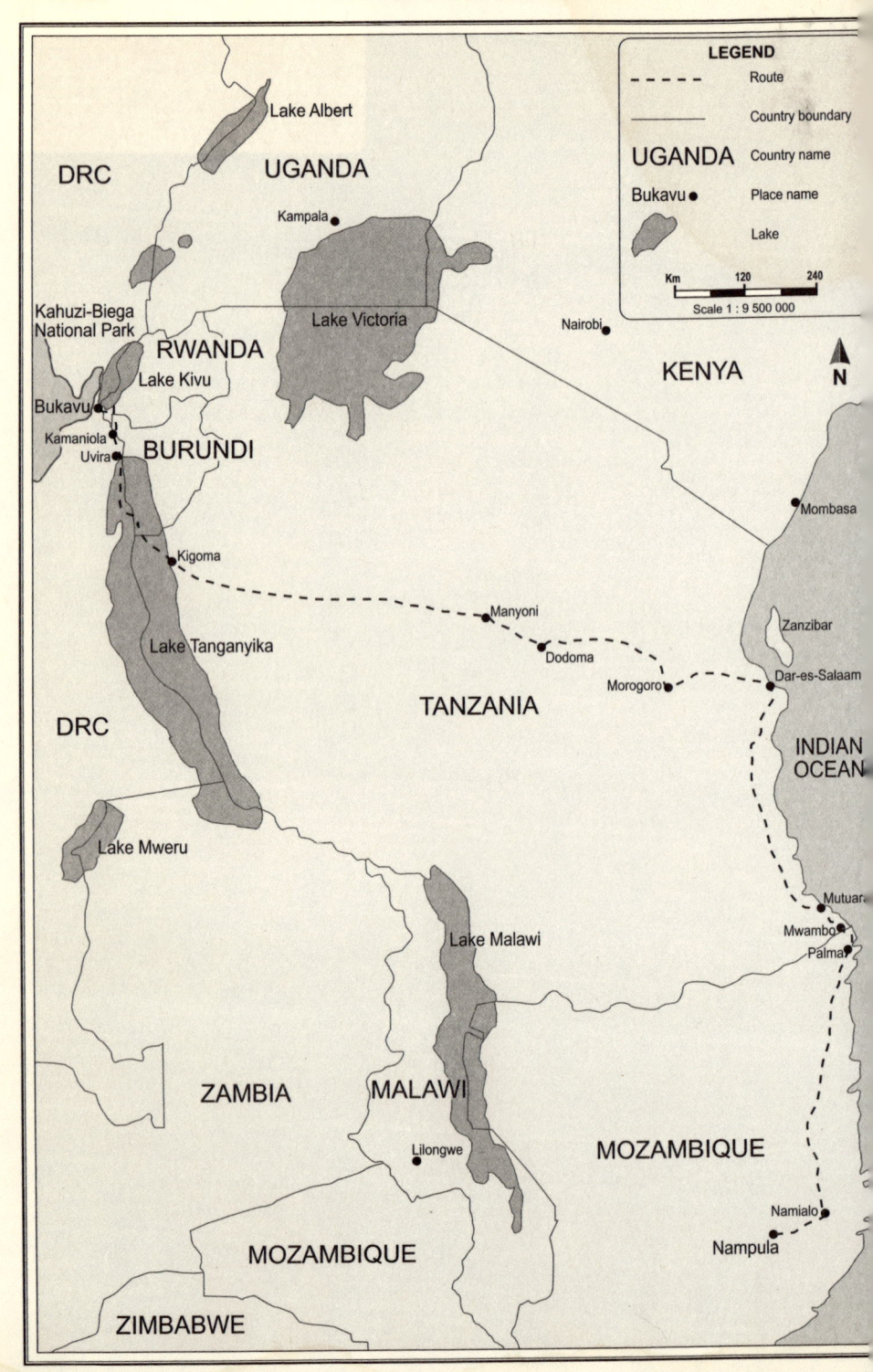

The Great Agony and Pure Laughter of the Gods

JAMALA SAFARI

UMUZI

BY THE SAME AUTHOR:
Tam Tam Sings (Poetry, 2008)

Published in 2012 by Umuzi
an imprint of Random House Struik (Pty) Ltd
Company Reg No 1966/003153/07
First Floor, Wembley Square, Solan Road, Cape Town, 8001, South Africa
PO Box 1144, Cape Town, 8000, South Africa
umuzi@randomstruik.co.za
www.randomstruik.co.za

© 2012 Jamala Safari

All rights reserved.
No part of this book may be reproduced or transmitted in any form
or by any means, mechanical or electronic, including photocopying and
recording, or be stored in any information storage or retrieval system,
without written permission from the publisher.

First edition, first printing 2012
1 3 5 7 9 8 6 4 2

ISBN 978-1-4152-0176-3 (Print)
ISBN 978-1-4152-0478-8 (ePub)
ISBN 978-1-4152-0479-5 (PDF)

Cover design by publicide
Text design by Chérie Collins
Maps by Rudi de Lange
Set in 11.5 on 15 pt Granjon

Printed and bound by Interpak books, Pietermaritzburg

To Willy Mwana-wa-Bene Kagayo and
all child soldiers in the world

KAHUZI-BIEGA NATIONAL PARK AND SURROUNDING AREAS

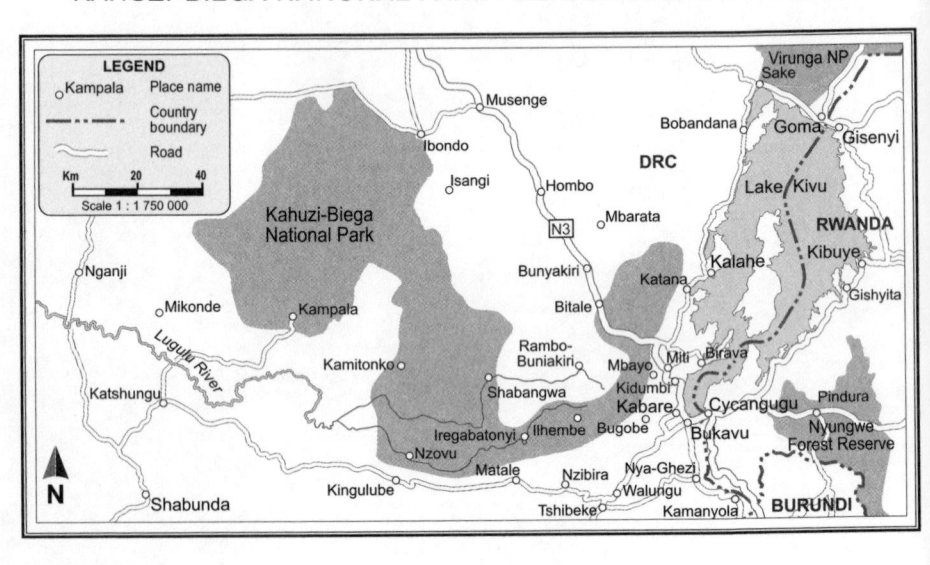

· Foreword ·

Thousands or more? No one knows how many exactly. Among them, Sudanese, Colombian, Rwandan, Burmese, Sri Lankan, Congolese … The list includes at least thirty countries. At times willingly, but most of the time abducted or forcibly recruited, child combatants are fighting for government armies, opposition forces, militias and paramilitaries in their countries or neighbouring ones.

The story of Risto is emblematic of many other abruptly interrupted childhoods. It embodies one story in particular, one that has left a scar on Jamala Safari's life. Jamala (originally from the town of Bukavu in the Democratic Republic of the Congo) and his family still await the return of their cousin. Theirs is a constant vigil, mourning with no closure. They have lived in hope and desperation, with unspoken dreams and terrors, ever since that day in 1996 when Safari's cousin, William Mwana-wa-Bene Kagayo (literally 'William Child of Others' in Mashi dialect), disappeared.

Almost fulfilling the prophecy of his name, the boy refused to leave town when the warning came to evacuate. Soon afterwards he became one of the first child soldiers (known as 'Kadogo' in the DRC) to join the rebel movement of Laurent Desiré Kabila, which later took over the country. Further than that, nothing is known of his fate.

Recounting the intricate psychology of a child combatant, torn between innocence and damnation, the loneliness among others in the same hell, the survival mechanisms, the challenges of rehabilitation and reintegration, Safari takes us into the land of desolation that is the lot of child soldiers.

Never found. Never buried. This book honours their memory, and especially William Mwana-wa-Bene Kagayo, whether he is walking somewhere in the lush forests of the Kivu, or whether the red earth of the region has already claimed back the blood of its child.

Elizabeth Mary Lanzi Mazzachini
Refugee rights activist, researcher and humanitarian worker in refugee operations.

April 2012

· Prologue ·

Sometimes Risto's father would say that man is the forger of his own history. In his hands lies the power to challenge and to change, in his feet, the conquering force, and in his mind, the driving compass. Therein is the essence of miracle and mystery. Good or bad, it will be the legacy left behind when he no longer has a voice to speak or strength to stand.

Many times Risto wished not to walk, not to touch; to stand still or find a cave to hide in. Then no footstep would be seen and his hands would leave no mark behind. If only that cave could be found, he would be in there right now; he would get in, close his eyes, clog up his ears, and ask rat and mouse to fill up the hole with soil. Then he would leave this earth, and sleep and sleep forever ... and peace would come to his spirit and soul. Sometimes he wanted touching, walking, but was afraid to put his foot down in the flooding river, in the stormy fire, in the ghostly mouth of the world.

In the end, he found himself on a fragile island: north, east, west, south, no path. All around him, children like him, raped and killed, many with hacked-off hands and legs, the young mutilated. And the war continued. Each day, moaning came from nearby.

Sometimes three or four would die in his street alone. He would hear people yelling, screaming at the announcement of death. Always the same, the story the same:

They entered our house, we wanted to give them money, but they said they didn't need le francs Congolais. Finally they locked us in a room. They took Mama and our sister in one room and Papa in another one. We heard Mama and our sister yelling and yelling, like birds whose feathers are being pulled out while alive. Later, it was cold silence. We heard a few shots. There was no sound in the house after the door was slammed. Half an hour later, when the neighbours came and opened the door for us, we were already orphans and without a sister. Papa was shot in his forehead. The neighbours didn't want us to glance at Mama and our sister. Their bodies were naked, blood spots were coming up north from their navels. Both of them dead.

Children went on playing. They were told never to go far from home because anything could happen, and their family might need to flee the town. They might hear something like a thunderclap, then a heavy hail-fall on the roofs. Then a big cloud of smoke in the sky, meaning a bomb had fallen on nearby houses. People would moan, weep, but no mercy would come their way. Guns and death had become part of their daily lives. That was how they lived.

This was Risto's hometown, Bukavu, where he lived, tried to dream, then refused to, as he knew there was no place his foot could walk to write his own history. Risto Mahuno, fifteen years old, with eyes older than his age. He had seen more than he deserved.

One could say that soccer brought healing to Risto. This was the only time his mind forgot his wish of finding a little cave where he could sleep forever in peace. Meeting his friends every day to play football, he felt the need to live again. No one remembered anxiety or felt fear when they played. They forgot their pain and time went on quietly. They played the way they used to play when Bukavu was still peaceful, with its green trees, children running up and down its streets like lost baby goats, and the taxi drivers driving twenty-four hours a day ... in those days, one would have thought that if the world was Paradise, Bukavu would be its capital city. That was just a few years ago, just yesterday.

It was a beautiful day in Bukavu. Soccer fever had infected the boys and they played the game under a hot sun. The sweat dripped off their faces into the dust. Then a frizzing silence consumed time, seconds became hours.

Something has happened, thought Risto, lying on the ground.

A great noise came from all directions. He heard women screaming and yelling, calling and searching. He was lost, confused between his memory and the reality he saw around him. Then he felt a little clearer, and he looked all around the open field where they had been playing. There was no goalkeeper, nor defender, nor striker; none of them were playing anymore.

Where he lay, Risto's ears heard a lingering noise like bee songs. He could see the goal posts. The goal stood empty. Ombeni the goalkeeper wasn't the real Ombeni who had been there a few minutes ago. He was in pieces. The scene was a butchery. Head and chest were apart, a hand here, a leg there, this here, that there. Risto's nostrils were too small for his breath. His body shook.

Their goalposts were covered in thick smoke, a house was burning, the nearby kitchen was on fire. There was no sign of Frank, Ombeni's older brother, only a hole two metres from the goal. It was the size of a palm tree.

'Come, come, come Risto,' a woman's voice called. It was his mother. 'Are you okay? Are you all right?' she kept asking. She shook too, but her voice was soothing.

'I am fine, Mama.' His body had no wound.

'Are you okay, my son?' she persisted, lifting him up onto her back like a precious golden basket. Risto did not like to be held like a baby on his mother's back, but there was no choice. A fifteen-year-old boy had become a little child. He wanted to walk, but his entire body trembled like a rootless tree hit by a rhino.

More and more people came to pick up their children, the wounded and the dead, to extinguish the fire; more noise followed. Some cried for the dead; others, especially children, were seized by fear, others were calling their relatives' names. It was chaotic, like being in an open-air market consumed by fire. The running, shouting, screaming …

The night passed. The story had grown, moving from the eyes of children on a playground to TV screens around the world. The news became a song. On the streets, it was a greeting for men, women, old and young people. At local radio stations, the news was repeated like a refrain, coming and going every thirty minutes.

'... Yesterday at about 2:30pm, a bomb that appears to have come from over the Ruzizi River on the Rwandan side exploded on a football field in Bukavu. Two young boys were killed and three are seriously injured ...'

The story hung in the air, coming back like a hiccup.

The sun rose with disregarding eyes, ignoring the bleeding canvas below. It didn't wink or cough at the sorrow of the people, it shone as if nothing had happened, and Risto didn't like it. Something had happened in his life that had changed the rhythm of his street's heartbeat forever. The sun had risen from the side of the front door of Mama Ombeni's house, where many people sat on chairs and mats, women weeping and singing while the men talked to one another.

Curiosity brought Risto to the scene. He felt it was his right to say his last words to his late friends Frank and Ombeni. He wanted to glance at their bodies to confirm what his eyes had seen the day before. He was quickly turned away with the excuse of his age. Too young to attend a mourning ceremony. Young children had to stay away while corpses were still in the house; that was what an old woman, one of Mama Ombeni's neighbours, told him. She wouldn't even allow him to go beyond her house, as it stood at the entrance to the place of the mourning ceremony. He wanted to insist, but the grey-haired lady with no teeth and a face tattooed with age hardened the banning order, her eyes fierce.

Mama Ombeni was Risto's neighbour; the house he lived in was about a 100 metres uphill from hers. Bukavu is a hill-town, and Risto was able to see some of the things happening that morning at her house. He sat astride a tree trunk at the edge of his mother's garden, watching, his feet floating as the tree was very tall. Sadness wasn't enough to describe his pain; it was beyond what a man could take. These two friends had been brothers to him. There was a taint of fresh blood in the air. He smelled it, and it made tomorrow unclear, cloudy. The faces of Ombeni and Frank kept coming back to Risto's eyes; the goalkeeper and the defender, the two brothers, his friends. Memories struck: his last trip with his late friends, a holiday to his grandmother's village, a trip that he would always remember.

· Chapter 1 ·

Risto's maternal grandparents lived in a village called Bugobe. It was so peaceful that many called it the Kivu's little Eden. There were fruit trees all over, and rivers that whispered at the foot of mountains covered with the greenery of ever-blooming trees. Ombeni, at twelve, was the youngest of the trio of brotherhood, while Risto and Frank were thirteen. Mama Ombeni considered Risto's mother as her older sister, so she was quite content when her sons told her that they wanted to accompany Risto on holiday.

His grandparents stayed in a big compound surrounded by fragrant indigenous trees. Inside the compound were three houses and two huts. One house was where Risto's grandparents slept, one was for their two children and relatives, and one had been built by their sons, Risto's uncles, as their lodge when visiting the village. Risto's grandparents had a special hut, a smaller one with a room where the fire never died; it was where the evening fire was usually set up. As special guests and spoiled grandchildren, they were offered the fire hut. The fire that never died was hidden beneath the ashes of a triangular stone fireplace.

In Bukavu, there were some fruit trees around the compounds, but here in Bugobe the boys couldn't even count the number of fruit trees. Banana, avocado, mango, sugar-cane and many more, there were all the things children dreamed of having in their yards. They were on the trees like birds, eating as much fruit as their stomachs could bear. Each one, after cutting down his own sugar-cane with a machete, brought them to the compound and washed them. Then the grown-up girls, their older sisters as they had been told to call them, would divide the cane into four pieces for each of them. Then it was time to chew the sugar-cane and suck the juice. No one would talk, silence would reign, disturbed only by the noise of chewing.

Their holiday was about mid-June, right after the final exams. Almost every tree had ripe fruit between its green-yellowish leaves, and all the trees were theirs.

'Climb on all of them,' said their grandfather, 'except for the papaya trees. They are too thin and weak.'

He warned them about the avocado trees; their branches were bigger, but easier to break. 'Just be careful,' was his refrain, spoken in a deep voice, his bald head reflecting sunrays like a mirror.

It surprised the three town boys to discover that everything that their grandfather told them seemed to be known by other children from the village. Many times when they saw something unusual or when they had questions without answers, the ones from the village had answers and explanations. They would be walking in a deserted place, to be surprised by Benny's insightful analysis of sounds and smells.

'Can you hear?'

His friends would pay attention in vain.

'People are talking. Listen.'

They never knew if it was murmuring human voices they heard, or the wind.

There was no need for the village children to wear a watch to know the time. They spoke to the sun and it told them the time.

'You have to stand in the sun, then look at your shadow; if you stand at the head of your shadow, then it means that the sun has reached the zenith,' said Benny when Frank was asking passersby for the time.

Benny went on to warn that midday was never a good time to go to the river or to be in the bush. It was the time that ghosts and evil spirits went to the river to swim and drink. Others went to the bush and the forest to hold their meetings. Being in these places could be dangerous for the living. They might carry bad luck or even death back to their families.

Soon the trio from town realised that the village children knew more than they did, and they learned to trust them. The village carried its secrets in the depths of its lulling nights and warm days, things that made it a mystery to the outsiders. For the three who slept under thatch on hanging beds above a fire that never died, these mysteries unfolded with the wise voice of the forest they navigated.

Benny became their best friend in the village. He was kind and intelligent, and he had the compass for the villages and forest. He knew many secrets, not just of the bush, but of the village too. He was a little bit slimmer and shorter than Risto, precisely three months younger than him. When they stood up to measure their height, the top of Benny's head reached the lower edge of Risto's ear if Benny stood on his toes. When they argued, though, Benny always said he reached the top of Risto's ears. Their grandfather told Risto that Benny was his cousin; he wasn't sure, there were many cousins in the village.

Benny soon left his family house and joined Risto and his friends in the hut. Whenever they sat around the fire at night, he told them stories and sang too. Each story had its own songs, and each song had its meaning. There were songs to sing only at night, and songs that couldn't be sung around noon or midnight. There was a song to be sung if one lost something that one wanted to recover, a song to sing when one knew that one's parents were angry and planning to punish one.

Benny's eyes lit up as he started a tale. 'Listen … you were sent for, and didn't come on time … you know a punishment is waiting for you. If you have been absent from home the whole day, take the kashisha flower, pull out a few eyelashes, and mix them together. When you arrive in front of the house, at the door, before you speak to any of your parents, you throw the mixture at the door. There won't be any punishment anymore! Your parents will just warn you, and sometimes they might even forget.'

'Are you sure?' asked Risto.

'Go and try it, you will tell me.'

The three boys were astonished by Benny's stories. He knew the answers to enigmas for which the boys had no answers. 'But who taught him all these things?' was the question that they couldn't help asking, when he correctly predicted rain on a certain afternoon in the dry season, or when he sang a song to call crickets in the bush, and the crickets came.

One morning Benny promised his three friends a special trip to a beautiful spot by the river for a swim, and many surprising things, including mushroom harvesting. The eyes of his three friends narrowed. Benny never planted mushrooms, and refused to believe that mushrooms could be planted by people.

'Tomorrow there will be some,' he said confidently.

The three boys looked at each other with doubt.

'How do you know that there will be mushrooms tomorrow?' Frank asked.

'I just know. You seem not to believe me.'

'We will believe you tomorrow if we find mushrooms,' Risto replied.

'Okay then, be ready tomorrow at 5am sharp. We will go to pick mushrooms.'

The three town boys slept with their eyes wide open, afraid that the day might wake earlier than them. The first rooster sang. Then the second one and the third, which, as Benny had taught them, announced 4am sharp. At 4:30, the lamp had chased away the darkness in the small hut. Risto grabbed his toothbrush and his small cup, filled the cup with water, and went outside to wash his face and to clean his teeth. He was surprised to see Benny coming from the barn where the cattle stayed at night.

'Where are you coming from?' he asked.

'From the cattle, I went to open up their compound. We might return late, better let them go in the bush alone; I will find them when I come back.'

Benny, like the other villagers, respected cattle very deeply. Cattle gave them milk and meat, and so they gave their cattle food and water.

'Where are Frank and Ombeni?' he added.

'Still sleeping,' said Risto.

'No, we are awake!' cried Frank as he came out of the hut.

'Are you ready? It is time to go,' Benny said.

The compound door flung open and swung slowly shut again as the four boys found their way into the cassava fields. The fields were wet with cold dew, a sign of the invisible dry-season rain that gracious heaven gave to the water-craving plants, a rain that softened soil and allowed vegetables to keep their green even in the baking sun. After five minutes, the boys were as wet as if they had been walking in the rain.

The cassava trees were taller than the boys, and as they walked slowly through them, they left the trees waving as if calling the land-owner to say that there were intruders in his field.

Benny warned his friends to walk cautiously, not to smash any trees, otherwise they would get in trouble. The owner of the field was a witchdoctor, a man who called thunderclaps and spoke with the wind. He might have been there in the fields; but he wouldn't cause any trouble if his fields were treated with care.

Benny stopped at a point where different fields met and split into smaller fields. Wild fig trees and shrubs grew nearby. The other three boys stopped too, eager to see which way Benny would take. The many footprints on the ground revealed that the place received many visitors.

'This is the place! Check near the shrubs. Everywhere you will find mushrooms, I promise you,' Benny assured them.

Everyone went to search.

'Here is one, two, and another one!' It was Benny, in a low soft voice, like someone who didn't want to be heard by many people. All the boys rushed towards him. Benny had three white mushrooms in his hands.

'How did you get them?' Ombeni asked, surprised and rather envious.

Benny laughed. 'Haven't you got any?'

'We have searched, but we can't find any.'

'You know what, this whole place is full of mushrooms; open your eyes and you will find them.'

'I won't go alone, I will follow you. You know where to find them,' Ombeni said, like someone who has lost something valuable.

Meanwhile, Frank was a little way off and keeping very quiet.

'Have you seen something, Frank?' called Risto.

'Two big ones,' he answered.

The boys ran to Frank's side. He had two big mushrooms, opened like umbrellas.

'No, no, don't pick that one!' Benny shouted as Frank reached out to pick another very small mushroom.

'You know, when you pick mushrooms, you can't take a small one like this,' Benny explained. 'It is the small one that calls the bigger ones. If you take it, you will never get mushrooms anymore. Leave it!'

Frank was reluctant to leave the mushroom, but did as Benny advised. He still had two big ones in his hands.

'Now Frank, you have to cut off a small piece of one of your mushrooms and drop it on this ground.'

Frank's eyes widened. 'Why?'

'Just do it, and then say, "Thank you, tomorrow I will come again,"' Benny insisted.

'To whom am I going to say that?' argued Frank.

'It is up to you; otherwise you will never get mushrooms here anymore. This land doesn't know you; this is the first time you have come to this place to get mushrooms. The land loves you, but you have to show that love as well, and thank the spirits of this land.'

Frank did as he was told.

The days went by as the moon appeared and disappeared, a fire-ball hanging in a blanket in a dark sky. The song of crickets was the regular evening lullaby in the quiet nights in Bugobe village. Risto and his friends became accustomed to the peaceful night pierced only by the whispering fire and the roaring of distant rivers. At dawn, they woke to the sound of the villagers' footsteps tramping the rhythm of daily life. Risto's holiday was a discovery of life without fear and boundaries. They went where they pleased and did what they wanted.

Months passed, and the school holiday was nearing its end. The sun's early gleam one morning announced already the rage it would have once it reached its zenith. As usual at that time during the dry season, the soil was hot, like a pot on a stove. It burned whoever wasn't wearing shoes. The town boys were used to playing soccer with their shoes on, but in the village, this wasn't the case. The village boys were shoeless and so the visitors were obliged to take off their shoes in order to be part of the game. Playing barefoot wasn't an easy thing for them. They could not stand the burning soil. They couldn't understand how the village boys played with such ease on such hot soil; maybe their skin was burn-proof, the town boys thought.

The boys' plan for that day was to bring the cattle to the river. There, they would swim and catch crabs. There were beehives to be harvested that night at Risto's grandfather's plantation. The meeting was set, the business of the beehives was not to be missed.

The way was long, and with the cattle eating whatever green leaves they could find, the journey seemed endless. Everywhere beside the paths, the leaves wore the same khaki colour that predominated in the area because of the dry season.

The warmth of the village was clear in the smiles of its people. Handshaking and news met the boys along the way; everyone they passed greeted them. They tried to be the first to greet people, as advised by Benny.

Here people knew even what one another ate; there were no secrets. The village was not like the town, where people went about with their own issues. Here things belonged to the whole village, to the community. A visitor was the visitor of the entire village. Everyone knew when a visitor came and where he was staying, and people came freely to greet him. If the visitor was a child, they would come with a bag full of fruit – avocados, bananas, plums, oranges, guavas, lemons. Others came with papaya, pineapples, sugar-cane. If the visitor was an adult, they would come with a calabash full of local beer, the kasiksi, or some kind of local banana juice, the mutobe, for example.

The boys arrived at the river before the sun reached its zenith. Risto thought it was a beautiful place, like a pilgrim site. The birds were singing as the river played music. The limpid water reflected the pristine blue sky above the trees. On one big stone in the river, the flowing water became a multitude of stars that disappeared and reappeared like mysterious lights.

They let the cattle wander in the pastures nearby, losing themselves in dances with their shadows in the river. Benny threw himself in the water and Frank followed him. But Ombeni and Risto stayed on the riverbank. They were happy to play with the water, but swimming was too frightening for them. They played ricochet instead, picking up small stones, throwing them into the water, and looking in amazement as water spurted up.

Frank and Benny enjoyed swimming, splashing, chasing one another. Sometimes they came up onto the riverbank, counted from one to three, and then threw themselves into the river like the stones that their two friends were throwing, but they splashed far more water.

Eventually they went a little further downstream, where the river narrowed through rocks. Benny said this was where they would catch crabs.

'Have you ever seen a crab?' he asked.

'Yes,' they replied without delay.

'Where?'

'At the open-air market and sometimes on the television,' said Risto.

The game seemed simple: lifting rocks at random from the narrow bed of the river.

'Many of these rocks are dwellings for crabs,' Benny told them.

They began the hunt, wading around, lifting rocks. Suddenly, something was moving underneath the rock that Benny had partly lifted.

'There is one! There is one!' screamed Ombeni as he looked on from the bank where he stood.

'Be careful with your finger, it can cut it off. Don't put it in its alligator pincers!' Benny yelled at Risto. Risto moved his hand stealthily towards the crab and picked it up by its back. Then he held its claws and legs. His fear vanished; he could examine every single movement.

He took a stone and hit the crab on its head.

'We don't treat crabs like this!' Benny exclaimed. 'We hold them and disable their pincers, that's all. Your way of doing things makes them suffer. Do you know the pain it is feeling now?'

'But you told me that it could cut off my fingers!'

'It still didn't deserve such treatment.'

'I didn't know, I am sorry,' Risto apologised.

'You know, God always watches our actions. If we mistreat his creatures, we will be treated the same. Like this crab, if we torture it, then the next time we come to look for other crabs, we will never find them; God will hide them from us. That is why if we catch one, we must treat it with respect,' Benny lectured while the boys hung their heads and stared at the motionless crab.

Later it was time to look for the cattle. Benny led them through the forest. He knew it like the backs of his hands. He knew how and when the river was born, and where it ended.

The boys walked towards unknown endings. They walked in secret leaves and dew. Sometimes, they felt peculiar temperature changes as they passed, somewhere else, an unusual scent. The things to discover were uncountable – different scents to smell, voices and echoes without owners. These were the secrets of the forest.

After some time, they reached the edge of the forest and soon the edges of some small farms. There were plenty of them.

'How on earth can these plants have green leaves in the dry season? The sun is shining at its peak; it is a dry season, no rain. How can these farms look so fresh?' Risto asked Benny.

'Risto, the village has it secrets. It holds them in its womb like the night holds its mysterious secrets from our faces,' Benny replied.

They found all their cattle and decided to retrace their path homewards. The sun was about to hide in its cave, its strength was already gone. After a long walk, they came across some cattle. Their own cattle diverted directly into this herd. The town boys tried to stop them, but Benny advised them not to waste their time. They were worried that they might not be able to recognise their own livestock as some of their goats and cows looked like the ones they had met.

The shepherds tending these strange cattle were a little way ahead of them. They had a camp near the mountain. Benny knew them, and as he approached them, they greeted him in their mother tongue. Laughs and jokes followed as the three town boys stood listening; they understood what was said, but weren't confident enough to talk.

'These are my brothers from Bukavu town, they came this side for a holiday,' said Benny proudly. The gleaming eyes of the shepherds revealed the questions that floated in their minds. There was a short silence, followed by whispers in a language that the town boys could not understand. By listening closely, they worked out that it was a mother tongue that had been twisted into a local lingo, a slang of some kind. Sentences were shortened, with words said in reverse. Surely this is some gossip, the visitors thought.

Benny finally bridged the gap: 'Ombeni, Risto and the other one is called Frank,' he introduced his cousins from town.

The shepherds looked at them, then spoke, with much laughter. The boys didn't know why.

'They understand Mashi, but they are not good at speaking it,' Benny explained to the shepherds, who switched to Swahili, the language considered the town boys' language. They spoke it very well, with only the Mashi accent revealing that these guys didn't grow up in town. The boys understood them perfectly.

Soon the shepherds asked Benny to compete with them in their sticks game. Benny agreed, even though his friends were unlikely to succeed in the village game.

'You are on my side,' he told the boys. 'It is about keeping the stick on the tip of one of your fingers without holding it or allowing it to fall. If it touches another part of your body, it means that your turn is over. If you hold the stick with your hands or if it falls, your turn is over. The longer you hold it on the tip of your finger, the higher the mark you get.'

The first time Risto got the stick, he wanted it to be the same colour as Benny's stick, a yellowish-black colour. He peeled off its bark and tied a spiral of banana bark around it before hitting it gently on the rocks in the shepherds' fire. It came up with a double colour, a snake-like curl of yellow around the black stick. The black mamba stick, he called it.

He took it to start the game. Ombeni decided not to play. There were three contestants on both sides. Benny rounded up his men, a song started, his friends grasped it within seconds; a song to sing when they would be juggling. Benny's advice was simple, 'Look only at the top tip of your stick and not at your fingers.'

A referee was there with his watch. Risto was the first to juggle, his song vibrating all the way to the top of the hill.

'A shepherd's stick does not fall, a shepherd's stick stands!' He repeated these words over and over again. His friends were afraid that he might bite his tongue. Finally his stick fell down.

'One minute and twenty seconds,' the referee announced, looking at his big clock-like plastic watch. Risto was confused; was his time a success or a failure? Nevertheless, he was happy; he felt he hadn't done badly for his first time. A shepherd from the other group took his stick: 'Two minutes, thirty-five seconds.' Then Frank: 'One minute.' On the other side: 'Two minutes, forty-five seconds.' Benny's turn arrived. He spat on his hand, and then he started with the song and the game. His voice sounded like soft waves on the peaceful Lake Kivu; it seemed to glue the stick to his fingers, floating it from finger to finger in a gentle rhythm. His eyelashes remained still. It was real magic. 'Eight minutes, fifty seconds,' the referee said at last. The last person from the other group started: 'Four minutes, ten seconds,' the referee announced.

The town boys couldn't hide their happiness, they had won. 'Viva, Benny, viva!' They were as excited as little goat kids just released from a pen.

It had been a long day, full of excitement and with many good surprises. In the bag that Ombeni was carrying were crabs and many other amazing things that they had picked up along the way. It was starting to get dark when they arrived home. Benny enquired about the harvesting of the beehives, and was told that the business had already started.

Ombeni and Frank were too tired for another adventure, but Risto went along with Benny.

There were only two men in the fields, one in his early fifties and one in his twenties. They shook hands after Benny explained that they were coming to help as grandfather had promised. The men's hands were as strong as iron, and they had twilight smiles, which glowed as the darkness hid their faces. The next step was to undress. The men wore only shorts, while Benny and Risto were in coats. The two men had four big basins, each of which could have swallowed Risto entirely. The two men in shorts lit torches tied to their foreheads and moved closer to the murmuring bees.

The beehives were in a small nyassi house. The young man started a fire on a small cloth soaked with coconut oil. He walked towards the beehives, and dropped the burning cloth in the small house. After a while, smoke started emerging. It disturbed the bees. Their quiet humming song became the endless roaring murmur of a lion. The two men approached and got their hands inside the hives. The buzz of the bees grew again to the hum of a strong rain; they flew in all directions. Benny went over to the hives to fetch some honey. He came back, his hands dripping with sweetness. He gave some to his friend to enjoy.

'Didn't they sting you?' asked Risto in amazement as he licked his fingers.

'Yes, but I couldn't feel anything,' said Benny.

The bees were all around them; Risto and Benny could feel them in the air as they stood in the dark. Risto wanted to run, but Benny advised calm.

The two beehive specialists were half-way through harvesting the first beehive when Benny shouted, 'Put on your coat properly!' Once they were finished, Risto and Benny would take the basin from them.

'I am going to help them to harvest the last beehive. You can come if you want, it will make us real men,' Benny told his friend.

Risto hesitated. The bee buzz was frightening; harvesting the beehives would be like putting one's hand in a glowing fire. Benny went ahead as Risto waited.

Time passed, and he grew impatient. Wasn't it his biggest wish to prove his manhood in the village, to be called a man, to do a man's work, to have a story to tell in town? A boy from town who wanted the crown of a real man in the village couldn't stay behind any longer; adrenaline was flowing and his heart was beating fast. His legs felt strong, although they shook a little. It was time to be a man in the village.

Risto covered his head and went towards the beehives. One big basin was already almost full of honey. He put his hands in the basin and tasted the pure honey. Benny, who was standing a metre from Risto, put his hand inside the hive and took out a layer of honey mixed with something white. These were the baby bees, and this was the best quality, he explained to his friend. The torch that lit the basin showed bees mixed in with the honey.

'Is this what we are eating? But we are eating bees!' Risto exclaimed.

Benny laughed. They were both excited; the bees were buzzing around everywhere. The rhythm was compelling; a hand in the honey basin, soon in the mouth, an amazing pleasure; Bugobe was truly a small paradise. But now Risto felt something land on his lips. Then he felt a sting.

'A bee on my lips! Help! Help!' he screamed.

He pulled it off forcefully, but a piece of the sting stayed behind. His lip became heavier than his head, hotter than a boiling pot on a stove. As if that wasn't enough, the buzzing sound of bees followed. There was singing above his head. Maybe the bees thought he was a real tree. He used his right hand to chase them away, then he used both hands while he screamed with all his strength.

'Help! Help! Help!' He started running, the buzz over his head, pain raining down on his head. His entire body was covered; he was done for.

He opened his eyes to see his grandmother nearby. Benny wasn't there anymore, and he wasn't in his room; it was his grandmother's. He could feel the pain in his lip; it was swelling. His grandmother took him from the bed and put him on her back like a baby to take him to the bathroom, which was a big hut with a straw roof close to the lemon trees. There, a big metallic basin full of water stood ready. She mixed fresh plants into the water and added dried ones. She took off all Risto's clothes, and made him sit in the hot pungent water in the basin. It was then that he saw how his body had swollen. His grandmother took a facecloth and used it all over his entire body. His body itched. Afterwards, she took him back to her bed. The next day when he woke, there was neither pain nor swelling anywhere on his body.

The month of September approached; school would be starting soon. It was time to return to Bukavu town. The boys from town had enjoyed the village; life here was limitless. What hadn't they experienced? They had been to the sacred silent river, they had played games and competed with the shepherds of the village, they had gone to harvest the beehives, they had done many things that made them wish to stay forever at Risto's grandmother's place.

The large yellow full moon shone, but never caught the attention of the boys in their hut, who sat quietly around the fireplace listening to Benny's stories. He had just finished a story when he jumped to his feet, startling his listeners.

'Oh! Let's go to Kaluli's house!' he said in excitement.

'Who's Kaluli?' Ombeni asked.

'Shhhhh!' he said. 'Let's go and get honey from his house.'

'No, I am afraid of bees,' said Risto.

'No, it is not at the beehives this time,' Benny explained. 'Kaluli offers food to his gods the first night of the full moon. He gives them honey, mashanza and kasiksi beer.'

'No, we can't go. If he does that, it means that he is a mufumu, a witchdoctor,' Ombeni replied.

'No, he is not. He only offers food to his ancestors and gods to thank them for their kindness in giving him a full moon. He can't kill us or make us sick. I often go there to eat that food, and nothing has ever happened to me. You know, a real mufumu knows everything that happens to his place. But Kaluli, he has never known it!' Benny tried to convince his friends.

But they forgot to ask: what if the gods found them eating their food? Would they take them to heaven or to hell?

'All right, but if something happens to us, it will be your fault,' Frank said.

Kaluli's house wasn't far from Risto's grandfather's place. But Benny said they shouldn't use the path that others normally used. They had to go through the fields behind Kaluli's compound to get there without being seen by anyone.

They set out across their grandfather's fields. All the huts at Kaluli's place were inside one big compound, except for a small one, which was close to a very big ficus tree. 'Kaluli should be on his way,' whispered Benny, so they stayed still hiding in the fields.

'This is almost his time; he will be here in a little while,' he kept confirming.

An old man appeared barefoot at the back door of the compound. He approached the small hut. In his hands he held a traditional basket made of creepers. He put the basket down, stretched his hands inside the small hut, and withdrew them holding a small tam-tam. He beat it gently while singing a song. He beat it over and over, then he danced, jerky movements around the small hut. He took a small kabehe, a pumpkin shell, and drank from it, then spat on the ground. He spoke, then turned his head towards the sky. He took things from his basket, exhibited them towards the sky, and put them down again. He took his tam-tam, he beat it, again he jerked around. At last he put the tam-tam inside the small hut, and left smiling.

Benny told his friends to wait a little while. Two people would have to stay while the others went to get the food. Risto followed Benny. They crept slowly up to the small hut. He peeped inside it; he could see different skins, most of them spotted, like those of leopards. The two boys took the different traditional dishes that were in the basket made of creepers, and crawled back to the cassava fields where Ombeni and Frank were hiding. The honey was in a large pumpkin shell, and the mashanza curds were in a dish made of a piece of wood hollowed out in the middle. They took all the food and drink except the kabehe of beer; none of them enjoyed strong traditional beer. The food was so soft that an old man with no teeth would have been able to enjoy it. Cooked meat, mostly livers. The honey reminded Risto of the night he was stung by bees, but this time he was safe; there were no beehives around. They finished the food, took back the creeper basket, and left, excited at their successful adventure.

As advised by Benny, the boy who knew the secrets of the village, each one scrubbed his hands with soil and chewed some leaves to freshen his mouth, so that people would not know that they had eaten something. They left the fields and walked back on the main path.

'When his ancestors or gods come, what are they going to eat?' asked Ombeni.

'Do you think they usually come?' Benny replied.

'And when Kaluli comes back, what is he going to say?' Risto asked.

Benny had watched Kaluli carry out his ritual many times, and after finding his food gone, Kaluli never questioned the gods or ancestors. Instead, he blew his whistle, he smiled, he clapped his hands, danced to the rhythm of his singing tam-tam, and thanked his gods and ancestors for accepting his offerings. Benny believed that eating what was offered to the ancestors or the gods was not a problem, as the gods and ancestors lived in living beings, in people, trees, rivers, winds ... whoever and whatever ate these foods became part of the gods, part of the ancestors. 'How do you know all these things?' Risto asked Benny as they sat on their beds, the glowing fire murmuring like a snoring child.

'Which things?'

'All these secrets. Whenever you tell us to look for mushrooms, we come back with some. You know where they are and when to go. Please tell us how you know,' Risto insisted.

'I just know it,' Benny laughed.

'No, there are secrets you are hiding from us,' added Frank, nodding his head like someone who had just discovered something.

Benny tried to defend himself: 'There is nothing hidden here. I have given you many secrets of the village and the bush. Why shouldn't I give them if they exist?'

'We are not saying that you don't want to tell us; we are asking how you know that this thing will happen here at this time, and this other thing there at that time?' Risto went on.

Benny was getting irritated. 'You know, children from the village are different from those in the town. Us, we have eyes to see, ears to hear, and hands to touch. But those from the town, their eyes are closed, their ears clogged, and their hands still.'

'No, no, we don't understand!' Ombeni exclaimed after concentrating hard on what Benny had said.

'You know what? I was born underneath an avocado tree, in a hut with bees, snakes, tortoises all around. I grew up on manioc farms, I played in rivers and hunted birds and crickets. This is my life. This is how I know where they eat, sleep and live.'

'Even us, we go swimming in the river, and we sometimes hunt crickets and birds,' said Risto.

'You said "sometimes". Me, I live with the river, fish and crickets.'

· Chapter 2 ·

These were among the fragments that floated in Risto's mind. His friends Frank and Ombeni had died and he would never see them again. He wanted to go and see their faces for the last time, to say goodbye to them, but he couldn't. The song kept coming back from the old tattooed woman's mouth: children are not allowed at funerals. She sat at the entrance of the path to Mama Ombeni's house, under a banana tree, blocking the way.

Risto remained astride the tree trunk. Why was he not allowed to pay them a last farewell visit, to drop his last tears? It was so unfair. Whatever the customs were, he considered these traditions unfair. They had shared laughter and tears, games and food, tales and music; they had shared the best and the worst times together. Why not allow him to sit next to the bed or sheet where his late friends lay, let his heart cry, his spirit meet theirs and say farewell?

Maybe the old woman had been sent to tell him to stay away because the sight of their mutilated bodies was unbearable. He remembered the day before, after the explosion, how he didn't want to look at the body of his friend Ombeni. He had been in more than three pieces, like a cow straight from the butcher's. He wasn't the Ombeni that Risto had known only moments before.

Later on, Risto saw a crow in the sky that had forgotten it was time to go to its nest. It was flying aimlessly, but without cawing, soundless. The chickens were rushing to their shelters as if the outdoors now belonged to something else. He realised that darkness had fallen; it was time for crows, chickens, children and adults to get to their homes.

The burial occurred three days after the bomb blast. The delay was because there was a serious discussion going on. Where would the two boys be buried? Risto overheard his father telling his mother that Mama Ombeni had objected to having her two sons buried in the town cemetery, the Ruzizi cemetery.

'She wants her sons to be closer to her,' said Risto's father.

'How can she think like that? Is that going to change anything? We are all affected by this tragic event, we are deeply concerned about her pain, but she shouldn't think like a non-believer. She is a Catholic, a Christian!' said his mother, her voice almost inaudible. She had lost it to the screams and cries of mourning. It was common for women to cry loudly at mourning ceremonies; there were some who believed if a woman didn't cry, it was because she could be linked to the cause of the death; she could even be a witch.

'What was decided in the end?' she asked her husband.

'To do as she wishes. The bodies will be buried in the open space behind her house.'

'Is that really wise?'

'There is no choice; we have to do what pleases her. And tomorrow the mourning ceremony will be over.'

The idea of burying the two late boys in their mother's yard didn't frighten Risto; but it left him adrift. He wandered between traditional beliefs and stories he'd heard, between customary practices and his own convictions. Maybe this would be a good way to always have them near him, he thought at first. But they wouldn't be human beings anymore ... spirits! Spirits! Eh! People usually said that spirits were harmful. They carried bad luck and many people believed them to be evil. No, it couldn't be! Not when they had been such good friends while alive.

Risto's father had once told him that if a person while alive had caused harm to society, particularly if he was involved in evil activities, his spirit could be harmful after death. His father often repeated a tribal philosophy: 'If someone dies, he becomes more powerful than those who are still alive. Even if he died as a child, he automatically becomes stronger than the adults he left on earth. He becomes part of a community that looks after us. And that community is not far from us; it is within us. When we walk, it walks with us like our shadow follows us. As we cultivate, it brings rain and protects the fields against parasites and insects. And that person sometimes appears and speaks to those who are still alive. But if that person's conduct was bad, he will become a whirling wind that sinks ships in the lake, an evil and unwelcome messenger. And if he carries on appearing, people have to chain his tomb and padlock it, so he won't be able to leave it.'

Risto knew that Ombeni and Frank were good children, beloved by the entire street. They would never bring bad luck to the community, he kept thinking. They would be there to talk to him when he felt sad, to protect him when he needed help. In his mind, Risto saw his two late friends drifting from him. At one point he thought they would appear to him; then he thought they were leaving him for far places. But surely they would stay close to him, he thought, if they were to be buried in the ground close to his house.

At around 10am, the singing became much louder, and the women's cries rose to the four corners of the street. The space became smaller as more people arrived. Everyone from the street had to be there. No excuse would have been accepted for being absent. If a family was absent, it meant they were not part of the community. That family would be isolated from the community, and no one would ever go to their aid if they had a problem. That is the Bantu culture; people are human through others.

As the two coffins approached the graves, the voices became wild, the songs intensified, the screaming and shouting pierced the eardrums like the sting of a bee. Ombeni's sister, Nkana, tried to throw herself in the grave on the right, but she was rescued at the last second by two young men who held her back. They had acted quickly, as if they were aware that this might happen. Her cries became louder as she fought to be released. The elders decided that she shouldn't participate in the burial until her emotions were less wild, and she was taken inside the house.

The two coffins lay in the middle of the circle created by the crowd in front of the two graves. One female voice started a very sad song, and then everyone joined in. People sang as they cried, they sang as they wept, and they sang as their tears dropped. Many were unable to restrain their emotions.

The priest stood up to give the homily. He preached for some time, but didn't blame anyone; neither the war, nor God, who should surely protect his people. Risto wasn't happy. He felt the priest was taking things too lightly; he spoke as though this was simply the way things were, children dying in wars.

'Everything happens for a reason; only the Almighty God knows why this way, and at this time,' the priest said. 'He is the one who gives and he is the one who takes away.'

After the homily, the process of lowering the coffins into the graves began; one by one, they passed through the hands of several young men. In each grave stood two young men, who took the coffin from four others above. Mama Ombeni, who had been weeping, started to cry like a child being burned alive. Almost every woman joined her. They howled until the priest begged them to stop.

At this moment Risto wanted to leave his station on the tree trunk, as he himself was sobbing too hard. But he wanted to see where his two friends would rest in the end. If he wanted to knock on their coffins, he needed to know where to stand to be close enough to their ears.

The priest asked the mother of the children to come forward and say her last words. She looked at the sky, then she looked into the graves. She opened her mouth. There was silence, as deep as that in the graves. Everyone was waiting for her words. Then without warning, she fell on the ground. People ran to her. The screams and cries intensified; the voices became so sharp, they could have opened the ears of a deaf person. Many of the women also threw themselves to the ground, yelling and weeping. They were like people competing in grief.

'Is she dead? Is she dead?' the crowd murmured.

'No, she is still breathing,' answered one of the three men who held Mama Ombeni. 'She has fainted, but she will be okay.'

Risto's father, as one of the respected members of the community, now addressed the crowd: 'Our souls and our hearts are wounded by this very tragic accident. We don't need a doctor to treat us, our pain can only be addressed by the Lord God. He has the answers to the impossible questions; only He knows why this is happening.' He looked at the crowds before going on, 'Our two sons passed away, only God knows why. Their mother, she is still alive. She is fighting with the unbearable emotion of losing all that she had. Only God knows how to heal her wounds. The bodies of the two boys have been in the house for three days; they cannot sleep there again tonight; we have to let them rest. This means that the burial ceremony has to carry on. We must call their sister to finalise the ceremony. The whole family is here, the whole community. These children were our sons.' There was silence for a moment, and then two women left to get Nkana from the house.

'Let's carry on with hymns, and together in our hearts, let us pray to God to comfort us and to comfort the family of our sister,' Mahuno concluded.

The singing started up again.

Nkana returned, weeping as she had been for the full three days.

'Nkana, we are here now to say goodbye to your brothers. As God sent them, he has once again called them. Say your last words and bury them in peace,' said the priest.

One young man, standing close to the priest, had soil on a spade, facing Nkana.

'My brothers, you have left me alone in this world. To whom will I talk to again? With whom will I eat again? My brothers, they have mixed up your blood and flesh. We couldn't recognise your bodies; why did you choose this death? The world hated you! You have left me in a desert of pain. You left me without life; will I survive? Go well my brothers, I pray to the angels to welcome you. God receives your souls! Farewell!'

She burst into tears as she threw soil into the two holes.

Uncles, aunts, cousins, friends and neighbours came forward one by one, each one with a goodbye message, to throw a bit of soil in the two graves. Then a crowd of men with hoes and spades started covering the graves in a hurry.

Afterwards, the songs carried on in slow motion, many women with voices almost inaudible from singing and weeping. There were even coughs from those trying to find voices they no longer had. Slowly people went back to their homes; it was like the end of a chapter in a book.

Risto was still on the tree trunk. Was he dreaming? Was it a story someone was telling him, or a play he was seeing? He jumped down from the tree. Yes, he was still alive, and it was all true; he had witnessed a real end to the story of his two friends. He would never see them again.

Peace was once again a visitor to the street after a long busy-noisy three days. No songs could be heard, nor crying. It was known that the following day, women would have to wash everything at Mama Ombeni's place very early in the morning. Food and drink would be served, and that would be the end of the mourning ceremony.

Risto's father sat on the sofa near his wife, who was holding their younger daughter, Zaina. They had finished eating. Usually, after the meal there was discussion, debate and storytelling around the table, followed by hymns and prayers before sleep. The house was very sombre that night, no stories, no debate, no discussions. Risto was impatient, waiting for one of his parents to lead the singing, but no one said a word. Then, with a deep, tired and sad voice, his father broke the silence.

'Yes … that is how life is, you can laugh with someone today and tomorrow you wake up and he is not around anymore.'

He kept quiet for a moment, took a breath, then he turned his face towards Risto.

'What I can tell you is to be careful. Do not go far away from the house; the situation is not calm in this country. I am talking to all of you, not only to Risto. Anything can happen at any time. And if it happens that we have to run away and find refuge somewhere else, and you are not close to the house, you may be left behind. So, whenever you play, play nearby. If something happens while you are at school, listen to the instructions of your teachers. When they tell you to go home, run here quickly.'

He remained quiet for a while, and then he asked his wife to pray.

An August sun rose from its cave. As usual in August, it was shy, maybe afraid of the wind that blew early in the mornings. There was still a bit of mist on the mountains and on the Ruzizi river, which links Lake Kivu with Lake Tanganyika. Children enjoyed the sun when it reached its zenith. At noon, the bell from the Catholic church could be heard. Anyone could recognise that time if they had eyes to see and could read nature, the way Benny had taught Risto to do.

As the day turned to afternoon, the buzz of children intensified. The noise came mostly from the games they played; singing and dancing, marriage songs and sewing competitions for girls, and soccer games and à la guerre for boys. The children created separate camps from different streets, and competed against one another. Each camp had its own dancers, singers, and a bride and groom, and judges would choose the best food, songs and dances, even which bride and groom wore the best outfits. Everyone enjoyed these competitions, including onlookers, but the parents hated it when boys acted like soldiers at war, screaming their songs and shouting the names of their enemies.

This was the last month of the holidays, and the noisiest. Come September, all the games would be forgotten and the street would be quiet and deserted again. But this was the last time for playing, and by mid-afternoon, the parents couldn't take the noise anymore; they sent the children to play elsewhere. But the noise of children playing was something that people missed when they went far from their homes. These sounds were the colours that painted the hearts of the people. Noise was medicine for their illnesses. It made the streets alive.

Buholo II Street, where Risto's family lived, was always happy and cheerful. When the children sang, Buholo II Street sang, when they danced, the street danced too. It wasn't noise; it was life. Often, older people stood to watch what was happening. They sighed in admiration; they would have wished to see childhood again, to play, and sing and dance like their children. These songs and dances healed burned hearts and wounded souls. It was rare to come across any case of heart disease in Buholo II Street. People were happy. They forgot about the war, they forgot about the soldiers, they forgot to worry about whether they would be invaded tomorrow.

At fifteen, Risto couldn't mix with the younger children in his street anymore. Instead, his home became a meeting place for young people of his age. His father had bought him a lot of games: drafts, mucuba, cards, dice, Scrabble, as well as a small radio so he could to listen to music and news. Risto especially loved mucuba. This traditional African game had thirty-two magical holes in which beans or marbles were moved back and forth during the game. This game was the old people's favourite; one had to be good at calculations to play it. Amazingly, some very elderly people were known as good players even though many of them had never been to school. They regularly won against the young people with tertiary degrees. With a little debate and talk of politics as the game was played, a day would go by as fast as a hyena being chased by a lion.

This was also a time for teasing and gossip. Risto was the victim almost every day. His friends began to tease him about the daughter of his neighbour, a girl called Néné. He never liked to hear her name coming out of the mouths of his friends. They never stopped fabricating stories about Risto and Néné.

'Oh, Risto, we heard that you sent a letter to her …'

'Oh, Risto, people saw you kissing her after you gave her a rose.'

All these were lies, and they irritated him. But there was nothing he could do except divert the teasing to another person, until they all turned to that person, and the day would go on.

One morning as he sat playing games as usual, he noticed Néné passing. Murmurs sounded. Provocative coughs came from Risto's friends.

Néné and Risto's eyes met and they both smiled. Her teeth flashed like lost diamonds in the night; it was a smile that took Risto's heart away.

She went towards Risto's family lounge. Everyone's eyes were on Risto. He swallowed his tongue. After a while, she returned back to her house. To avoid any comments his friends might make, Risto concentrated on his game. Not five minutes had gone by when Néné's voice vibrated in the air.

'Risto! Risto! My mother is calling you.'

'What for?' Risto asked.

'I don't know, but I think she might send you somewhere.'

Risto stood up, reluctantly leaving a game that he was close to winning.

As he approached Néné's family house, she came out and confessed that her mother was not there.

'No, I am lying ... my mother is not calling you,' she said, a bit afraid and shy.

'Then ... so ... why?'

'No, it's me,' she looked at the ground. 'I am going to Labotte, I don't want to go alone. Would you mind coming with me?' She looked back up, and this time her eyes met Risto's. Then they both looked aside.

Risto nodded his head in agreement. Sparkling smiles shone on their faces.

Labotte was one of the most beautiful places in Bukavu. It was like a land that was about to be stolen by Lake Kivu, but then the entire landscape had fought for its rescue. It remained suspended above the water. From far away on the south mountain, one could see it like a string floating on the waters of Lake Kivu. Fresh breezes blew from both sides. Fishermen and their boats danced to the rhythm of the gentle waves of the lake, a lake that slept like a tired mother after a long day tending to her children. The fishermen, in happy songs and chants, floated with their boats and canoes on the quiet Lake Kivu. Its peaceful breeze was so beautiful, like a grandmother singing lullabies to her grandchildren.

Firstly Risto and Néné walked to the bus stop, and then they took a taxi to Labotte. This time, Risto's friends would have good reason to create stories about the couple. But what they were saying was something that he didn't want anyone to talk about: the love he was feeling for this beautiful girl. Risto's heart skipped a beat whenever she smiled, showing the small gap between her teeth and her dimples ... Oh, if beauty were a mother, Néné would have been her first daughter, he thought. The sun rose in her eyes! She walked with the grace and rhythm of a Congolese zebra! He felt special whenever he was with Néné; truth be told, he was deeply in love with her. Was this trip going to be an opportunity to tell her that his heart was dying for her? He had wanted to declare his love to her before, but his mouth had never allowed him to go ahead with the plan of his heart. This time he decided to use this opportunity.

They walked together side by side. It was difficult for Risto to start a conversation. They usually only talked about school. This time he wanted to talk about something else, to offer her his friendship, his love. But he was shy. He couldn't make eye contact with her. She also didn't allow it to happen. If their eyes met, they both quickly looked aside and carried on walking.

What is she going to think of me if I don't talk to her? Isn't she going to think that I am afraid of her? Risto argued with himself. He wanted to show Néné that he was strong, that he wasn't shy. But what if she refused him? He would be miserable.

But maybe she has the same feelings; maybe she loves me too, he thought.

Risto looked at her again; their eyes met, and he felt relieved.

· Chapter 3 ·

Six months had passed since Ombeni and Frank had been killed and buried, and a new wind buffeted the whole town of Bukavu every day. It was a never-ending whirlwind in people's minds, strong at night and weak during the daylight. Everyone was afraid.

Bukavu's peace had been broken by war and fear. Whenever a mother left her home for her daily job, or for the market, she left the responsibility for her children to the adults remaining in the neighbourhood. If anything happened, they had the right to make decisions about those children. The echo of heavy firearms banged in people's eardrums. Even when it came from afar, it made life uneasy. Each day, the news filtered through and added to the uneasy air. Each night Bukavu slept uncertain of the morrow: tomorrow was an unborn ghost that haunted everyone's sleep.

At last, the news no one wished to hear blew into the hearts of the Bukavian people. The region had been invaded. The news travelled from lip to lip and house to house. Anything could happen at any time. Bullets lit the dark skies of Bukavu as they flew back and forth between Congo and Rwanda. It was terrifying. How could a bullet cross the Ruzizi River and reach a home in Bukavu? Or cross in the other direction until it reached a home in Rwanda?

These things weighed heavily on Risto's shoulders, becoming a shadow that took his appetite, his smile and laughter away. The question he always had in his mind was whether the next house to be hit would be theirs. Sometimes the exchange of bullets came as a rain-like sound, of hailstones on the roof; sometimes it was like two metals crashing and colliding. Risto lay among the banana trees, as the entire family had been advised to do by their father. He was afraid, hanging in an endless earthquake. The shooting echoed inside his head and left him feeling that his heart had been pulled from his chest. Now and again, he would put the palm of his hand on his chest, so that he could feel if he was still breathing. He had heard that one could die without knowing it, so he kept checking that he was still alive.

At first, the noise of firearms made children afraid. Whenever it started, they cried and ran in all directions. Later, they grew used to it, and would shout, 'Shoot another one!' They did not cry anymore. The shooting, the deaths, had become a part of their daily lives. There was no longer any difference between greetings and shootings.

The people's prayers were not answered; the South Kivu region had been invaded. An official message came that people should evacuate. Soldiers arrived, setting up their posts in the streets. Their tanks were bigger than some of the houses in the neighbourhood; some of them walked on four feet like elephants. At first people opposed the evacuation, but one shot from a tank made a jam in the streets and paths. People fell with their bags on their necks; children's cries burst towards the skies.

Risto's father was at work when the town caught alight. With their mother, Risto and his two sisters followed their neighbours, their eyes and ears turning behind, hoping to find their father. With tears falling from her eyes, Risto's mother followed the steps of her friends, walking in a multitude of people like ants. Her friend followed another friend, who in turn followed a friend. Nobody knew where they were going. They travelled aimlessly, following the mountains around Bukavu town. No one questioned the destination; everyone followed the same path, each person filling the footprint of their predecessor. The guns were heavier and sang rhythmically in the air. Their echoes came from different directions.

They walked past dead bodies, burning houses, wounded soldiers, wounded civilians. Risto thought about his late friends Ombeni and Frank, then was distracted by the cries of a lost child. He shivered. The crowd was as large as that at a soccer tournament. To keep count of their children, mothers would shout the name of each child, from the firstborn to the youngest, and every one would answer loudly. The noise of guns combined with the cries of children was deafening. Bullets whispered a quiet but violent song that people often only grasped after fatal words pierced innocent bodies. The song of the bullets came in a wind that carried many voices, those of the dead, the dying, those fighting death and those escaping death, and when it became very loud, people fell down on their stomachs with no wish to open their eyes again. Then the bullets would fall, not very far from where they were lying. For some, it would then be time to bury their loved ones, for others, a time to build crutches for their own bodies, but the journey carried on and on to the unknown destination.

On the third day of the journey, the songs of the guns could no longer be heard. Risto, his mother and his two sisters were alive and very far from Bukavu town; they were in the Luhoko village in the heart of Walungu territory. The woman they had followed, the friend of their mother, had been heavily pregnant when they first set out. On the journey, she had given birth to twin children. There was no clinic to go to. Everything – the labour and the birth – happened along the way. Generous villagers had given them food and a lot of fruit without questioning. It was the spirit of the people of the village to help.

The news had come that the pregnant woman needed to rest. The entire group stopped. The pregnant woman was taken in by the villagers and offered a small straw hut. Then everything turned into a grown-up women business. From where the curious children watched, a frenzy of activity could be seen at the hut. Two women, with plastic basins in their hands, ran to the pregnant woman's hut. It didn't take long before some shouting could be heard. Apparently there was not enough paraffin in the lamp they were using. An old woman emerged from the hut and ran like a buck. One of her loincloths fell off unnoticed. She went straight to another hut a few metres away and came back with a working lamp.

Later that afternoon, the news came that the journey couldn't go on; the pregnant woman had given birth to twins. Songs burst into the air. The villagers gave the new mother the small hut where she had given birth, and offered other huts to Risto's family. Many other families were hosted by volunteers from the village. Some who had family members in nearby villages decided to carry on.

Eventually, reports came that war had ended and peace had returned to Bukavu. Displaced people started returning home. Risto's family and the entire group that had found refuge in Luhoko village decided to go back home too. The twins were two months old when the party set out on the journey. The refugees thanked the villagers for their generosity and warmth, and promised to stay in contact.

Bukavu had changed. Was it wearing a mask, or did it have another spirit in its body? The people said it was a new country, and indeed it was. It had new people with new tongues, new ideologies, many new things indeed. These new things had captured the attention of the media. The country was in the headlines across the globe.

Something else surprising had happened. Teenagers were now more rare than gold. And those who were visible had deer eyes on their backs, ready to run whenever suspicious or sinister stories emerged of the kidnapping or militarisation of children. They looked with resistance and insistence at each new face. An unfamiliar face was a dangerous one; it made them run. The story was that many teenagers had joined the new army.

Some of Risto's schoolmates now wore an army uniform that slowed their movements and made them look like puppets wearing their masters' clothes. The uniforms these boys wore swallowed their spirits as well as their bodies; they were slaves to a uniform they would never be able to take off. Their youthful age raised questions about their decision to join the fighting. Only later was it revealed that boys like these had not chosen freely. They had been forced into violence, in secret ways they dared not pronounce.

It had been only a few years since the country had changed from Zaire to the Democratic Republic of Congo; now there was change again. There were new leaders, a new army, new soldiers. Risto was confused; he had many questions that even his father couldn't answer. Was it a new country? Who was in charge? When he heard about the many different militia groups that had risen, he wondered who protected whom, who guarded whom. Some of his friends had joined the most feared army group, the Mai-Mai. They had mystical powers; they couldn't be defeated and they couldn't die. Bullets wouldn't penetrate their bodies; they would would tear their clothing and then fall like little plastic balls hitting a concrete wall. Knives would bend and machetes would bounce off their magical bodies. They were tattooed with lion blood and crocodile scales, and had the spirits of sacred forests and fearsome ancestors to protect them. They wore talismans of feathers and bones around their necks, and never washed in rivers or let the rain fall on them; they never ate food that had been cooked by women, and were not allowed to steal. They had many rules and principles. They were there to protect people from foreign invasion, Risto heard.

But they were not the only ones with the goal of protecting people from outside armies; there were many others: the Movement of Liberation from This, the Movement of Liberation from That; Patriotic Front for This, Patriotic Unity for That. Risto was shocked to learn that the army in his town was not part of the national army; the militia that 'protected' them was a rebel army. All the militias wanted to get rid of 'the rebel army', but they were rebels themselves, according to the national government in the capital city of Kinshasa. It was confusion, curse and chaos.

Bukavu had changed from a peaceful town with the joyful noise of happy children to a fearful town with the silence of fear and confusion pierced only by screams of mourning. The afternoon dances of children had changed to the thunder of soldiers' footsteps chasing unhappy children. High-school and university students were seen as the troublemakers; they wanted to own their own history, to write it with their own blood, and so they became the targets of the rebel movement. They vowed never to allow the rebel movement to settle and rule, never to allow them to give the Congolese people instructions or to implement new policies. These students embarked on strikes and marches many times each month. They protested against foreign armies, against daily assassinations, and called for freedom of movement and freedom of speech. The more they marched, the more they got arrested and shot, the more they were forced to join the rebel army, and the more they diverted into the Mai-Mai movement.

Days became uncertain, and each dawn gave birth to new fear and pain. Gunfire became the evening song in the streets of Bukavu. Armed burglars in military uniforms took over from the police nightshift. They visited houses as if they owned the town; so many lives were taken each night. The newspapers were full of reports of missing teenagers, who had been taken from their streets and homes. Later they would be found in military uniform.

Risto's parents decided to send him away to escape the situation in town. He had no choice; he would go to Bugobe, to his mother's village, until things calmed down. But it felt like treason to leave Néné behind. Though their mouths spoke little of their relationship, their hearts' beating depended on it. They could not bear a day without a glimpse of the other. But the order to leave the town was not one that Risto could defy. He packed his bag in tears, berating himself as a coward. He would leave behind half his heart to save his own skin; he wept as he waved goodbye to Néné.

Risto found Bugobe with a timid smile breaking out from between its grinding teeth. It had been a long time since he had visited his beloved village. His last visit had been a breathtaking one, and its memories were still fresh. Bugobe was the place where he had discovered the mystery of villages and their forests. He had heard invisible shadows talking, he had heard the voice of nature and the songs of silent nights. He could still see the face of his old friend Benny, the boy who knew the sleeping room of the moon and the different voices of the universe's soul.

But as soon as he arrived, he realised the Bugobe he saw was different from the Bugobe he had known. He was surprised to be unmet and to walk alone on his way from the bus stop. Had they forgotten he was coming today? Usually when Risto visited Bugobe, many villagers waited for him, mostly young boys waiting for gifts. This time his gifts were lying in his bags. It wasn't easy to walk and carry all his bags. Every now and again he stopped to rest. After he had stopped many times, he saw Benny coming towards him. He greeted Risto in a rush and took a few of his bags.

'I was about to die with these things,' said Risto, but Benny didn't respond. He seemed preoccupied, quiet. They crossed the village, but to Risto's surprise, he saw no children coming for the usual hugs and greetings. The few people they passed by greeted them hastily and passed in a hurry without handshaking, their smiles lasting no more than a few seconds. It seemed like the village wasn't happy.

'Are you well, Benny?'

'No.'

'Is that why you are so quiet today? Is there bad news?'

'No,' Benny answered.

'I feel like the village is not happy, like there is something that is not going well here.'

'People are very busy. You know, Risto, life has changed in the village. We only have life during the day; the night is something else.'

These words captured Risto's attention. He stared at Benny. He knew Benny as the face of the village; whenever he smiled, the village smiled. Now the village was scowling. There was no sound of pestles pounding, or of young girls singing; everything was as quiet as midnight at a cemetery.

'You see, it is only 2pm, but there is no one in the village. Everyone is out with their children; the whole family goes to get anything they can from their fields and farms to bring it back to be near their houses,' said Benny quietly. 'You know, the farms, those near the big forest on Donga and Mlangala, they are looted each evening by the militias.' He took a breath and looked at Risto, waiting for a reaction. Risto tried to look unconcerned; he had seen a lot in town.

'Do you know the militias?' Benny asked.

'No, I have only heard about them,' Risto answered.

'Huh! The militias!' exclaimed Benny. 'These people are looting our fields. They have invaded the Birava and Kidumbi villages. They are inhumane! They have looted families and raped the women and even the little girls! They have killed people and taken young girls into the forests as their wives.'

'Are you sure of what you are saying?' Risto's face changed.

'Risto, the militias are wild. People from those villages are in Bugobe as refugees. Many of them witnessed these horrors.'

Risto couldn't believe his ears. There was no peace in either town or in the villages. He had run away from a war-zone into a battlefield!

'So, the people of Bugobe … you are not afraid?'

'No, no … we are far from them. They won't come this side. Before they can arrive here, the soldiers of the new government will intercept them.'

'So, you guys this side trust the rebel movement? How can you call it the new government?'

'No, we don't trust them. But they are the ones who came to rescue the people in those invaded villages. And they are the ones who control the region.'

'Even so, they are killing people in town! They are looting homes. You know, I am running away from them, that is why I am here right now.'

Benny looked at Risto with surprise.

Soon they arrived home. No one was in the compound. Risto went behind the hut his grandmother used as a storeroom and came back with cassava. It was still wet and covered in black and white mould. He went back to the hut where he had dropped his luggage; the fire was hidden underneath hot ashes. This was one of the secrets of the village he knew from his last visit. He revived the fire and put the cassava on it. Benny sat on a stool outside.

'Take this piece, man!' He threw Benny some cassava that he had cooled after taking it from the fire.

'You said you don't trust the new government, the rebels. Why then do people from town send their children to join them?' Benny asked, agitated.

'No, people don't send their boys, no!'

'But that is what we heard on the provincial radio station.'

'The radio station is run by the rebels; they say what pleases them! No one wants to join their army!'

'Maybe you don't know, Risto, but many young boys are joining the movement. Some of them are working at different posts in the nearby villages, on the road to Mwanga and Birava ...'

'You know, Benny, the truth hasn't been told. From what I know, young boys are not joining the movement; they are being kidnapped and forced.'

Benny went very quiet, perhaps because of the news Risto had told him, or perhaps because he had trusted in the rebel movement. Maybe it was the chaotic state of both the town and the village that made him sick at heart. Risto examined his mind to check whether there was any exaggeration in the news he had given Benny, but all he had said was true. Those young teenagers whom the rebel movement claimed were happy to serve the movement were morally and spiritually tortured. They didn't join the army willingly; they were forced into it. And those who fled were in trouble. Risto had witnessed this in town; he had seen runaways caught in his street, and all their ribs broken by the beatings ordered by the commander of the battalion. The following day, the victim would often be found dead from his injuries.

It was getting late. The sun was on its way to its hut to sleep. Benny and Risto went to find the cattle nearby. They were being kept in a very large, enclosed compound with stagnant water all around.

'Why do you have to keep the cattle enclosed?' asked Risto.

'We can't go very far with them,' said Benny, while throwing stones at a goat that didn't want to respond to his calling. 'Sorrow and fear have invaded the village, and made it small. We can't go far to cultivate, we can't go far to pasture our cattle. Those militias are very bad people. In the Birava and Kidumbi villages, they would loot whatever they found in the pastures and in the fields. If a shepherd said one word, he would be brutally killed. If a woman was found in the fields, she was raped by a dozen men. Imagine! Now we are afraid to go far from home. We have to stay near the village. Here at least it is safe.'

That evening, Risto's grandmother arrived home much later than usual. She had gone with her friends and their children to harvest the fields near the Birava and Kidumbi villages. The crops were not yet mature, but the villagers feared that if they were left any longer in the fields, they would be harvested by the militia.

'Everyone has heard what the militias are doing. They don't leave anything for you if they enter your fields,' she said. Risto ran into the kitchen to help her. She wanted to chase him out.

'The kitchen is not for men, it is a place for women,' she said. If Risto's grandfather were to find him in the kitchen, he would be cross with his wife for allowing the boy to stay. But Risto insisted. He saw the heavy basket she carried, he saw that she was very tired.

There was a pot on each of the four fireplaces. Fireplaces were traditionally set in a triangle made with three stones, with burning wood beneath. His grandmother's fireplaces were different; they were in pairs, two by two. Each pair of fireplaces combined had an odd number of stones – five each, instead of six, each sharing one stone. So the pots stood close together, almost scraping against each other.

Risto's grandmother set up the mortar and pestle, wanting to pound cassava leaves. Risto took the pestle. 'This isn't a man's work,' she said again. He insisted again. Eventually she gave him one pestle, keeping two for herself. The mortar was very large. She started a song as the pounding started.

Pounding work was like a dance. Whenever people pounded cassava, or its leaves, or maize, the pounding work had a rhythm. The song went with the rhythm of the pestles. The pestles were like sticks and the mortar was a drum. Risto's grandmother sang her endless songs in her dialect, Mashi. Eyes closed, pestles in hand, she sang recital melodies. Her songs freed fugitives from a heartless universe. They were like fishing nets picking up lost ancestral relics. The mortar awoke the spirits while the grandmother sang her lulling hymns. Her body boiled and sweated. Her litany navigated the epics of kingdoms; the history of the great Kivu fishermen came to life again; the silhouette of a hero hunter murmured.

'O, Grandmama, just pray, just sing, Grandmama,' Risto whispered to the travelling soul of his grandmother. 'You baptise my heart with sacred verses, priceless perfume.' The ancestors travelled in his swelling veins. Then his grandmother's girlhood songs echoed out: how shepherds danced on the mountaintop, how they had cooked banana and cassava over campfires, how the smoke had pierced her bones and flesh. The past was gone, but history lived on. His grandmother was the breath of history; its blood filled her veins. Her songs were living remnants of the ancestors resting in sacred shades.

She was lost in the world of her words. Then her voice changed, becoming sad and melancholic. She sang about her son who had died very young. He was bewitched by the jealous spirits of her neighbours. He was a pretty boy, whose smile was like sunshine. Then the bad spirits grew jealous of the treasured boy. His departure to an unknown world left his mother in pain and mourning. But he was at peace, the handsome boy. He rested in peace with his ancestors. Then she sang about the invaded villages. She asked why people with wild spirits wanted to invade them. She called for God and the ancestors to fight for them. Her songs rocked Risto in a bath of joy and sadness. She stopped singing only when the cassava leaves were ready to be put into the hot water boiling on the fireplace.

The deep voice of Risto's grandfather rumbled outside; one could tell that he was still on his feet. Risto went outside to greet him. His grandfather took him into his hut and presented him with a kabehe with local banana juice inside it. He knew that Risto never drank beer. The old man took a swig from his own kabehe. He looked at Risto, then asked how his family was. Risto replied that the family was doing well.

His grandfather took another swig, and then tried to smile. 'I heard that you had run away from town?' he said. He tried to joke: 'A man can't run and leave his sisters behind, but you left yours.' Then he grew solemn. 'The situation of the country is very bad. Especially for us in the great Kivu. I am coming from the villages near Birava and Kidumbi. There is a thick cloud covering our horizon.'

The old man explained a lot of things. The peace that they had been living in was slowly ebbing away. Bringing it back would require many years, many generations, maybe. 'In the other villages where I was, there are different taxes that the local population has to pay. One militia group comes to the market to take what it can as tax, another passes through the villages in the afternoon for another tax, another one at night for another tax, then another one comes to loot at night, and so on. It is impossible to live. It is bad, but worse for women. They don't sleep in their houses at night anymore; they pass the night in the fields so that when the militias come, they just loot the houses and cattle. Otherwise …'

His grandfather didn't finish this sentence, but Risto knew what he meant. The old man went on, 'There is no peace in town or in the villages. We don't know who is fighting whom, and who is protecting whom. All of them say that they protect the people even as they are carrying out crimes against the same people. But they won't come this side. We will just look after our cattle and see how the days pass.'

· Chapter 4 ·

The night in the village was not as peaceful as usual; the constant footsteps of people passing by stole Risto's sleep away. When he blinked, he saw little sparks of light in the hut; it was morning. Benny came in from letting out the cattle.

'Did you hear how people were moving up and down the whole night?' he asked Risto.

'Yes, where were they coming from?'

'They were people from the villages near Birava and Balaga. They ran away from the militias.'

'Did the militias attack them?'

'No, but they received news that the militias were going to attack them last night.' He changed his tone and opened the door of the little hut. 'And you know, it is not only people from the villages that are coming here to Bugobe. I have heard that there is a bus bringing people from the town on its way.'

'Are you sure, Benny?'

'Yes.'

'Who told you?'

'A lorry arrived from the town early this morning. The news was given by the people who came with the lorry.'

Risto thought maybe he would see other boys from his town. He and Benny walked towards the bus stop. As they reached the small bumpy track that led to the bus stop, they saw a group of five people coming from the opposite direction, carrying luggage.

'The girl on the left walks like someone I know,' Risto said.

'These are people from the village; you don't know them,' Benny replied, laughing.

'I'm sure it is someone I know from Bukavu town,' Risto insisted.

'No, these people are from this village; I know the one wearing the white top.'

They approached the group slowly. There was one young woman, one teenage girl and three boys. Suddenly Risto realised that the teenage girl was someone that he knew very well; it was Néné. His heart pounded with an excitement that he could not explain. He felt like running to give her a big hug, to hold her tight in his arms for a few minutes to let her feel his heartbeats. He wanted to tell all that he had always wished to tell her, how much he loved her. But again, he thought of what people would say, and this weakened his resolve.

Instead, as Néné approached, he wondered which was the right word to say, how to greet: should it be a kiss or a hug, a handshake or waving? He felt like the entire world was looking at him.

Néné had a big bag on her head. She smiled as she saw him; he returned a shy smile.

'What are you doing this side?' Néné asked.

'What are you coming to do this side?' he replied.

As Risto finished introducing himself to the other people, he found himself before Néné, who had put her bag on the ground. Benny was talking to the others and answering their questions. Risto, in spite of his search for a moment to say all that he had in his heart for Néné, found himself once again speechless. His eyes had to speak the unsaid words of his heart. He would fix his eyes on Néné, then look aside as she bit her nails and smiled to herself.

'Oh … let me help you!' He jerked forward, realising that Néné needed his help.

She gave him her bag as they walked together.

'Are you coming on holiday?' Risto asked Néné.

'You sound like someone who doesn't know what is going on in town!' she replied.

'I thought only boys were targeted, not girls …'

'Things were tense after you left. Students and pupils marched in town for the release of the spokesperson of the student organisation. The mayor and the governor refused to listen to them, and then they declared the march illegal. The students and pupils didn't want to disperse. The soldiers shot at them, they replied with stones. The windscreen of the governor's car was smashed. The soldiers chased the students and people everywhere. There was a rumour that a raid was planned for tonight. And you know if someone is jailed, he is automatically taken to be a soldier; you know how badly they need them. So, young boys and even girls have started to leave the town.'

They said goodbye to Néné and her friends as she entered the compound of her relatives. Risto promised to visit her in the afternoon.

'How do you know that girl?' Benny asked, smiling as he looked at Risto's face.

'She is a friend from home.'

They both smiled.

'She is beautiful ... eh?'

Risto responded with laughter.

'A friend? Are you planning to marry her?'

'At fifteen? Come on, Benny! We are still too young to think about marriage. We are just friends. Maybe one day, if God wants, we can get married.'

'I wish I could see that day,' Benny laughed.

The sun was very strong that day. Risto waited for its fierce rays to soften before visiting the person his heart was yearning for. Néné was staying only five compounds away from Risto's grandfather's home. As Risto approached, he saw her with one small drum in her hand and a big pot on her head; she was going to the well for water. He ran towards her quietly, slowing to a stealthy walk as he approached her from behind. Then he put his hands on her face, covering her eyes. As she fumbled, she lost control of the pot and it fell onto Risto's foot.

'Oh my goodness!' she screamed.

'Sorry! Sorry! Oh, my foot!' he cried out.

She turned around to see him. 'I didn't know, I am so sorry, Risto.'

Risto was holding his left foot, which had been struck by the pot. Néné knelt down to look at it.

'I'm sorry, sorry ... I didn't know. I know it hurts. Please ... sorry ...' Her eyes were on Risto's face, her soft voice showed her great care.

'No, it was my fault, my stupid games!' Their eyes met, then a sweet silence seized the moment as they both looked at the ground. He could feel the moisture of her breath as she had knelt close to him. For a few seconds he inspected her beautiful eyelashes, her light brown skin and her reddish lips. His heart pounded, the usual sign whenever he felt the urge to declare his love to Néné. Then she looked up at him again.

'I'm fine, it was my stupid game, my fault. I'm fine,' Risto said.

They both stood up, laughing.

'You will have something to tell my grandmother today. You know how she respects this calabash!' Néné's grandmother never allowed anyone to take her calabash, except for her beloved granddaughter. It was the oldest pot she had; she had received it from her own grandmother.

'If you break this one, it is like breaking the whole house,' Néné added.

'Why did you take it then, if you could break it?' he asked her, smiling.

'No, I have to take good care of it.'

Her grandmother wanted water straight from its source among the rocks, to be kept in that calabash as it cooled down; this gave the water a very natural smell of rock.

They walked for a while in silence. Risto held the small drum and Néné carried the calabash steady on her head like the women from the village, walking without touching it.

'Where are you going?' Néné broke the silence.

'You don't like that I am walking with you. Should I go back?'

'No! People will laugh at you when they see you with the drum.'

'Even if they laugh at me because of you, is there a problem?'

She looked around as he spoke and replied, 'I don't understand the people of the village; they classify some jobs for women and others for men. I don't think they see that the world of today is changing; there is no job that is only for men or women anymore!'

'How did you feel the day I left town?' Risto asked, changing the subject.

'I felt lonely. I thought maybe I wouldn't see you until school opens in September.'

'Did you choose to come to Bugobe?'

'My parents told me to choose between my mother's village and my father's … I chose this side.'

She looked into Risto's eyes as she said these words.

They reached the village tap, where there were only a few children playing with the water. There were two taps, one for water from the dam that was situated in the mountain of Bugobe, and another one for the water straight from the rocks nearby. Néné was slowly filling the containers as Risto stood distracted by the games the children were playing. Néné put the palm of her hand against the tap to give the water more pressure. As the pressure built, she splashed water at Risto.

'Néné, stop it! No, stop it!' he screamed with laughter. Néné was laughing too.

When he came closer to the tap, she ran away laughing. Risto ended up filling the containers for her.

'It is boring in the village when you are not allowed to go to the fields. My grandparents want to spoil me; they don't allow me to go to the fields with the others,' she said as they made their way back.

'Will they be friendly if I come into their compound?' he asked, looking at the mountain-top.

'They know you as a grandson of the village, they can't complain.' Néné was like a real village girl; she spoke the local language, Mashi, fluently and walked barefoot. She carried her shoes in her hand and walked with her calabash on her head; it was in perfect balance. Risto carried the drum until they reached her family's compound.

Here, Néné offered him some mangoes and bananas. She put the fruit in a traditional creeper dish and covered them with a small cloth, a sign of respect. She also brought Risto a plastic cup of banana juice. They sat and ate together, sharing the banana drink, in a heavenly silence, sometimes nervous, with blinking eyelashes whenever their gazes met along the corridor of their shy looks. They both looked aside whenever this happened. Néné tried to hide her smile, but her dimples still showed. It was something that Risto longed for and loved to see, her smile, her dimples. Whenever she smiled, he felt a strong and mysterious current of water travel through his veins, and he always smiled back. They could have sat the whole day, looking at each other endlessly. Then came stories, like a tortoise leaving its cave in the midday sun, stories from school, from their streets back home, gossip about their friends and even their families; all these stories made them happy. They wanted to stay there, looking at each other and giggling, forever. Maybe this is destiny, each one thought in the secret chamber of their heart.

This was one of Risto's happiest days. He had sat and gazed at someone worthy in his life, someone special to his heart. He had seen how she laughed and smiled when she looked at his face. He understood now how much she would have missed him if she had stayed in town.

The evening soon arrived. The moon shone brightly as Risto's heart danced with happiness. He thought a lot about the next day, he meditated on the affectionate words he would whisper in Néné's ears when they next met. He thought about love poems he had read, romantic books he had read, romantic words he had heard in movies. Impatient to see the night end, he ate quickly. In his excitement, he told Benny that he was preparing the sweetest words he would tell Néné the next day. Benny just laughed; he had the wisdom of the bush and forest, but he was illiterate about love; it had never been part of his world. Maybe one day he would see the heavenly, smiling face of a girl dying for him and understand.

That night, Risto didn't have any trouble sleeping; the bed pampered him. The thoughts about his sweetheart were lullabies; they rocked him like a baby in a cradle. He slept in peace and happiness.

He was woken by a huge noise nearby. Then he heard a detonation.

'Gunshots!' said Benny in a fearful, low voice.

'Yes, I hear,' Risto answered, shivering.

'Another one!'

'Yes, I am listening,' Risto's ears were popping out.

He felt a hot breeze pass through his body. His heart pounded. He was in urgent need of the toilet. Both boys remained silent and still, listening. They couldn't guess what was happening and where. They heard a noise outside; this time near their compounds; the mooing of cows and the bleating of goats amplified their fear; pigs grunted and chickens cackled; something was happening. From afar they heard whistles and drums being beaten, then screams followed; it was a code. Risto didn't understand, but Benny, who had the village in his soul, did.

'We have been invaded,' he said, in a voice cold with hopelessness.

Risto's heart beat like a drum, it was about to burst in his chest. He tried to contain his breath, but it came harder and faster than before.

'Risto, Benny, wake up! Wake up! We have been invaded! Wake up!' It was the voice of their grandmother at the tiny window of their hut.

'You have to run ... wake up! We are invaded! Hurry up!' her voice repeated.

Risto put on his shirt quickly and opened the door. He was barefoot. Benny followed him.

'Run into the fields, my children, run!'

The noise was coming closer to their compound. Now it was coming from their closest neighbour. A few shots followed. They ran in the direction of the fields.

'Eh! Do not move! Stay where you are, or I'll shoot you!' A fierce, deep voice came from the fields facing them. They stood still, shivering. A man appeared in front of them. Then another one, then another, then another. It was a group of very strong men, gigantic with untidy beards, scraggly uncombed hair and ragged clothes. They held guns and machetes in their hands.

'Go back!' one of them ordered.

Risto's feet couldn't reach the ground; he was floating. He couldn't feel his body, his heart was about to burst. They turned and walked back. On the other side of their compound, the door swung as it was kicked off and knocked to the ground. A group of people entered abruptly, while outside of the compound, the lowing of cows intensified.

'Get out! Get out!' ordered the strange men as they entered the huts.

'This is our whole family, Papa; there is no one still inside,' the grandmother pleaded.

'Shut up!' they told her.

The soldiers went behind the main hut and came back with ten cows and six goats. A loud boom frightened everyone.

'Oh, my God!' It was Benny; he had received a hard knock. He was already on the ground. One of the soldiers had hit him with the back of a gun.

'Do you know me? How dare you stare at me like that! Are you a Mai-Mai?' the soldier asked Benny.

'Papa, he is not. He is still a child. Forgive him, Papa,' the grandmother begged, almost dropping tears.

'Carry this!' They threw a bundle of clothes wrapped in a pagne at Risto. They belonged to his grandparents; he was being ordered to carry clothing and possessions that had been looted from his beloved grandparents. The soldiers added a dozen new pots from his grandmother's house to his bundle. They gave Benny a ten-kilo bag of sugar, cooking oil and many other things they had taken.

'Let's go!' one of the men ordered.

Risto's grandfather begged them to leave the children. He told them to take all his cattle, everything they wanted, but to leave the boys. The soldiers refused. Grandmama ran into her house and came back with money. They took the money; then a giant shirtless man held a knife against the old man's neck, threatening to kill him. 'All the money,' he demanded. The old woman ran back into the house, two soldiers following her. When they came back, having taken all the elderly couple's savings, it was time to go.

'Your children will come back,' they said, as they left the compound. Risto's grandparents followed, insisting, weeping, negotiating for the release of the boys. The shirtless soldier got irritated and threatened to shoot the old couple if they kept on following them. Risto and Benny left them standing still, tears on their grandmother's face, her hands pointing out the bastards to God who was absent from the scene.

Risto had faith; he believed he would be back in a short while, so he did not cry. He knew that they might go very far, but he believed in Benny, who knew the forests like the back of his hand. As soon as they were released, Benny would lead the way home.

Outside the compound was yet another desperate scene. The crowd was very large. There was a long queue of young boys loaded with baggage, cattle and soldiers all around them. They followed one another like a community of ants. Risto walked behind Benny without talking; he could hardly breathe and was still floating. He heard a female voice crying out, and saw that there were young girls in the crowd that had been rounded up. He suddenly remembered what was said about the militias, that they took young girls into the forests and turned them into their wives. He felt sorry for these girls, but there was nothing to do, they had to walk.

They walked fast, without rest. A cold breeze froze their melting bodies, which were sweating from the heavy baggage and giant steps. The journey seemed to be endless, with only the moon lighting their path. They were ordered to walk silently and without talking when passing other villages. But Risto soon realised that most of the villages they were crossing were deserted. There was no smell of life in any of these villages; a daunting eeriness yawned from each house they passed. They went on walking, walking, in a long queue, the cattle following. There were no more villages to pass; no path was clear ahead of them. Their bodies were tired and torn and wept in an endless sweat of pain. Their bodies created a path through the choking creepers and thorns of the forest. They hurt Risto's feet and bruised his back and face, but he was too afraid to cry. The soldiers' reactions were unpredictable; he buried his tears in his heart.

They walked through the forest until near dawn. There was no rooster song, there was no human trace; it was creepy in the dark forest as they kept walking deeper into it. Risto was getting very tired. Some of the soldiers were behind with the cows, sheep and goats, others were with their captives. The soldiers had told each of the young boys to look after two animals and at the same time carry the looted luggage. The fatigue was unbearable. Eventually one boy asked for rest. They stopped. The shirtless soldier looked at the boy with contempt and spat on the ground.

'Eh, boy! You pick up those things and keep walking!' he said, his eyes lit like a lion's. The boy kept crawling along. But his load was very heavy and he was very, very tired. He started groaning. He looked younger than Risto, maybe thirteen or fourteen.

'Come ... you need some rest; I will give you rest,' the soldier said, taking the bags from the boy's head and passing them to three other boys. Then he chased the two goats the boy had been looking after into the flock. The soldiers ordered the rest of the group to keep moving. They walked while Risto left his eyes behind. He saw the boy standing in front of the soldier. The sound of shooting hit his eardrums. As Risto looked back, he saw the boy falling down like an uprooted tree. He lay still on the ground.

Risto felt an electrical current passing through his entire body, then settling in his spine; his heart pounded faster and harder than before. In slow motion, he saw the image of his two late friends, Ombeni and Frank. Death was certain and brutal, it was coming, it was happening right in front of him, he could smell it. Maybe he would never see his grandparents or the rest of his family again. He was afraid that death was calling; he could force himself to walk for a day, but not for two. And when his strength was gone, he would be shot in the same way; his body would feed scavengers for a few days, and then he would be gone, leaving a hole in the heart of his family.

His fatigue disappeared and he walked faster. The soldier who had shot the boy caught up with them. He seemed normal. He wasn't anxious. He didn't talk to anyone. He went on looking after the flock without any bother. Nothing had happened, it seemed.

Bruises were burning their bodies; the members of the militia were also feeling the pain. Two of them took up their machetes to clear the way, cutting down shrubs, creepers and thorn trees. It was hard to get through the forest with baggage on their heads, each looking after two animals, barefoot in the thorns.

Risto had been scrubbed by many wild plants and carried thorns in his bare feet, but he swallowed his tears. His whole body was scratched, his legs, his hands, his face … wherever he was scratched, that body part swelled and itched painfully. He wanted a rest, but feared how it would come, and where it would leave him. He decided to walk until death found him walking and staggered on like someone with unequal legs.

· Chapter 5 ·

They arrived at an open space in the middle of the forest. The sun showed that it was around midday; Risto could step over the head of his shadow. The place hosted a few mud huts with straw roofs and a few tents with international NGO names on them. There were little children and very young girls with the drawn faces of old women. They wore dirty, untidy and cheap clothes. A few soldiers were hanging around, relaxing in slippers. Risto's whole body was sore. The captives were told to sit on the ground; they waited impatiently for their promised release, but not a word was said.

Some soldiers disappeared into small huts visible in the surroundings; they did not go with the looted luggage, but with the little girls they had brought. Suddenly a noise erupted, male voices arguing in a language that Risto couldn't understand; it was not one of the local languages. They shouted like two dogs fiercely fighting for a bone. From nearby a giant man, dark with an untidy long beard and uncombed hair like the rest, appeared with three armed soldiers. He seemed to be a chief, as the two quarrelling men fell silent as soon as he spoke.

'What is your problem?' he asked with authority.

'I came with my wife, now he says she is his. It is my sweat that gave her to me,' the tall one explained to the chief.

'No! Last time I gave him the wife that I got in the Gabale village. I had three. We agreed that the next time he got a wife, she would be mine for one week. Now he refuses to give me the girl he got today,' said the shorter one.

'Where is the girl?' asked the chief.

'In my hut,' said the taller soldier.

'Bring her here.'

Two of the chief's men went to fetch the girl.

'Do you have a wife?' the chief asked the taller man.

'Yes, I do. But last time, when I came with three, I gave him one.'

'No! The one he gave me didn't come back when she went to fetch water.'

'Okay, what you have to do is this: as your friend doesn't have a wife, you give him this one. He has to pay you. Next time, he has to do his best to find you one.'

The tall soldier left muttering to himself. The two soldiers who had gone to fetch the girl came back with her.

It was Néné. She was to be exchanged like a cheap piece of goods.

Risto's heart began beating louder than a tam-tam. He felt like jumping up and tearing the chief and his men apart, but he knew he was powerless before such cruel people. Out of fear, he swallowed his tears.

Néné was barefoot. She wore a short skirt and a vest that showed her young breasts visibly pointed in front. They looked like her sleeping clothes. She was weeping, and kept wiping her tears with her hands. She stood in front of the group of soldiers like a little chick in front of elephants. She was still a little chick, a very small girl.

'I don't want to hear your noise anymore. Take!' The chief pushed Néné towards the shorter soldier as if he was handing out a toy. And the soldier left with her.

'Eh, Kadogo!' the chief turned to the boys huddling on the ground, addressing them with the dreaded word for child soldiers. A Swahili word, meaning 'small', it held a more frightening meaning in the rebel movements and in the militias. Kadogo were child soldiers trained for one thing: killing. And their killing was brutal and heartless.

'Don't dream of going back to your villages; we will enjoy the work together here. We have a lot of things to do. You will have food for free; if you want women, you will have them for free. Life is great this side. We will train you and very soon you will be young lions. We have some of your friends here, who came from other villages, and now they have become commanders of great missions. They have found the life they dreamed of. Don't worry, you will enjoy this place.'

He stared at the boys, trying to look each one in the eyes. There were eight of them, six who were younger than eighteen, and another two who looked older, maybe in their twenties.

'Dare to run away from this place, we will cut off your running legs and your ears. Never ever try that!' he emphasised. 'No one has ever escaped; if you try, you will be killed. You follow the rules of your commanders here. This is a military command; there will be no objections.' He looked at the boys with fierce eyes.

'Who among you knows how to use a gun? Who knows?' No one's hand went up.

'Right, you will be trained. Give them meat to cook,' and he left.

Risto was in pieces; his heart was consumed by a volcano. Why didn't he stand up to the chief? Why didn't he speak or fight for Néné? He had promised to fight for her, whatever it took; now she was in the captivity of lions. He had betrayed her. He felt he was a worthless coward. He wept inside. Why didn't I speak? Was I afraid for a life that will not be worth living? The life of a child soldier? Terrorising people like myself every day? Risto kept asking silent, agonising questions. He felt that he should do something, but what?

His cousin Benny was nearby. They hadn't exchanged a word since they had been kidnapped. Risto looked over at Benny; his tears had drawn a highway down his cheeks, running one behind the other and disappearing in his half-open mouth. His pain was written on his face. He must have been thinking about his parents. Maybe asking himself why he had gone to spend the night in Risto's hut; if he had stayed home, maybe he would be sitting in the village at that moment, telling people what he had heard.

Risto's thoughts went back to Néné, the men fighting for her like wolves fighting for prey, her body and soul in the hands of a devil who was happy to take pleasure from the anguish of a small girl. He pictured her face, he knew she was crying. He could not stop himself imagining what she was enduring. Had she asked for forgiveness for sins she had never committed, begging the man to free her? Had she fought until she had no power left? Had she cried to heaven and earth, and cursed them when there was no answer?

He thought about her big, dark-brown eyes, her shyness with men, how shy she would be in front of that cruel man who had declared her his wife. Her vivid smile would be gone now, along with her virginity. Naked in a small hut in front of a naked man almost three times her age. A man who had barely washed for months, a man without a heart or a soul that could feel the misery of a young girl who had never before known a man.

Risto knew Néné would be asking herself which cursed wind had blown her to Bugobe. He knew that she had chosen to come to Bugobe because of him. If she had stayed in town, or gone to her other grandparents, even if she had been taken by the rebels, her parents would have gone to see the governor or the commanders, paid money to ransom her. But here, there was no such option. There was a chief, but everyone did what they wanted; and if a man quarrelled with his comrades, he would go off and start his own militia group, taking more children from the villages and making them his disciples. So Néné was in the hands of an evil man who didn't have to report to anyone, not even to God. He was a devil, and in his small hut he had made his own hell for Néné. And it was all Risto's fault.

Benny still sat near his cousin. His tears had dried. It was obvious he had been crying since they were taken from the village; his swollen eyes showed as much. Risto guessed at what was on Benny's mind. He knew the forest very well, so he was probably thinking about running away. It was a crazy idea. These people were cruel, as careless as wild animals. To them killing was simply a game. He saw how they had killed the young boy who had said he was tired. The soldier had killed him and no one among the group had even asked why. It was as though nothing had happened, as though the man who had executed the boy had no feelings of regret.

If Benny were caught, he would be tortured; the soldiers had promised to cut the ears and legs off anyone who tried running away.

Long ago, Risto's father had considered this. One night before the usual family prayers, he had told his children that if at school, the rebels kidnapped them and forced them to join their army, they shouldn't refuse or run away. They should rather first agree and show willingness to join. Then after they had built up some trust with the rebels, they should start plotting to flee. It was good advice for Benny, Risto thought.

Risto's mind was diving into deep thoughts when he felt Benny nudging him. A group of soldiers, young and old, were coming out of the forest. They stank with a rotten smell; they had not washed for months. 'Ah, Kadogo!' they cheered as they passed.

The boys still waited for the meat that had been promised by the chief, when more soldiers arrived. They seemed maddened by an unknown drug. This group of soldiers carried heavy sticks, guns, machetes and other dangerous and unusual weapons; they sang in a frenzy, and danced with rage.

'Stand up! Stand up, Kadogo! Stand up, sons of bitches!' a few soldiers shouted as they hit the captives with their sticks. The beating intensified as the soldiers kept on screaming at the boys.

'Two lines quickly, two lines, I say!' one of the soldiers shouted as he beat Benny's back with his stick. The boys quickly formed themselves into two lines, while the soldiers began singing and jumping about. As the boys did not know the songs, they clapped their hands and danced uncertainly, following the soldiers' movements. The songs had little meaning, and were mostly full of swearing, except for a few that spoke about fighting hard, till their last drop of blood, until the country is freed, until their country is given back to them.

Now and then, one of the soldiers would jump forward and brandish his gun in the air. He would shout words in a foreign language, then crawl on the ground like a soldier on the battlefield; he would make as if shooting an enemy, and then his fellows would shout with joy, and the man would start jerking around and then dance with his gun pointing in the air before going back to the others. Their dancing and singing made them drunk with power, especially those who were hallucinating from the cannabis they had taken.

Suddenly, with a shout from the soldier who had called for two lines, every soldier stood still, firearm upright, silent and listening.

'Lieutenant!' the man screamed.

'Yes, my commander!' A man rushed forward and stood at attention in front of him, firearm still held upright.

'You will train these Kadogo.'

'Yes, commander.'

'It's your duty to give them the hearts of lions.'

'Yes, commander!'

'At ease.' The commander, whom the boys came to know as General, left with two men on either side of him.

The soldiers told the boys to take off their shirts; they were given to one soldier to keep. Before they would be given food, they were told to start jogging. They were taken to an open space that had been created by hacking down the forest trees and bushes. The boys were told that they were receiving REI training, the same as for the feared French Foreign Legion, and that they had to imitate the leg movements of their trainers. They went left and right, they did the half-turn, they learned how to stand to attention and salute, and to shout fiercely at a person standing an inch from them.

Hours passed, and still the meat promised by the chief was not yet there; meanwhile the running and singing intensified. As the boys ran, those who could no longer run fast were beaten. One of the boys could no longer stand it; his body had weakened, his hunger was unbearable, he fell on the ground. One of the trainers beat him, but not even this could raise him to his feet. This was seen as a sign of disobedience.

'You are a young lion!' the trainer screamed. 'You should prove this to everyone. Boy, military service is never sweet, it is always bitter. Son of a bitch, your mother is not here.' He kept screaming at the exhausted boy as he tried to force himself to stand.

'I close my eyes, I open them, you should be running with your peers!'

But still the boy could not rise. And so, an order was given to each boy to go find a stick in the forest and come back within five minutes.

'I mean a stick that can correct a disobedient boy,' the trainer stressed.

When they returned, the boys were ordered to strike their friend on the ground twenty-five times each. Risto wanted to plead for mercy for this boy, but he imagined what his own fate would be if he did so. Instead, he did as he was commanded. As the boy lay on his stomach, Risto gave him twenty-five blows, this village boy, his countryman. He was the sixth to do so. By then the boy had no strength to scream; he hardly moved as the blows fell. Risto imagined his pain, his suffering, and felt the guilt of beating a brother, an innocent boy. The eighth boy in line said the victim was dying, and refused to beat him further. The fierce eyes of the lieutenant shone, and like thunder coming with no announcement, he punched the refusing boy, felling him to the ground. Then he took a gun from one of his soldiers, and bayoneted the refuser in his back where he lay. He called for a machete, and commanded each of the boys to cut off one of their friend's body parts.

'Do as I say, or your friends will do it on your body,' he said, laughing, as if torture and death brought him a lot of joy.

Risto was the unlucky one to be given the machete first; his peers looked at him with pleading eyes. He knew the lieutenant was not playing games, that he would be the one to be cut in pieces if he didn't do as he was commanded. The bayoneted boy was screaming, begging for mercy, when Risto took the machete.

That night, the boys were praised by the soldiers and called by their new name, young lions. But they could not shake the shame, guilt and self-hatred they felt. The first boy to be beaten also died in the night, and the helpless killers were left to mourn and bury their dead. In just one day in the forest, they had become demons, killers of the most gruesome kind.

Stomachs were still empty the following day but this didn't stop the soldiers from waking the boys at 5am. The promised meat had never arrived. Instead, each of the boys had been given three large cooked bananas alongside a few beans on a plate. They had built their own sleeping shelters with sticks and wild thatch from the forest.

As the whistle blew, each boy forgot his empty stomach and tired body, and went running at his wildest speed. Two lines formed quickly, songs and dances followed. The boys were still without their shirts. Razorblades were given to a lucky few, pieces of broken glass to others; these were to be used for haircuts. A bit of soap foam was used on the head to speed up the process. The cutting was done by the trainees, one on one. There was blood, pain, but no crying; punishment awaited whomever shed tears.

As they stumbled around their makeshift camp, being taken through different training activities and duties, the rest of the soldiers enjoyed a kind of festival. Cows were being slaughtered at a fast rate, Congolese rumba and Ndombolo music could be heard from every corner, men were playing cards, bottles of Primus and Amstel beer and stereo players at their feet; others giggled as they related their killing and raping exploits to their friends.

The boys had gathered that their training was to be swift and intense, as there was a high risk of attacks by rival militias and other rebel movements. So they had little rest, little food and little water; they went shirtless and barefoot in a damp tropical forest populated by mosquitos of every kind. Escaping fatal punishment was no guarantee of survival in a forest where malaria or typhus could knock one down at any time.

And indeed they experienced fatal punishments. One could be beaten to death for a mere mistake. Risto had been beaten for accidentally pointing his stick, which represented a firearm, at one soldier.

'Son of bitch, you want to kill me!' the soldier screamed as he released his blow in Risto's face.

'Sorry, sorry, I wasn't—' Before he could finish, another blow followed.

Risto did not cry. They had been told that they were not children, therefore no tear should ever be seen on their faces. Instead, Risto saluted the soldier and left, blood weeping from his arm.

Another rookie received fifty lashes for calling a captain a lieutenant. He was first harangued before being beaten by the captain himself.

For each slight mistake, there were punishments: punishment for not standing straight in line, punishment for still chewing after hearing the whistle, punishment for a weak saluting position, punishment for this and that – and all these could lead to serious injury or death. But Risto endured and lived through them day by day.

There were harsher punishments the day of shooting training. Fortunately for the rookie boys, they were not the guinea pigs used for the exercise that day. Instead, to their horror and repugnance, the chief commander brought them three captured poachers.

But first, they had learned the five critical positions for shooting. It was the first day they had been allowed to touch a firearm. They looked at it scrupulously, as they knew only too well that it was a deadly machine. At that point, the training shifted to French, as the trainers said they had also been taught in French.

'This is the best inheritance we got from our Belgian colonisers; thank their bloody asses for this toy. Without them, we would never have learned how to use this toy!' One trainer screamed these words as if he was drunk.

'Kadogo, you will thank us for teaching you this skill,' said the other trainer.

'The skill of killing,' the one who spoke like a drunkard added with laughter.

There were many beatings that day as nervousness shook the boys' bodies. They knew the damage a gun could cause, and the vicious and eternal stamp that comes from using one in their culture, so they trembled as they touched it, as they learned how to manoeuvre and master it. The roaring of the trainers made them tremble even more.

'ONE. Position du corps!' The trainer would scream these words, and a trainee boy would kneel down or take one step forward.

'TWO. Tenue de l'arme!' The boy would grip the gun tightly.

'THREE. Viser et épauler!' The boy would pick his target, looking through the sight.

'FOUR. Couper la respiration!' The boy would stop breathing as he focused on his target.

'FIVE. Action du doigt sur la détente. Tirer!' And the boy would shoot at a wooden figure.

It was while they were still learning the possible positions in which they could hold the gun that the chief commander, the General as they called him, arrived with a group of soldiers who were dragging three bleeding men. The three men were naked, and one was still holding a trap. These men were villagers who, because of the increased insecurity and militia looting of farms in the surrounding areas, had gone into poaching as a means of surviving. And indeed one of the three men confirmed this in his testimony when he was interrogated by the General. He said they had been setting traps for mountain gorillas when the soldiers had seized them.

The speaker, who looked to be in his late forties, cried like a little child as he swore he was innocent of any spying. He poached for the survival of his family, he said. He confessed that he had foreign buyers who requested live baby gorillas and even dead gorillas, and this had brought them to this part of the forest.

The story of the pleading man was like a joke to the ears of the General; he laughed so hard that the vigour of his mirth caught the other soldiers, and they too lit up as though they had heard the funniest story ever.

There was a sudden stop in the General's laughter, followed by an intense silence. Now he was serious. He called for three guns, then he called for volunteers among his Kadogo. None came forward. His eyes burned with anger. Risto feared what might follow this anger; he volunteered. A smile sparked the General's face.

'You are trained to become young lions, to teach idiots like these three here to learn never to go behind our backs and spy for our enemies.'

The General prowled around the three boys who had been given guns.

'I heard that you have already had your first killings, once by machete and once by beating. Wasn't it fun?' he laughed. 'Now, you three are lucky to be the first to learn how to kill with a gun. It's simple and easy, easier than killing with sticks. You do what you have been taught: you take a position, you hold your gun, you focus on your target, then you take action. Simple, easy.' He demonstrated this with a gun that he had taken from his bodyguard. 'Go on, one by one, you aim at the forehead. Go ahead.'

Benny stared at Risto with disgust as Risto did as he had been taught. He didn't understand why Risto had been the first to volunteer, and this hurt him; he felt like vomiting.

The three men leaned against trees a few metres from where Risto and the two other boys took their shooting positions. The men's eyes were closed; they were taking their last breaths, saying their last prayers as Risto and his two colleagues focused on proving that they had truly become young lions.

The first man was shot in the neck. He kept moving in agony, so the young rookie fired a second bullet, forgetting that bullets were expensive, and that one bullet meant one life. He got punished for that. And the body remained still, lifeless.

The second boy, shaking hard, lost one bullet in the air. He was severely punished, with a hundred blows and three days and nights of walking naked. But the loss of his bullet changed the fate of the poacher. Instead of being executed, he was tortured and mutilated by two other Kadogo and then released to go and warn villagers against spying. The man left without ears and without one of his arms.

Finally it was Risto's turn. As he pulled the trigger, a bullet flew, a shot was heard, a forehead exploded, a man cried out, a body fell, and praises were heard. Risto had become a true young lion.

Days passed by as the village boys grew into little guerrilla soldiers.

Their clothes had been given back to them. They had learned how to use guns. They had seen how easy it was. They had familiarised themselves with the environment; they knew where the well was, and were the ones sent to bring water and sometimes to do the laundry. There was little trust, though; there was always someone to escort them with a gun when they went to fetch water.

They had learned that a good soldier is awake like an owl, ready to fight at all and any times. A good soldier has acute senses, with an additional sixth sense for instinctive judgements. A good soldier has to listen, and execute the given commands. A good soldier never questions, never cries, even if it is his commander who dies. An army has never been a widow; there are always other commanders to take charge.

They had been told the secret of the jungle: if you want to survive, show no mercy to a stranger. Whoever was not part of them was their enemy, and his fate was death; he was to be killed immediately.

The boys had almost no weapons, except for the machetes a few of them held; others had heavy sticks in their hands. Some had no weapons at all, and carried the baggage and herded the livestock. It was up to each boy to find his own weapon.

'If you kill an enemy, his gun is yours.' These were the words the commander spoke as he caressed his untidy beard. 'No killing means no gun, and you remain vulnerable. It is up to each one of you to get his own firearm.'

It was an equation with ten unknowns; a barehanded boy could not seize a gun from a fully armed and trained soldier – it was foolishness. But the message was simple; they were little Kadogo with lion hearts. And a lion was a king, and powerful.

It was early morning; the camp had settled into a routine. Risto was among the boys supposed to fetch water and wash laundry. They gathered clothes from the General. Two soldiers followed them like a rabbit's tail. Risto had some clothes and a drum that belonged to Néné's cruel husband, a man called Amani, which means 'peace' in Swahili. Risto carried the man's stinking boots, socks and sweaty clothes. They arrived at the well. First they washed the clothes, then they hung them out on the branches of trees before they themselves bathed in the river.

Risto dedicated his time to the shirt he had been given to wash. Benny was there and swimming, but not as he had done in the village; he was still in shock. All was visible on his fragile face. Indeed, all the boys were in shock. The lion-heart tag was in reality an attribute that frightened them, haunted them. How they could come to carry that lion heart, that evil spirit within them, so soon, was the question that confused them all. Killing was evil, a disgusting, shameful thing to perform, and they knew this, but it was still the only way to survive. This was what hurt them, what shocked them, and made them feel evil.

As Benny sunbathed on a rock, he stared at his cousin and best friend Risto, now a stranger to him. Benny no longer saw the Risto he knew, the Risto of tenderness and laughter. He could not believe that Risto had volunteered to perform horrible executions, to torture a human soul. Twice he had been the first to hold the fatal tool. All was confusion and agony for Benny.

So between Benny and Risto, like between all the rookie boys, talk ceased. They communicated with distrustful eyes and suspicious looks, as if the person next to them was an alien predator. They all suspected each other while hiding the traumatising pain of being a child soldier, afraid to show any weakness. The reality was that, in secret, each one cried, each tried to confess his sin to his God, but each knew that he could never be forgiven; he was evil, he was a killer.

When the two boys returned to the camp, each one headed off to return the clothes they had washed. Risto went to a hut at the back of the camp. There was no proper door to knock on, only a cloth curtain. He coughed to announce himself.

'Who's there?' a female voice called. It was Néné.

Risto was careful; maybe the cruel Amani was listening within. 'I have brought back the clothes. All of them are washed, no soap remains.'

'Don't worry, he is not here.'

Néné said her words with a soft voice. She moved to the door frame and looked out at the high trees and creepers that surrounded the camp. The little hut had a low roof; it would have been impossible for Risto to stand straight in it. With the soft wind blowing, the curtain in the doorway danced like a marionette, letting a curious eye peep inside. Risto saw a thin mattress with a dirty cover, once white, now khaki.

Finally Risto dared to look directly at Néné. She wore a new red loincloth with an old white blouse. The blouse was too big for her, leaving her clavicles greeting the skies. She was barefoot. She looked down at herself, at what she wore, then looked at Risto with eyes full of tears. He didn't have a word to say.

'No news from home?'

'No.'

She kept quiet, a heart-devouring moment.

'How are you doing?' he asked, and immediately felt stupid for asking the question.

'You can see my misery on my face; I am helpless.'

'You are strong,' he said, looking at the ground.

He sucked his lips, then showed a shy smile. She tried to smile back at him. It was difficult; tears filled her eyes instead. She tried to hide them by staring at the tall trees all around, but still they came. Suddenly she burst into tears, but even then she tried to keep her voice low as she wept. Risto could bear it no longer; he embraced her as she cried. She sobbed silently into her fingers, which had taken on a dry dirty-white colour.

As she stood in Risto's arms, she seemed to remember something that kept her floating in thought for a moment. She took off her small plaited bracelet, held it tight to her chest, then tied it onto Risto's right arm. She began crying again.

'Sorry, Néné. Please don't cry. Be strong. This will end. We will get over it,' Risto begged her quietly; a loud voice could mean death to both of them. But he knew he was lying to her and to himself. There was no hope of liberation from the hands of these people. It was just a way to keep her faith alive.

'Can you see how much thinner I have become, skin and bones only!' She showed him her slim hands.

'You cry every day, I know.'

'I would rather die than stay in this shack with this cruel man. But he has told me that if I stop crying every day, he will allow me to visit my parents. So I try to stop sometimes.'

Oh, what a crazy hope! The girl was naïve, Risto thought to himself.

They could hear voices coming closer.

'There he is. Go! Run!' she told him as she released herself from his embrace and quickly wiped away her tears.

'I have dropped off your clothes,' said Risto to a face that didn't have time to turn and look at him.

No word. No answer. He walked past Néné's tormentor.

· Chapter 6 ·

Risto was ready. He wore smelly plastic shoes taken from one of the rookies, as well as his dirty white socks. He had borrowed them for the long walk ahead. It would be very long, he had been warned. The General had chosen him and Dumbo, another young Kadogo, as well as others among his soldiers, to go to the mines.

He went to report to the house of the General early in the morning. The men emerged with brand-new equipment; the commander of the mission, Lieutenant Kurega, had a radio, a GPS and a compass.

'Don't come back here if any one of those things is not with you!' the General warned the soldiers.

Risto was handed a new gun.

'Take care of it, bring it back.'

They began walking and disappeared into the forest, heading towards the mines in the Kalahe district, northwest of the Kabare territory. It was only then that Risto understood that the militia was based in the Kahuzi-Biega National Park. A few curious chimpanzees peeped timidly through the bushes at them, while birds' songs eased Risto's sore heart.

He was ready for any assault; he held his gun ready while Dumbo walked brandishing his machete. As they passed the chimpanzees, Kurega told them that the animals made good meat. The boys only replied, 'Yes.'

They crossed swamps and climbed high mountains, sometimes crawling. It wasn't an easy journey. They followed paths marked only by the footprints of people. Each split in a path was an equation to solve, a frightening dilemma; any wrong move could lead them into the territory of other militia. But the map saved them many times; the foreign militia knew the forest better than the locals did.

It was midday when they arrived at the Mbayo mine village in Kalahe. They arrived at a small business centre in the village; a very straight, narrow road ran between a few straw and iron-sheeted houses. The road served as an open market, with tables surrounded by a considerable crowd of villagers. A few soldiers in uniforms were hanging around, relaxing. They greeted the men with Risto and Dumbo; they seemed to know them. The language changed into a foreign one; the five soldiers with Lieutenant Kurega sniggered with their colleagues as Risto looked around the area, familiarising himself with it. The crowd was mostly made up of elderly people selling their crops. The villagers seemed unconcerned; they seemed to be in another country, busy with their activities.

A few metres from where villagers exhibited their merchandise, a barricade blocked the passage to a brick house with an iron roof. Two bored soldiers sat outside while three others stood like president's guards manning the barricade. When Lieutenant Kurega approached, he was welcomed with a king's salute. The bored soldiers stood like statues for a few minutes while the lieutenant spoke through his radio.

Risto was very curious to know what had made his group willing to travel for more than four hours in these vicious conditions. He followed Lieutenant Kurega into the iron-roofed brick house he had commandeered. A bodyguard stood by the door, and a group of soldiers sat inside. They spoke in Swahili. They spoke about holes and money, holes and diggers. They were giving the chief of the militia a report on coltan and gold. The commander of this cohort was named Kahimya. In spite of his long beard, he looked cleaner than the other soldiers. He held a radio in his hands and was surrounded by a triangle of three bodyguards.

Kahimya took Lieutenant Kurega into a chamber where they spoke quietly. Minutes later, the lieutenant came back and ordered Risto to find young men who could carry heavy loads through the forest; they would need very strong men, he was told. Risto didn't know where to start and who to bring, especially if he thought about what their fate could be. He lurked around the market for a while before coming back alone. Inside the house, he found sacks of unknown products lying on the floor of the house. The lieutenant was furious when Risto told him that he could not find any strong boys.

'If you can't find any boys to carry these bags, then you will have to carry them yourself, and if one falls, or you get tired, I'll blow up that stupid head of yours!' Kurega screamed at the top of his voice as he smoked some cannabis. Before five minutes were up, Risto was back with six young men who were older than him, and who looked physically stronger than him.

This time, there had been no arguments and excuses. All he had done was to point his gun at each man and order them to follow him. The villagers knew that simply coughing at the wrong time could mean death at the hands of the militia, and had learned never to hesitate for a second when called. With militia men, killing was even simpler than greeting.

Kahimya was still reporting to Lieutenant Kurega when Risto returned with the young men.

'At each hole, they are giving half of what they extract each day. But those mining gold, they hide what they get. We have zero tolerance for this. If we hear that they got a certain quantity of gold in a hole, and they don't want to pay half, we take everything they have.'

Kahimya looked at Lieutenant Kurega, who didn't seem impressed. He took a breath and carried on, 'Last week, I ordered the killing of a man who didn't want to give half. It has given a lesson to others.'

'To whom did you give the market?' Kurega asked, his eyes narrowed.

'Donald McField, that white man.'

'From Satellite?'

'Yes ... his company. Remember we signed a contract with them last year?'

As chief of the mission, when Lieutenant Kurega spoke to his counterpart, the whole hut kept quiet.

'Are you sure no one takes it somewhere else?' Kurega asked, still with narrowed eyes.

'There is no other place to go. How and where would they pass with it? Our boys are everywhere with roadblocks.' Kahimya smiled, letting his counterpart know how strong and tough he was down there in the Mbayo mines.

'They are obliged to sell to Satellite only. That is the only choice we have given them; whoever tries to sneak it through the forest gets caught by our boys. They get good punishment.' Kahimya's eyes spoke the same tongue as his mouth.

'So how much do you have? How many kilos?' asked Lieutenant Kurega.

'More than fifty kilos of cassiterite, more than 200 kilos of coltan, and a portion of gold,' Kahimya replied, scratching his palms.

'We have taken six young people to transport it to headquarters in the Kahuzi-Biega Park,' said Risto's commander.

'I don't think they will make it. These things are too heavy for so few men.'

'We'll have to make them remember to be strong.'

Lieutenant Kurega's final words were a warning to Kahimya to look after the business; the daily taxes were very important and were not to be held back; he reminded him that they all reported to the hierarchy above.

As orders were given, the six young men bent their bodies to lift what seemed like small bundles of a grandmother's delicacies; to their great surprise and that of Risto, each small sack required the strength of a warrior in order to be moved. After Lieutenant Kurega had warned them, with curses, that the bundles were not their grandmothers' bags of beans and potatoes, and that a falling sack spelled death for its bearer, each one gathered his strength and put the bag on his head, perspiring all the while.

The soldiers left the house, walking together to the end of the village before entering the bush. A fifteen-minute walk led them to the edge of a big stream, which dispersed into many small streams. They followed the main one. Soon they came to a wide-open space. Risto realised that it was a mine, with dozens of tunnels.

A small crowd of young people was busy, some with hammers and chisels breaking rocks, while others were pounding and crushing rocks in an iron mortar. Still more were busy with different sorts of rock-breaking and searching activities. There was another group of younger children, aged maybe ten to fourteen, with plastic basins and sieves, a few of them holding hammers with which they scraped heavy rocks.

Lieutenant Kurega, like the inspector of a ministry, walked under the guidance of Kahimya, who whispered to him in a foreign language. Workers quickened their pace; those with the heavy hammers pounded as if their arms were made of steel. Even the smallest children sped up their sieving movements with a vigour that would have broken any world record. No worker dared gaze at Kahimya for more than half a second. As he passed them, they worked with concentration, almost without breathing, as if they had become robotic machines.

Risto was terrified when he peered into one of the tunnels; it was limitless. Darkness would not allow him to see where it went, until a few men with metallic basins and torches on their foreheads emerged sweating. They looked like the dirt they worked in. This was a coltan mine with its unstable rocks, always ready to fall on an unfortunate body. Soldiers lurked around, watching every single move the workers made.

The group headed back through the forest, travelling snaky paths through everlasting green foliage, crossing streams and water sources of many sorts. The soldiers saw abnormality in any thing that moved. With vigilant eyes, they kept scanning each movement of trees, of tall bushes, of birds and playing monkeys. It showed how much, even though they had become the owners of this park, they were still afraid of it, afraid of the unexpected visitor it might carry in its hidden corridors. They questioned the reason for each monkey sound, why some monkeys screamed so loudly, why the birds made simultaneous movements, and why a bird sang in a specific way at a particular time.

After a while, there was a halt; Lieutenant Kurega gestured for each person to get down and crawl. There had been a loud noise followed by an immense movement of bushes, which had stopped when Kurega and his crew halted. A certain kind of bird signal could be heard again and again. Lieutenant Kurega looked through his binoculars, irritated as the trees in front of him blocked his vision. He gave instructions, dividing his team into three groups. Three soldiers remained behind watching the young men who carried the luggage. Lieutenant Kurega and two other soldiers took the second front line, while the two Kadogo, Risto and Dumbo, were sent forward.

Risto and Dumbo went on crawling on their stomachs and knees. They pulled themselves along with their elbows, sweating, but ready to destroy whoever might be trapping them. Each boy felt comforted by the presence of the other, but when Risto remembered that Dumbo did not have a gun, just a machete, he realised how risky it was to rely on Dumbo to protect him if attack came from that side.

Suddenly, a crackling was heard behind, coming from the group that had remained behind guarding the luggage. The noise scared a group of baboons ahead of Risto and Dumbo. They made a huge racket and left trees moving and swinging. Kurega hooted like an owl, a signal that things were fine and under control. Then he instructed Risto to move forward. With the departure of the baboons, there were no more strange noises or suspicious movements. Risto stood up; he walked towards where they had been expecting to find enemies, and instead found a stand of tender young bamboo where the baboons had been eating. He imitated an owl song, and the lieutenant and his three soldiers appeared.

Again there was a noise coming from behind. One soldier was shouting ferociously. He came forward pulling one of the carrier-boys while waving his gun. 'This rat has swallowed one bead of gold!' the soldier screamed.

'Where is it? Where did you put that gold?' another soldier screamed, a knife in his hand.

'No, no … I don't have any gold! I didn't take any gold,' the boy pleaded with falling tears.

'He should shit here, we will see it!' shouted the man, his knife getting closer and closer to the boy's throat.

'Where is that gold?' Lieutenant Kurega asked as he pulled back the soldier with the knife and made a sign to the one with the gun to lower it.

'Chief, I didn't have any gold. What I eat usually comes back into my mouth, then I chew it and swallow it again ... just like ruminating. That's what happened.' The young man was crying.

The lieutenant ordered calm and commanded his group to keep moving. He knew he was the only one with gold; he was keeping it all in his bag, and even though the practice of swallowing gold and diamonds was common among people of this area, he knew the boy had no gold with him.

But on this side of the world, death was the easiest way to punish and control the villagers. The militia wanted to be feared and revered. Killing was the best way to achieve this. Without the intervention of the lieutenant, the boy would have been killed and his body left for scavengers and other wild carnivores.

Late that night, the group of soldiers and boys arrived at the militia headquarters in the Kahuzi-Biega National Park. The young boys who carried the luggage were lucky to be released, but the idea was simple: they would be needed to carry the luggage again.

The owner of the plastic shoes wanted them back, but Risto refused. He hadn't worn shoes for a month; he couldn't give them back now. On the journey, they had protected him from wild thorns. He would give them back after he got himself his own pair. The other boy began shouting at Risto, but Risto threatened to blast out his brains if he carried on disturbing him. He had a gun, while the owner of the shoes had only a machete. They were people of the jungle, and they applied the law of the jungle. Fight for survival was the motto.

Risto had built his small hut with his cousin Benny and another two Kadogo. It was typical of the militia camps, which had shaky shacks of bamboo and mud. None of the boys could stand up straight in the little hut. Dry grass and straw covered the floor, which was at the same time their beds and seats. They left a small hole in the front wall so they could check who passed by. Risto still had only the blood-spotted shirt and shorts that he had been wearing when he was captured. But he also had a pagne that Néné had secretly given him to use as a blanket.

Two days after the trip to the mines, the General announced that they would attack the villages near the Kahuzi-Biega National Park. He called everyone to the open space in front of the huts and addressed them: 'For those with firearms, take care of your bullets. One bullet, one enemy, otherwise use knives for any other work.' He paused, then added, 'Do not come back if the gun does not come with you.'

It would be a tough and dangerous mission, as it would be far from the forest and near the camps of the Mai-Mai, as well as those of the main rebel movement that controlled the town of Bukavu. But the soldiers were not afraid; they had had better training than the Mai-Mai, and they had fought many times against the main rebel movement that occupied the South Kivu and other regions in the eastern Congo. A lot of Mai-Mai were village boys who had taken guns either because they were forced to, or because they were willing to protect their territory. They did not have much training, but relied on ancestral beliefs and magic.

The main rebel movement, which occupied the town and the surrounding area, was a well-trained army made up of soldiers from neighbouring countries and a few Congolese.

The nearby villages were deserted, and the families that still lived in the area were very poor. They no longer had cattle. No cow, no goat, no sheep, no chickens, no rabbits, and even guinea pigs had become rare, while their fields were empty.

The evening was cold. The moon shone and a gentle breeze blew as they walked to their destination. Risto was in the first line of soldiers. It was his first time on a mission. It was the first time he would turn on his people, traumatise families and break their hearts. He was a real young lion now. The General was fond of him. He had seen Risto volunteering to shoot the poacher, and he had done it so well, using the one bullet, one person method and hitting his target accurately. He had seen Risto getting what many soldiers failed to get right, striking the forehead of a person standing some distance away. Even better, the killing of the poacher had not seemed to bother Risto; he was fine, as calm as if nothing had happened. Those were the kinds of soldiers the General wanted. This was why Risto had been given a firearm and selected to go on the mission.

Benny had been selected too; he would be among the carrier-boys, as he had no gun yet.

There was no sign of life in the first village. The huts were empty; there was a creepy smell in the air; total eeriness reigned. They passed the second village. A small hut fumed a whitish smoke; they moved on. They met a young man with a machete out walking. They questioned him about what he was doing outside at night. He explained that he was searching for a banana tree for his sick father, who craved fried banana. Trembling, he revealed that people didn't sleep in the village anymore; they slept in the fields far from the main paths, or they left in the evening for other villages. He went on to show them the way to the other villages, and was released as they approached one of the villages he had spoken about.

Risto, with three other soldiers, led the way. They hung around in the cassava fields, watching for any movement from the huts of the village. The order went out among the militia; no one was to be allowed to enter or leave the village. As some of them surrounded the village, others went door to door, knocking them down. A group of soldiers went into the compound. Close by the cattle screamed.

'Everyone out! Everyone out!' an authoritarian voice shouted.

Minutes went by as women cried helplessly. Two female voices pierced the sleeping village. A male voice rose up in protest, and another one could be heard shouting, 'Shut up! I will kill you!'

The first group of soldiers returned with cows and goats and made their way back up towards the forest. Another group took over the watch from Risto and his crew, and they rushed to the nearest compound. Here was a sight that was horrible to see. A girl who looked about thirteen was lying on the ground naked and shivering, swimming in what could only be her own blood. Another older woman, maybe her mother, was still in the hands of two soldiers. At first she tried in vain to release her naked body from one half-naked soldier as the other one watched with two guns in his hands, but now she lay barely moving and sobbing.

Risto's companions seemed willing to take on the woman once the other two had finished. A man who seemed to be the father of the family was on the ground. His hands and legs were tied, and he lay still in a bath of blood. Risto rushed into the house. He snatched a bag hanging on the wall; there were clothes inside. From underneath the bed he took two pairs of shoes; he needed them badly. On a table stood a small radio and batteries. He picked everything up and left. As he went outside, the little girl was struggling to move; there was blood on her stomach and over her legs.

He left the compound and took a position outside, close to a path that led to the side of the forest. The second group of soldiers passed by with more cattle. Benny was among this group; he looked after the herd of cows and goats. He had a machete in his right hand and a stick in the left. They made their way towards the mountains.

'Follow me, follow me, Kadogo!' a soldier shouted at Risto.

'And my bag?' Risto asked.

'Drop your dirty bag and follow me, I say!' he screamed.

Risto followed him. They crossed three compounds and reached a fourth.

'These bastards have run away from us, I will show them,' muttered the angry soldier.

He went inside a big rectangular house, which was surrounded with huts. Then he came out again and went into a hut on the left. Smoke began issuing from the rectangular house and the hut. The soldier came to Risto with a twist of straw on fire.

'Take it, quickly. Put it on that hut there.' He gave the burning brand to Risto and pointed to the neighbouring compound. Risto did as he was told. He took the brand and lit the straw roof of the first hut, the second one and the big one in the middle. Then he ran from the compound as the whole place sparked with flames.

A rifle sounded from down near the business centre. Then people shouted. More shots followed. Trouble was in the air. Everyone was alert. The soldiers who were in the compound came running.

The General was already at the scene.

'Get ready, we have to respond,' he said. 'We stay in our positions.' He knew the enemy was the Mai-Mai.

The soldiers squatted down in the cassava fields close by the village while the General went to speak to another group that had positioned itself on a small hill. The shooting continued. The first bullet in response came from Risto's neighbour, a soldier with a Kalashnikov who nearly deafened himself. Risto needed the toilet, but remembered he was in the front line of a battle. He felt dizzy. Little fires flared out in the direction the Kalashnikov noise had come from; these were enemy bullets. The moon shone, but he could still see the red tracers of the bullets as each side fired on the other. There were sometimes screams and hurrahs from down in the valley as the enemy fired their weapons.

Risto lay on his stomach, his eyes focused down where the shooting was resounding. A few soldiers came from the hills, crawling down and spreading all over the wide cassava fields. Risto was shivering, but kept his position while his gun watched the movements in the valley. He was thinking about the number of talismans, gri-gri and mystical spirits a single Mai-Mai would have, as well as the dozens of tattoos engraved on his body. He had even heard that some Mai-Mai left their bodies behind while their spirits went to fight. He kept quiet, shaking as he lay in the field.

The fighting intensified. The crackling got closer and closer. As the Mai-Mai fired, they sang and screamed. Risto's AK-47 was ready, his finger on the trigger. He hadn't yet fired a bullet. He was sweating. Suddenly, a huge noise erupted down the valley, followed by a lot of smoke. A fire appeared on a small hill. After a few minutes, the noise of bullets came from that direction. There must have been Mai-Mai positioned there. Risto imagined how they would scream 'Mai' meaning 'water'; the place would burn to ashes, but they would walk out alive. They never died.

More than thirty minutes had gone by. A group of his soldiers descended quickly, running in the fields, then throwing themselves to the ground. They shot as if it was the end of the world. Risto put his fingers in his ears to soften the noise.

The cassava bushes ahead of Risto were waving. They were fifty metres away from him. He stared, scrutinising each leaf as it moved. He sighted his firearm on the moving leaves. It seemed as though no other military eye saw the movement; the others were focused on what was happening in the valley. The cassava bushes kept waving. At a distance of about thirty metres, a head emerged, like a chameleon in slow motion. It was a man with a gun. Risto couldn't wait – he pulled the trigger. Four bullets left. A scream. Each soldier's gun now followed his eye. Risto breathed deeply as sweat dripped from his face. He couldn't believe his eyes. The wounded man tried to move, and he fired again. This time he struck the man's head.

Risto remained in his position, unable to move. The soldiers who were close by went towards the still body. One picked up the dead man's gun and fired down the valley, but there were no answering shots. This caused vivid fear in each soldier's mind. From their experiences of fighting with the Mai-Mai, they had learned that when a fight stopped abruptly like this, it was the time when the Mai-Mai would find their powers through rituals and sacrifices. The soldiers feared their return.

Risto pulled himself to his feet and went towards the path to regroup with the other soldiers. The chief said that they had to start moving: 'We have to go back in the forest; their return will be fierce. This is the time of their satanic rituals!'

Three soldiers were losing blood. One from his right shoulder; he had covered the wound with a cloth. Another had a cloth that dripped blood wrapped around his right leg.

'Look at that rat!' screamed an angry voice.

Someone was running down the main path towards the valley. He was still within range. His movements seemed familiar to Risto. He moved his head from left to right as he ran, just like Benny did. It was indeed Benny. A soldier cursed and fired several shots at him. Benny fell down.

Risto wanted to run towards Benny, but he knew he would suffer the same fate. But how could he see someone killing his brother without intervening? How could he leave the body of his brother abandoned in a field? He had to do something, but what?

The crackling of guns erupted in the valley once again. Reinforcements had arrived, or maybe the Mai-Mai had reconnected with their world of spirits and power. The General ordered his men to leave some of the cattle to save time, and to return to the forest as fast as possible. Risto held his looted bag on his head while he carried his gun on his shoulder. They ran quickly.

Every step he took, his heart questioned his love for Benny. He had been his best friend. They had enjoyed happiness and pain together. They had thought they would die together. Now he couldn't even fight to bury him! He couldn't think of saving him! He thought of how many times he had betrayed his friends, his dearest friends. He remembered Néné, and now Benny, a brother who had showed him the mysteries and pleasures of life. He ran with his heart breaking.

· Chapter 7 ·

Risto mourned Benny alone in his small hut. He was alone in a jungle of wild beasts. He imagined how he might take his revenge on the soldier who had killed his cousin. Maybe it would happen when the two of them were sent somewhere. Risto would let the man walk in front of him, then he would kill him the same way he had killed the Mai-Mai soldier; he would pull the trigger, force a few bullets into his head. He thought it would be a good idea to stalk Benny's killer. To know his roster, which day he was on night watch, at which position, and with whom. Then he could hide and wait until the man started his shift. With his AK-47, he would open fire and blow off the man's head. He would even shoot whomever the man was on shift with. Of course others would hear the shots, but it would take them time to work out what had happened. They would probably believe that it was the work of a Mai-Mai spy.

Many soldiers disturbed his mourning day with unneeded congratulations for being the hero of the mission; he had killed a Mai-Mai, one of the demons of the forest, as they were called. They praised him, called him a brave lion.

Risto thought about the Mai-Mai he had shot. He wasn't supposed to die. They couldn't die. Maybe he woke up after they left? Maybe he had violated the Mai-Mai rules – by robbing someone or eating the food of a woman. Maybe he had slept with a woman or forgotten his talisman, and that was why he died.

In his shack, he kept his fire going, mixing wet and dry wood to produce a smoke that prevented those who came to bother him with endless messages of felicitation from staying longer than a minute. His mouth and nose also became a chimney, but for cannabis smoke. He had not smoked it before, but now as he inhaled, he saw the world floating like a fallen leaf on a dancing river, and it made his pain float away. Soon he was smoking more than a camp of cannabis addicts could finish in a day.

He was no longer Risto; he began to believe that what the Kadogo had been taught during the training was true. Killing a man was easier than killing a goat. With just one bullet, a man was down, no matter the weight of his body or the strength of his talisman. Risto felt invincible with his gun; he became proud of his ability to use a single bullet to take away a life. He imagined a world that he would soon rule with his gun and his cannabis, how important he would be with his ability to kill with only one bullet, the respect he would earn as the strongest of all the Kadogo.

Already he had begun to forget what had happened only a few days earlier. He had forgotten his life. He had forgotten where he was and who he was with. He had forgotten his pain and his fear. He had forgotten his past and his future. He had forgotten with whom he had come, who was still with him, and who wasn't. He lived in the present. He was neither happy nor sad. He was just there. He took his gun and his cannabis everywhere he went. These were now his only friends, the only ones he needed.

Bisi, his housemate, wanted to know where Benny was. Risto shouted, 'Shut up! If you say his name again, I will shoot you! It's none of your business where he is.'

Later, he threw the borrowed plastic shoes back to their owner; he had his own now, and they were leather. When the owner dared to complain about how dirty they were, Risto took a bayonet and threatened him. The Kadogo started complaining that since Risto had been given a gun, he had become too proud. Risto knew that he had earned his gun; he had proven his bravado, he was a favourite with the General.

They had already conquered the valley of Birava and the surrounding villages. Sometimes Risto was based in Birava for days. People feared him. It was what he wanted; he was not interested in games or jokes. He ran for his gun whenever he was upset. The others gave him the name 'Buhanya', a Mashi word meaning misfortune. That was what he had become: it was unfortunate to have a problem with Risto. If anyone said a bad thing against him, Risto would beat that person until he called to his ancestors.

Soon the chief and his entourage began to assign the cruel tasks to Risto. He was the one they called to carry out punishments, to beat whomever didn't want to pay taxes. He was the one to burn a house if someone from that village had run to give news to the Mai-Mai or the main rebel movement.

Even among the Kadogo, he was the one to punish and to restore order when needed. Whenever he saw someone with a watch or nice clothes, he took them away. The chief praised his charisma and strong spirit, giving him a share of the loot from raids. It seemed as if Risto no longer cared about people, or their weeping and protests. When they cried, he smoked cannabis or drank beer, and then he became fiercer than before. But there was one thing he would not do: he would not take the little girls they captured and terrorised and use them. If anyone questioned this, he would wave his gun, and that would be the end of the matter.

One day Risto was sharing beer with his comrades at the Birava market. Two soldiers arrived dragging a man in his late thirties. He had refused to carry a fifty-kilogram sack of cassava powder that the soldiers had taken from the open market. The man had pills in his hands; he said his daughter was very ill, and he was in a hurry to give her the medicine he had bought her. The chief ordered Risto to handle the situation.

'Rat, put the sack on your idiot head, or I will blow it up with one bullet!' shouted Risto. He had taken to imitating the ferocious voice of the General despite his youth. His voice alerted people all around the market, and they watched. The man put the sack on his head, but after a few steps, he fell down. Risto took a stick and beat the man, but the General was not impressed. He wanted Risto to shoot the man so that other villagers would see and be afraid. For a moment, Risto pretended not to see the gestures the chief was making.

Suddenly, shots sounded; another soldier had shot the man in the head. Blood flew and spattered Risto's face and clothes. The man moved helplessly on the ground. Risto shot him twice in the chest, and he lay still.

In a split second, Risto's entire journey since he had entered the forest revolved in front of his eyes: from the poacher he had killed to Benny's death. The scenario was unbearable. He ran quickly for his beer, then his cannabis.

Néné had become a woman. She wore a loincloth that made her look like a prematurely aged village woman. She had few clothes; most of them were too big for her. Sometimes she tried to smile, but it hurt her bones and flesh; she cried most of the time. It was unusual to see her walking around the camp, but she craved a real bath, so she had decided to go and bathe at the river, like everyone else. She was tired of washing at night from a small bucket. As she walked, trying to forget that she was in the forest, abducted by human monsters, she heard a voice calling her. She looked around, but didn't see anyone. She felt a gentle tap on her left shoulder.

It was Risto. 'I have been following you, calling your name, but …'

'I can't hear, Risto … my pain and suffering have taken all my senses. I only feel, hear, see and touch pain … can't you see?' Her voice carried the moisture of anguish, it was empty of breath. Risto's cruel lion heart never appeared when he saw Néné; with her, he was always tender and kind. That day he was even weak; feared as he was, the careless, tough Risto broke down in front of Néné when he saw her wet eyes, when he heard the sadness in her voice. He held her tight in his arms and felt her heart beat in unbalanced cadences. He had no calming words for her, no healing story to recount to her, no songs of miraculous healing that could soothe her; all he had as therapy, a moment's relief for her pain, were his warm hands and his heartbeat.

So he tried his best to let Néné feel his heart beating, as he felt hers.

And she held him tight in return because he was indeed the only comfort in her life.

Néné thought that Risto's tears were a response to the misery of her appearance – her torn, ill-fitting clothes that left one shoulder greeting the skies, her shoeless and dirty feet, her dry skin. She looked like a skeletal old woman. She wanted to tell him about all the internal pain she felt, all her suffering, but then she imagined the burden of it on his soul. He, too, was a slave like her, a child soldier, a prisoner of monsters. She feared the terrible stories of her life with Amani would become yet more ghosts to haunt Risto.

She had indeed many painful stories to tell. Her daily suffering in the little windowless hut would destroy any human soul, the cruelty her body endured: the pain of Amani's fingers inside her, as he searched for sources of pleasure that could keep him going all through the night. He wanted to be aroused all night long and pleasured all through the day. And so he tried any trick that could harden him so that he could climb back on top of her. He would finger her, he would tell her to turn this and that way, he would swear all kinds of swearing, he would penetrate her with pitiless force, forgetting that she was just a little girl, then he would scream with joy as Néné cried with pain. There would be bruises and bleeding, but Amani wouldn't care. Even little she was always dry, Amani, who had neither tender hands nor sweet stories, would rush quickly to satisfy his selfish desires, leaving Néné bleeding and wounded.

So she wanted to tell Risto all this pain that slept in her heart like an unnoticed fire in a savannah, but in the end, she could not speak. Instead, she held him in silence, listening to his heartbeat.

Footsteps echoed, but neither Risto nor Néné had the strength to release the other. It was Amani, with Lieutenant Kurega and three other soldiers, walking past on patrol. Amani glared at Risto as the boy saluted Kurega. His fierce eyes carried rage and jealousy. Néné left in a hurry for the river. As the group passed Risto, he regretted not having his gun. He made a second promise to himself: to kill the devil Amani.

'You have to wake up, you must go to Mbayo. You know the programme.'

'Yes ... but I am not feeling well,' Risto replied.

'Stop with your story, the chief calls you.'

'I understand, but I am sick.'

'Eh! I'm not joking with you! Go yourself and tell the chief you are sick.'

Then silence. Risto was alone in the hut; Bisi had gone to patrol the forest. The programme had been set a week ago; that morning they were to go to Mbayo village to collect taxes of cobalt, gold and cassiterite. But Risto's last patrol had left his bones shaking; a terrible rain had caught them in the heart of the forest at night. He had returned with strong fever. Now his mouth was bitter and he was dizzy. It was malaria.

'Risto, the chief says you must wake up. He doesn't like lazy people,' the voice rose up again outside the hut.

Risto tried to stand up. He leaned against the makeshift wall and ducked outside. Here he found Amani, the husband of Néné. He was there with two other soldiers and two Kadogo.

'Where is your gun?' asked Amani.

'What for? Is it yours?' Despite his weakness, his hatred for Amani was visible in his eyes and voice.

'I asked you, where is your gun?' shouted Amani, his expression wild. Risto examined the faces of the others; he knew the two Kadogo, and the two other soldiers seemed familiar. He remembered; they had tried to send him and Bisi to fetch water one day. He had refused, and had promised to shoot them one day.

One of them went inside Risto's hut and came out with his gun.

'You must go to Mbayo today,' pronounced Amani.

'Don't you see how ill I am?'

'And you carry on arguing!' Amani's last sentence was followed by a blow.

The rear part of the gun splashed blood; Risto felt the earth turning at 250 kilometres per hour.

'Stand up, you must go to Mbayo,' shouted Amani, fiercer than ever, while pulling on Risto's shirt to make him stand. Risto twirled. Another knock to his head, then a punch. He was on the ground.

'This boy is proud. One day he promised to shoot us,' said one soldier.

Punches, blows and kicks followed like raindrops. Risto lay motionless.

· Chapter 8 ·

Risto wanted to open his eyes, but they were too heavy. He wanted to talk, but his mouth couldn't open. He spoke, but no one heard him. He called Bisi at the top of his voice, but Bisi never responded. He felt hot; there was a sheet covering him. He wanted to take it off; he tried with all his power, but his hands wouldn't move. He heard people talking nearby; how could they not hear his voice? He called again. He screamed and screamed. No one answered. He became angry with Bisi. If he could hear Risto screaming and was not answering him, then he deserved punishment. He would shoot Bisi when he got up, he thought.

He tried to lift his legs, but they hurt. His hands felt sore. What was happening? Was he still dreaming? The time of dreaming was over, he told himself. He wanted to wake up once and for all. He couldn't. He fought and fought, but he couldn't. No one spoke anymore, the place was quiet. He knew Bisi had run away because he was scared of Risto.

'Risto … Risto!' It was a female voice. He had heard it somewhere before; he wanted to open his eyes.

'Risto, are you okay?' the gentle voice asked again.

There was a great flash of light. He closed his eyes, then opened them again slowly. He was in a large room. Then the light became softer, someone had diminished it.

'Risto,' the voice said again.

'Yes. Where is Bisi?' Risto asked.

But no one answered. Instead, the person next to him brought her ear close to his mouth.

'Where is Bisi?' he asked again.

She didn't answer. Her ear came even closer to his mouth.

'Sleep, sleep, Risto,' she said as though she was speaking to a little child. She covered him with the sheet up to his neck. He was powerless to resist.

Time passed; the silence was unbearable, also the heat. Risto knew he couldn't stay in bed the whole day. He fought to wake up, but his body was powerless and full of pain. He managed to move a little. The same woman sat close to him on his bed.

'Risto, it is me, your mother. Can you hear me?'

'Water.'

This time she heard him.

'Where is Bisi?' he asked, as she brought him a glass of water.

'I will tell you later; first drink, my child.'

He wanted to lift himself and sit, but it hurt.

'Wait …' she told him.

She lifted his head gently and took the glass in her right hand. She let him drink slowly.

'Where am I?' asked Risto, when he could speak again.

'In the hospital at Panzi.'

'Where is Bisi?'

'Who is Bisi?'

'The boy who lives in my hut. He should go and get my clothes. He left them at the well yesterday.'

'No, you are in the hospital, Risto. You have left that other place; there is no Bisi here. You will get other clothes. Don't worry.'

'I want to get up.'

'No … you can't. You are badly wounded. You have many broken bones.'

'But I want to go to the toilet.'

'Wait, wait.'

She left quickly. The room was big, full of patients, but most of them were resting or sleeping. The few who were sitting stared at Risto.

'What is that for, Mama?' Risto exclaimed as his mother returned with a tin basin.

'You said you wanted to go to the toilet.'

'Yes. Help me to stand up.'

'No, you can't stand up. You have to use the tin.'

There was someone behind Risto's mother, a man.

'Not to pee, but ...' he said, trying to explain his need.

'Yes, I understand.' His mother looked at his face with pity. 'We will help you.' She pulled the sheet down, and then she lifted him as gently as she could. It was supposed to be a time of relief, but it turned into an episode of great pain as Risto's bones moved and he cried out. Afterwards his mother brought a wet cloth to wash him.

'You haven't washed since you came here; it has been a week now.' She smiled at him. 'I am happy you can speak. How do you feel now?'

'I am okay. How did you reach this place? Did they allow you into the headquarters?'

'No, we are not in the forest. You are in the hospital at Panzi. Sleep; rest a bit. We will talk later.'

Risto didn't want to sleep; he wanted to talk. But if he kept talking, maybe something would go wrong, he thought. He couldn't sleep either; the pain was too strong. He wanted to scratch his legs. There was a flea in his wound that he wanted to take out. But he could not move. It was maddening him. Pain flashed in heartbeat rhythm from his hand as well. He had a fever. He wanted to weep, but he saw people staring, whispering into each other's ears. Risto asked his mother to pull the sheet over his head. As she lifted up the sheet, he saw that he was wearing a green gown without underpants, his entire body wrapped in bandages. Mercifully, he drifted back to sleep.

When he woke the next morning, Risto saw clearly that he was in hospital. At last he understood he was no longer in the Kahuzi-Biega National Park; he remembered what had happened. One night, he had had a fever. Bisi had gone to patrol in the forest, and had left Risto's clothes at the well. Amani, the so-called husband of Néné, had come to his hut early the next morning, bringing two Kadogo and two other soldiers. Risto had been dizzy; he had had to lean against the wall to go outside. Finding him weak, his enemies had grabbed the opportunity and had beaten him. He had tried to resist, but his dizziness wouldn't allow it. Many punches, a hell of knocks, kicks and blows had followed. He had cried and screamed. Then he was down. Then … then … nothing. This was all he could remember.

He tried, despite his pain, to push the sheets away from his face. There was a strong light.

'Risto, how are you? Something to eat?' It was his mother; she was nursing him.

'A bit better. No appetite.'

'The doctor said you have to eat.' She looked at him with a begging eye. 'Banana, milk, tea … just something, Risto.'

'Maybe … banana.'

She peeled a banana and held it out to him.

'Give it to me, Mama. I will try myself.'

'Don't hurt yourself. Hold it by the peel, as you haven't washed your hands.'

He slowly bit into the banana.

'Here is another one,' his mother smiled.

'Water to drink.'

His mother held a cup again.

'How do you feel now?'

'Much better, not as sore anymore.'

A deep silence consumed the time as mother and son looked at each other. Risto realised that his mother had become very thin. But her eyes still held a spark.

'I thank God to see you talk.' Her teeth flashed as her smile made a gap between her lips.

Despite his pain, his mother's shining smile made Risto want to cry with joy. But then ghosts flashed into his mind. He was back in the forest; he could hear flying bullets and see Benny running and running, only to fall. Tears ran from his eyes. His mother came close to dry his face and to comfort him, but the news Risto whispered tore her apart. First her eyes shone, then her mouth widened wordlessly, then she held her shaking face in her hands and sobbed. She tried to hold back her cries, but the magnitude of her sorrow was too great to be contained by her mouth. She called Benny's name, and in her dialectic tongue, she asked the heavens why only her children should suffer and die this way. All eyes in the room were on Risto and his mother, and a nurse came to lead her outside.

A day had passed since Risto had opened his eyes. The story of his recovery had travelled beyond the spheres of family and friendship. Many did not know whether to rejoice or to grieve that of the two boys, only Risto had returned from the forest alive.

Landu was one of the many touched by Risto's story. He was a distant cousin the same age as Risto. His family stayed in Burinyi village. It produced a lot of gold, coltan and cassiterite, like many other parts of South Kivu, and for that reason, it had attracted many armed groups. Each group wanted to control the mines, and each militia used children as soldiers to work and fight for them. Landu was a runaway child soldier. He had served in a Congolese militia controlled by Major General Simba Kali. No one knew Simba Kali's real name; he had taken a ferocious name, 'fierce lion', as a form of psychological intimidation.

Landu had worked for Simba Kali as a carrier of looted goods and as an informant in the market. Landu had managed to escape while his platoon was under attack from another militia. He had walked many days and nights and ended up in Bugobe village. From there, he had relocated to Bukavu to rebuild his life. Risto's family had agreed to take him in and pay for his studies. As soon as he heard the story of Risto, he felt deep pity for his cousin and wished to contribute to the restoration of his life. He believed they had many things in common: a beautiful childhood, ugly teenage years, and hopefully a future to look forward to.

Landu volunteered to take over from Risto's mother at the hospital. Besides the on-duty nurses and the doctors, families preferred to send their own person to look after the sick in hospital, to be a 'guard' as they called them.

The first day that Landu sat by his cousin's bed, Risto slept all day and barely noticed his new friend, except at those moments when he needed something. Landu responded obediently, and showed care in everything he did for Risto. The second day, after a morning of quiet, their conversation grew in the afternoon. Risto had many questions; this was what Landu wanted, he wanted to connect with his cousin, he wanted to help him at this difficult time. He guessed at some of what Risto might have endured, and he knew how hard it was to rebuild after such experiences.

'So, how many days have I been in here?' Risto asked, as Landu brought him a glass of water.

'About ten days.'

'Ten days? A long time ... which hospital is this?

'The hospital at Panzi. That ex-military camp of Panzi, remember?'

'Yes, I remember. Tell me, how did I reach this place?'

Landu stared at Risto's face, then looked away. 'I don't know ... but what I have heard is that you were found by poachers in the Kahuzi-Biega National Park. You were unconscious, with wounds all over your body. They thought you were dead, then they saw your chest moving. No one thought that you would survive. It is a miracle to see you alive.'

The story amazed Risto, but he kept quiet for a moment.

'Yes ... I only remember being beaten up by Amani and his friends. They wanted to kill me.'

Landu stayed quiet, wanting to hear more of the story, but Risto had no more to say. He realised that he had started a story that he didn't wish to speak about.

But his journey from the Kahuzi-Biega National Park to the Panzi hospital was indeed a miraculous one, as Landu had said. Since the day Amani had caught Risto holding Néné, he had wanted to devour the boy in a passion of hatred. He saw Néné as his personal property, and didn't plan on sharing her with some rubbish Kadogo. But he knew the General's eyes were on Risto all the time, and also that the boy was never without his AK-47. So it was a perfect opportunity when he found Risto weak and unwilling to go to Mbayo village. He and his friends beat the boy swiftly and brutally, and as soon as they believed he was dead, they carried him deep into the forest and dumped him, knowing that the scavengers and other carnivores would thank them for a great meal. Amani knew that once Risto's absence was noticed, the General would believe his young lion had tried to escape, and no investigation would be made.

It was a group of poachers coming to check their traps who found Risto. First they thought he was dead and were about to leave, when one of them saw his chest moving. His colleagues could not believe that someone with so many wounds could still be alive. Even if the boy was still alive, surely he was on the point of death. But it wasn't in their culture to see a man in dire need of help, even if he had only minutes to live, and to leave him alone and unattended. Their moral code obliged them to take him to the nearest place of help.

They carried him to the nearest village clinic, which was eerily empty, as most of the doctors and nurses had fled the insecurity and violence of the countryside. An exhausted nurse was looking after a woman with a complicated pregnancy, which was beyond her humble ability to manage. An ambulance came only once a week, and the pregnant woman could no longer wait. So a farmer took both the pregnant woman and Risto to the Panzi hospital in his pick-up truck. Everybody believed that both patients would die before they had travelled one kilometre beyond the village, but it was as if death was afraid to come into their bodies, and they made it to the hospital alive.

Soon afterwards, Risto's mother was visiting with her church group, to offer prayer and comfort to the sick and dying. She could not believe her eyes when she saw the unconscious face of her son in one of the rooms. She sat by his side day and night, praying and singing to him, urging him to wake up.

'So ... who is Amani, and why did his friends beat you? If I may ask?' Landu was hesitant.

'How is my uncle and the entire family back in Burinyi?' Risto asked, trying to run away in his mind from the forest and the story of his beating.

'They are all doing fine ... just living under fear every day. Burinyi is full of militia too ... so one fears for one's life each second.'

Landu rolled up the sleeves of his shirt. He had two dark marks on his left biceps. He pulled his shirt up, showing scars that ran in an almost straight line across his right ribs.

'All these ... I got them in Burinyi,' he said with a smile that intrigued Risto. He was suddenly curious about this man who exhibited his marks and scars.

'All these, I got them in battles.'

'Who were you working for?' Risto asked.

'Simba Kali was my general.'

'You escaped? You were not shot at?'

'We were losing the battle, we had lost our platoon commander and his assistant had been wounded ... I knew it was my chance.'

They remained silent for a moment, as if each one was remembering his own battles.

'I heard that you lost your cousin Benny in battle in the forest.'

Risto remained silent for a moment, then made a sign of acknowledgment. Landu wanted to hear more about Risto's journey; he knew that talking was the only way one could heal and come to terms with the horrible memories, but Risto seemed reserved, shut off.

He went on to tell Risto about his own experiences in the forest. He was one of hundreds of children in Burunyi who had joined the Mai-Mai movement in order to remain alive and to protect their families. A family who did not have a member who was a soldier was vulnerable to victimisation. Landu spoke first of his experience as a carrier of looted goods and an informant in the market. Then he spoke more slowly of his history as a fighter, a rapist and maybe even a killer. He had fought many battles, but had never come face-to-face with any of his victims; he never knew if his bullets had taken lives or not. His greatest regret was being involved in the rape of a girl in a village controlled by rival militia.

After this long litany, he told Risto how he had come to terms with his terrible journey: 'I never wished to commit any atrocity; I was forced to do so. So I shouldn't blame myself. I have come to understand that I am not a naturally evil person. We human beings are born to do good, but corrupt environments try to change our nature. But if we get a second chance to be who we are meant to be, we should reclaim our natural identity and be good people again.'

Risto listened with great interest. He could relate to Landu's story. He could feel this shared connection with his cousin, and wished he could talk about his experiences too, but he was still afraid of what Landu would think of him. His crimes were far worse than Landu's. He regretted that he could not open his mouth to utter a single word to trace his journey in the forest. His history was so dark that it would frighten the strongest of human souls. How could he begin to tell a story of so much evil, so much betrayal and so much pain? There were so many loads on his soul that he knew he would never be free. He thought of Benny over and over, wishing he had had a chance to talk to him, to explain that he was not evil, that it was the forest that had changed him. The law of the forest had hardened his soul so that he could survive. He wished he'd had time to tell Benny that he was still the Risto of their youth, the innocent boy who wished nothing more than laughter over the wonders of life and the mysteries of the village. But Benny had died holding onto the image of the cruel Risto, the young lion with an evil soul. This thought haunted Risto.

But he was able to open up a little; he shared with Landu his happier memories of his early childhood. It was still too painful to think of Benny and their life in the village.

As Risto and Landu spoke, their sick neighbours and their visitors looked at them as if they were new masterpiece paintings; their eyes stared, as their mouths whispered to each other. Risto knew they were the subject of gossip. 'Do people know that you were a child soldier?' he asked Landu.

'Some, but not everyone.'

'In our street?'

'Yes, they know.'

'What do they say?'

'I've shown them my scars and told them about my bad experiences in the forest. They feel pity for me; many see me as brave for escaping.'

Landu's story did not take away Risto's fears. Their experiences were different; they had worked for different militia groups. His had been a foreign militia, and they were the most evil of all; many people knew and hated how the foreign militia treated people who lived near the forest.

'So … you said people felt pity for you … even when you told them about the rape story?'

'No, I didn't talk about that one.'

They looked into each other's eyes. Risto understood that even Landu was still afraid of his dark past; it was impossible to share all, he told himself.

'So, what are you doing now?' Risto asked.

'Studying. I am carrying on with high school. I want to become a journalist,' said Landu with a vivid smile.

How could Risto have known how many months he had spent in the Kahuzi-Biega National Park? Days and nights there were all the same. A week, a month or months were just days and nights in a row; the only difference was when there was a moon, and when there wasn't. There was no Easter, Christmas or New Year in the forest. Today was no different from tomorrow. They went to the well, they washed clothes, they went to patrol the forest, they returned to their huts, they ate their stolen meat, and they did the same again the next day. The story was always the same. Some days they killed people; that was the only thing that made any difference to their days.

As the forest had no calendar, the hospital had none too; there was neither day nor night in the hospital. Risto closed and opened his eyes to the flash of a strong light. He asked that the lights be switched off at night. Some of the patients in the ward agreed, but one man, who was hidden in a small kind of house, refused. This man cried like a baby every day. He didn't want the lights to be switched off for any reason. Every single hour he called his guard, but would say only, 'I want you to be here.' Sometimes he would ask his guard to scratch him somewhere. But the guard could not do so; the man's whole body was wounded and bandaged. He had been involved in a car accident that had burned away most of his skin and flesh, so the doctors had built a toy house around him to protect him from flies. He was like a tortoise; the toy house was like his shell, with only his head sticking out. People called him 'the tortoise man'.

Nearby was another patient, as strange as his untidy bed. He didn't talk to anyone. He was always quiet. He only spoke to the doctors. They said he was paralysed. He was a gold-digger. He had been in a mine tunnel with his torch attached to his head, his dirty clothes and his basin, searching to become a rich man within a week; then he found gold, a really big piece of gold. He decided to leave the site, come down to Bukavu, and buy a house near Lake Kivu in the centre of town. He was nearly out when the tunnel collapsed around him; stones fell and buried him. Other diggers came to his rescue. He was saved, but paralysed. His gold was taken by one of his rescuers. He lay on his bed thinking about how he could have been a rich man.

Risto's father came often to visit his son; his best friend Papa François was always with him. Despite their constant arguments about culture and customs, modernism and the lifestyles of their people, theirs was a good friendship that looked more or less like a brotherhood. Mahuno was a family man, deeply rooted in his African heritage, and he never stopped telling Papa François that he was part of the lost breed of the continent, the uprooted Africans who had been left halfway between worlds by Western culture. Papa François hated the African 'football families' of ten children, and disliked the African courtesy of people looking on the ground while somebody talked to them. As a fan of Western culture, he introduced himself as Papa François, even to his own children. He refused to be called Baba Mao, his traditional name, as his firstborn was called Mao. Both men, however, shared a dislike for the unstable political landscape of their country and the troublesomeness of the Great Lakes region. They also hated the new, so-called 'rich boys', who never ceased taking each other to court because of land disputes or paternity rights.

The two visited Risto frequently. They always came with unfinished discussions about Africa versus the West.

'I always like your opinion, young man,' Papa François would say whenever Risto made a comment that favoured his argument. He would tell Risto's father, 'Your boy should study politics. These are the people who will save this continent from our brainless politicians who have been unable to create intelligent and strategic international policies that would benefit the continent.'

'François, I am very proud of my boy. Don't you think he is the new Renaissance man?' Mahuno would respond as they both laughed and patted Risto. It seemed as if they shared him; they were both his parents because of the love they showed him.

· Chapter 9 ·

Risto could move both his hands and legs with less and less pain; his mother would have slaughtered a cow for celebration if she'd had one. Risto's father brought him geography books, world history books, a few novels and a small radio so he could listen to the news.

The number of his visitors increased. At first it was between four and six visitors a day; now it grew to ten or fifteen. On Sundays, they came in their dozens. Some of them didn't even get a chance to see him. Each one came with something in his or her hands: foufou or ugali with Sambaza fish, the most special fish of the Kivu region, taken from the lake. Others came with foufou and meat, or foufou with different types of vegetables. Others brought Sombé – cassava leaves pounded with spices. Some brought bread and fruit, and some came with money. No one would have paid a visit empty-handed. It would have been a sign of discourtesy, unless one was experiencing terrible financial problems. Even if one brought just one big avocado or one juicy mango, it would be enough. The hospital didn't provide food for the patients, so patients relied on the food brought by visitors or made by their relatives. Visits and food to a patient were also a debt to the patient and his family; if that person got hospitalised, he knew these people would visit him with food too.

Some people came to visit Risto's neighbour empty-handed, and the boys couldn't understand it. Didn't he get even two sweet potatoes? As more visitors came, and more food was delivered, Risto donated some food to others in the ward who didn't get any gifts from their visitors.

Landu was very happy when he saw church representatives coming to visit sick people. When he heard that even prisoners were fed by religious people, he was amazed. There is always a stranger without family or friends who needs help, he kept repeating. He knew that each Sunday morning, patients received visits from religious people who came to pray for them. Many believed that diseases came from Satan and other people possessed by evil spirits, which needed to be thrown out by prayer. Maybe it was someone's last hour on earth, maybe their disease or wound couldn't be cured, and those patients had to be prayed over. They prayed for the delivery of those with sin, for those who didn't know God to be saved.

One morning, the tortoise man in his toy house had made Landu laugh until he cried. The tortoise man was always afraid – afraid that a jealous aunt had bewitched him and caused his car accident. After he dreamed his guard was chasing him with a knife, he refused to eat the food the man had cooked, even though he was his own brother. That day, he had called a pastor and told him of his fear, that he felt he was about to die. The pastor told him that if he had faith in God, he wouldn't die. He argued, asking the pastor how many saints had died while they had faith in God. He asked the pastor where Peter, Luke, John and all those other people in the bible were. They had died even though they had faith. Was his faith bigger than that of all those people? The pastor prayed for him anyway.

The day came for Risto to stand up for the first time under the watchful eye of a nurse. Landu held the crutches for Risto as his mother came with a wheelchair. Risto no longer wore a green gown; he had changed into a boubou made from a piece of cloth brought by his mother. The boubou covered his remaining bandages without hurting him.

Risto refused the wheelchair; he wanted to show his family that he could stand up, like a hero. He stumbled and a flash of pain went through his bones; he felt dizzy, then leaned on his mother's shoulder. Her celebrative voice was in each onlooker's ear. She told everyone how her son, who had once had little hope of walking, would soon walk again. She became even more excited when the doctor told her that her son might be able to leave the hospital within a week.

Risto was torn between happiness and fear. If freedom from a hospital bed meant liberation and a return to normal life, it might also be his ticket to hell, or even a journey along suicidal paths. What if he bumped into someone from Birava village, someone on a business trip, a family visit, maybe even running away from the militia? What would happen to him if his past was exposed?

Risto sat on the grass outside the hospital beside Landu and his mother, the green grass his seat and bed. The world seemed different; it was quiet and clean, peopled by loving and caring people. He looked at the streets, the hills; things seemed brand new again. Only one week was left before he would go back to those streets. Would he reconnect with his old friends? Would they welcome him? Darkness was falling; the hospital bed was calling.

Landu was fast asleep beside his cousin when Risto's body, like a melting iron bar, burned him; his sweat was as hot as steam from a boiling pot. His entire body moved in an endless earthquake.

'What is going on, Risto? You are burning up!'

'Call the nurse, I am dying,' said Risto, shaking.

Landu couldn't run fast enough. Suddenly a towel soaked in cold water shocked Risto's face. It started to take the malaria fever from his skin and brought him a bit of relief. Landu came with another soaking towel; he took off Risto's robe and spread the towel over his chest.

Risto felt the bed moving, turning. His head was about to explode. He had escaped the rage of the militia in the Kahuzi-Biega National Park, only to be killed by malaria. He closed his eyes, waiting for death. Nearby, a voice was speaking urgently to a nurse. The nurse approached Risto and asked how he was feeling. The nurse had lost his senses, Risto thought; couldn't he see how badly he was suffering?

'Carry on soaking him; it will help,' the nurse told Landu.

This time it was as if Landu had poured a bucket of water onto Risto. The cold wet towels dripped; the bed was a pool of sweat and water. The nurse came back. He gave Risto an injection and attached a drip.

Risto felt low. The hospital had become a tiresome place. Visitors were no longer very regular. Many knew that he was supposed to have left the hospital by now. He had discovered a nice spot to spend the late afternoon, a bench in the garden of the hospital. He sat here to watch the moon take over the day from the sun. His wounds were almost dry, but he still had a permanent bitterness in his mouth and no wish for food. His malaria was at the verge of disappearing, surely it was a matter of days, but the doctor wanted to keep a close-eye on him nevertheless.

Risto sat on his bench looking at a young girl in the garden playing with a baby. The baby boy, bare-bottomed, was crawling; he couldn't walk yet. The girl would throw a ball, and then the baby would crawl quickly to retrieve it, screaming with joy.

The girl looked over at Risto and smiled, and he humbly returned a smile. She approached him, her eyes looking aside.

'Sorry, may I ask you something, please?' she said with shy courtesy.

'Yes, no problem.'

'Did you see a pastor here before I arrived?'

'A pastor? No, but it is not easy to know if a person is a pastor or not.'

'I don't know if you are from here and would know him ... he preaches early in the morning and prays for sick people in the hospital rooms.'

'I don't know which one you are talking about, we are visited by more than three pastors a day, and they are not the same each day. But I haven't seen anyone looking like a pastor out here today. I am sorry.'

The girl's Swahili was spiced with the Mashi dialect, and her discoloured, torn loincloth made her look like a villager. Her slippers were hooked on with wires, and Risto wondered if the wire didn't hurt her toes. Her naturally chocolate skin seemed to be craving lotion; it had gone khaki. The baby playing on the lawn was barefoot.

'Was there something important with the pastor?' Risto asked.

'Yes, we had an appointment here.'

'Pastors have a lot of people to see, maybe he met someone else ... be patient.'

She stared at the sky, as if to say that the night was approaching.

'When were you going to meet?'

'At 6pm.'

'He might still come. It is not yet late, we still have the sun.'

The sun was setting over the mountains in the west, in the direction of Kabare territory.

'Oh, such a cute boy! Where is his mother?'

The girl looked at him as her face changed. She sucked her lips for a moment. 'He is my baby.'

She passed her left hand over her face like someone drying sweat, but it was tears she was wiping. The answer hung in her mouth; she wasn't proud to be a mother. Risto was quiet; he understood that she hated who she was.

'I dreamed all my life of furthering my studies. I wanted to go to college, to get a degree, I dreamed of becoming a nurse. But the dream was thrown away and burned to ashes …' She lowered her face to dry her tears.

It had always been very difficult for a young girl who fell pregnant to carry on with her normal life in the South Kivu. Often a girl would drop out of school, unable to cope with the gossip and bother coming from her classmates. Some school principals would not allow a pregnant girl to remain at her desk, fearing she might become a distraction to her class. The girl would be marginalised, stigmatised and finally rejected. Her family would often believe that she had disgraced them.

The girl had stopped weeping, but her eyes were still dropping tears, 'My name is Mina. I am not from this town; I am from Kalahe village where no one lives anymore except those bloody armies. Right now, we are staying in the village of Luhoko. Yes, I dreamed of becoming a nurse one day but today I am nursing the child of a snake. Whenever I think about this, I feel like … but I don't have the heart of a killer. If I had, I would have thrown this child into the forest or the lake. This child is a curse, a shadow that my heart carries every day.'

Risto, who had at first thought he might cheer Mina up, was now sweating. Her story made him deeply uncomfortable, and even worse, there was a third person hovering. His voice echoed on the wind's rhythm, it whirled. An ironic and horrible laughter followed when he saw the person behind Mina. The voice, the laughter came from his mirror image, a Risto whose body floated in the air.

'Kill her, stab her … she knows all about you,' taunted the other Risto.

As he stared at himself, Mina continued her story, explaining how her family had given everything they had to the militia. But the militia wanted more. Mina was thirteen years old. Five men, three times her age, left her unconscious on a moonless night, naked in her family's yard. She became bitter as her dreadful memories overflowed. 'Oh, the cruelty of these dogs! Why didn't they kill us so that we don't have to live like this? Will we ever regain our dignity? My shame is here, in this child with his five faces – who is the father? How can I ever know?'

'It's you she's talking about. It's you she hates,' said the ghost Risto, with his nasty laugh.

Mina's cries were like calls for Risto's death. He didn't deserve to live; he had stood by, even helped, as this had happened to his people. A breeze passed, and for a moment, a freezing silence cooled the garden. Risto saw the ghost-Risto holding the little baby in his arms while the mother, Mina, leaned on that ghost's shoulders.

That night was unusually cold. Risto had covered himself with sheets to call sleep, but no sleep came. He wanted to forget the story of that day. He begged for the lights to be switched off, and this time even the tortoise man agreed. He begged for absolute silence, and it was given. The silence of the shuttered room became indescribably eerie. He desperately needed deep sleep. One hour passed; he was still awake with his eyes closed. He avoided thinking; he wanted his mind to remain blank. When something would appear in his head, he would open his eyes to let it go. However, something refused to leave him, making the night unbearable. He opened and closed his eyes quickly; there was something hanging around that he couldn't see, but he could feel, the echo of a female voice crying. Perhaps it was Mina, the girl he had met that evening? The echo seemed to come from far away, maybe from the mountains. A voice came on the breeze, carrying a story. It cried and mourned, growing louder and louder.

'Can you hear it too?' Risto asked the tortoise man's guard, who seemed to be staring at him in the dark.

'What? Are you dreaming?'

The voice he could hear faded, but now Risto felt the staring of a strange figure. The story of little Mina had awakened ghosts from his past. Risto threw back his sheets, restless in the quiet room, with everyone else asleep. Only the tortoise man moved in his shell made of cloth. Risto took the glass of water from his bedside table and drank, then sat on his bed.

· Chapter 10 ·

Risto's sisters surrounded him. The youngest, Zaina, was in his arms; she leaned on his chest and looked at her sister Pendo, who stared at their brother as though he were a newborn child. They examined every single scar. They would run fighting to give him the glass of water, or plate of food he had requested. Advised by their parents, they avoided asking him questions about his mysterious time in the jungle of the Kahuzi-Biega National Park.

Every day since their brother and Benny had been kidnapped by the militia, they had cried with their mother, thinking they would never see him again. They had missed him, but their mother had helped them by driving them to work hard at their studies. She had become very strict and wouldn't tolerate the slightest mistake. So both girls had done well at school.

Landu, who had arrived in Risto's family to resume his studies, had become a best friend to Risto's two sisters, and this had helped the ache of his absence a little. He was kind to them, told them beautiful stories and played the most beautiful tunes on his flute. The gentleness of his melodies, the tenderness of their rhythms, and the peace they brought to the heart of each listener was what had sealed the great friendship and strong brotherhood between Landu and the girls. He had become so attached, so close to the entire family, a visitor would have thought that he was born and raised with them.

Each evening, the family looked forward to Landu's musical performances. He mostly played his own compositions, except for a few ballads he had learned from his teachers. He played his flute in many different ways, his fingers caressing the instrument as he let his breath transform into sweet melodies of great magnificence. The beauty of his melodies had led Zaina and Pendo to become background singers. They sang to his melodies, whispering at first, then with angelic voices. And this way he had contributed to the healing of the family; his music brought hope of a better tomorrow, and his presence gave them the love that they needed. Of course they missed Risto, but things would have been worse without Landu.

Zaina told Risto in a sad and soft voice that Néné didn't live in town anymore. She had been kidnapped by the foreign militia; no one knew if she was still alive or not. Pendo gave her sister a fierce look; she wanted Zaina to stop her stories. The younger girl stopped speaking and looked down.

'She is alive,' Risto said sadly. 'Maybe one day she will come back,' he added, even though he did not see how this was possible.

His sisters looked at one another with amazement, but did not say more.

Days passed by as Bukavu, the town where a story travels like wind, gossiped about a child soldier, a militia boy who had come back from close to death. The supposedly secret story travelled the streets faster than a storm; it caught each ear along its way. A wife would tell her husband, he would relate it to his closest friends, who would in turn recount it to their wives, who would debate it in the open market of Kadutu.

Néné's mother came to ask Risto questions about her daughter. Each one of her words carried tears, and when she thought about the fate of her daughter, she tore at her hair, pulling tufts out. Risto didn't know how to describe the situation with the militia; it was torture to recall, and he wept at the horror of it. Eventually, he told Néné's mother how her daughter cried every day in the forest, how they had been taken, and how he had been rescued. He didn't have words to describe the evil man who had taken Néné as his wife; and because he did not want to kill the woman with the full story, he said little, trying to keep his account as broad as possible. The few words that Risto did say made the woman mad with grief; she threw herself to the ground, screaming. She cried out, imploring, why this had happened to her, to her daughter? Risto didn't have an answer; he had the same question, and he never knew who to ask it of.

Two weeks after arriving home, Risto was still barely able to leave the house. The experiences he had when he went out frightened him. Twice he had left for the market, but was unable to finish his shopping. He could not explain why. He had sensed an omnipresent person following him, but whenever he looked behind him, the person hid. He could tell no one about the creature in empty streets and corners; it might make them wonder about his past, about his healing, or perhaps they would think he was going mad; no one would take him seriously.

Risto's mother wanted him to meet people, to talk to his friends and to visit family members. She wanted Risto to start a new life, socially and mentally. She was particularly displeased because he kept postponing visits to his uncle at the last minute.

This time, she was serious; the visit to his uncle had to take place. He was a successful businessman who stayed in the Avenue du Gouverneur, one of the richest suburbs in Bukavu. Risto knew what he needed to avoid along the way; eeriness and empty paths and gossiping women who hung around the streets looking for slander and lies. The plan was simple; in order to avoid walking and talking, he would get a moto-taxi.

The main road was about a hundred feet from his home; he waited there for a moto-taxi. It was a sunny morning. The first moto-bike passed, the motard leaving a cloud of black smoke behind. He didn't look around. He had a fat woman on his bike. Another one passed, a young woman on the back. It was moving more slowly than the previous one, perhaps because the customer had a child on her lap. Two women who saw shouted at the woman with the baby and her motard. How could she carry a child on a dusty road with a crazy motard!

Motards were cursed every day by elderly and conservative people. They were hated for their way of driving, and the noise and trouble they created in the streets and roads of Bukavu. The roads had merely the colour of tar, covered with a thick layer of dust, but the motards didn't consider it dangerous to speed along these so-called roads. They would drive as fast as they could in the dust, hooting a horn that could destroy a person's eardrum. They cared less about getting fined by the police. What mattered to them was the attention and esteem of other motards. Each motard wanted to be known as the master driver, and so they never respected the laws of the almost non-existent roads. They would make up roads where roads never existed, and passed where this was forbidden. Even in the midst of many people in a narrow space, they would pass, hooting insistently, while pushing and knocking human bodies.

For the elders and all true Bukavians, the most abhorrent thing about the moto-taxi industry was its growing popularity. Many women now used moto-bikes as their preferred means of transport, even though their husbands and fathers judged this unacceptable. They could never understand how women could bear the reckless driving of the motards. The design and size of the motorcycles themselves left women in an uneasy situation because of the clothing they wore. Most women wore pagnes or loincloths which easily left their bodies exposed once seated on the moto-taxi. Men thought this was intolerable. And the danger of an accident was always imminent. The motard would drive fast, racing against the wind, and the customer could cry and curse and scream, but the motard would not slow down until the final destination was reached.

The motard who stopped for Risto was young, as most of them were. He wore fashionable expensive pants, shoes and a shirt, with a brand-new cell phone hanging from his neck. This was typical. Motards used the money they earned to show off to girls and to impress their colleagues, showing that they were not afraid of spending. Each motard wanted to show that he was a cut above the rest, and richer than his peers.

'Where to?'

'Avenue du Gouverneur,' Risto said.

'300 francs Congolais.'

'No, 150 francs.'

'Make it 250,'

'I only have 200.'

He had more, but bargaining was like a genetic disease in this part of the world and Risto couldn't help it.

'Where to exactly?'

'The third house, near the governor's.'

'Fine.'

Every ten seconds, Risto passed a motard and his client. This wasn't the case before he had left Bukavu; there had been a moto-taxi revolution while he was away. He realised that he had spent a long time in the jungle and hospital; many new things had happened. The motard hooted as he reached one moto-taxi station and held down his clutch to make a loud noise. His colleagues hooted back. The wind was stinging Risto's ears and eyes. He had to clear them with his hands.

He heard a voice singing his name. He looked all around, but could only see motards and their clients, taxis and private cars, and a few people walking. No one seemed to be singing. Then he saw her; a young girl, fourteen or fifteen years old, with a child on her back. She wore old-fashioned clothing. She was neither on a moto-bike nor in a car, but she was moving fast – she was being carried by the wind. At first she was in front of them, then she fell behind. She yelled at Risto, she cried and sometimes sang. Then she was in front of them again.

'Do you know her?' Risto asked the motard, slapping him on the back.

'Eh, stop it, stop it! Know who?'

'The girl with the child on her back?'

'Where did you see her?' The motard held his anger in his teeth.

'Look … look! Look in front of us!'

'Am I not looking in front of us? Do you think I am looking behind? Eh, man, one more time and you are off my moto!'

The girl had gone and the voice had died. Even so, a mysterious creature was drawing closer to Risto. He could feel its breath on his neck.

'Okay, okay, drop me here!' he yelled in the ears of the motard.

'This is Nyawera, we are close to Avenue du Gouverneur.'

'No, no. Drop me here. Drop me, please!' He was desperate to jump off the motorbike.

The motard stopped and drove off after Risto had paid. The omnipresent creature was still there, behind Risto's back; this time it was spying on him. It was following him, Risto could feel it. At first he thought it was a man, but then he felt it was a woman. But why was he or she following him? He felt insecure. He needed to get home as soon as possible. There were many routes to take, but at each corner, he was afraid that the person would be waiting for him.

Risto decided to stick with groups of people, not to be alone. He took a seat among a dozen people on the CINELAC company compound. Some of them were eating, others discussed politics, and a few others watched the motards at the moto parking lot of Nyawera.

Half an hour passed. It was around 2pm. Risto bought ten bananas; he dropped three in the hands of a blind man who sat close to the wall. He hated the rebel movement, the blind man kept shouting. He would use whatever means he could to defeat the rebel movement that divided the country. He was patriotic and ready to die for his country. Risto sat and listened to the tirade. Then he heard a man's voice whispering in his ears.

'Go, give the medicine to my daughter, she is very sick.'

He was startled. He looked around; no one was close to him, so he pretended that nothing had happened while his eyes went east, west, north and south. No one else in the crowd seemed to have noticed. He shook in agitation, looking in all directions.

'My daughter is very sick, give the medicine to her. You did not let me give her these pills. Go, go, she needs her medicine.'

The voice shook Risto's bones. He wanted to flee and took the road that headed up around the main building of the Institut Supérieur Pédagogique, but was confused about the direction and soon found himself back at the point he had started from. He went to the edge of the Avenue du Gouverneur; the traffic was too fast for him to cross.

He went back again, this time following the road going to the high school Atheneé D'Ibanda. This didn't seem safe either, and he found himself back among the people endlessly debating politics. No one in the crowd seemed interested in his crazy movements, except for a shadowy mysterious creature that peeped from a faraway corner. He had taken almost all of the six roads that split at Nyawera junction, but none of them seemed to be right; and besides, they all carried mysterious blinking eyes in their corners. Risto was lost in his own town. He jumped into a taxi, the fifth passenger in a white Toyota Corolla. The driver was heading towards the Atheneé D'Ibanda. They passed by the office of the Mayor, la Mairie as they called it, and headed down Feu-Rouge.

'Where do we stop?' the taxi driver asked; two passengers still remained in the taxi.

The woman in the front seat said she wanted to be dropped off at Feu-Rouge.

'Where are you going, driver?' Risto asked.

'Eh! Where are *you* going?' The driver stared at Risto in his rear-view mirror.

'No, I want to know your last destination.'

'The lady will stop at Feu-Rouge, then you will remain alone.'

'Then where will you go?'

'Eh! Eh! I am working, boy, don't waste my time. Where do I drop you?'

'I am going to Buholo II.'

'Damn! Didn't you see the taxi for Buholo II? You are in a taxi of the Nyawera-Nguba line.' He laughed, and shook his head. 'Where are you from?'

'I am from here, a Bukavian,' Risto answered.

'How can a boy from Bukavu get lost in a taxi? I will drop you at Place du 24, you can take a taxi to Kadutu there. Do you know Place du 24?' Now the driver was making fun of Risto; anyone from Bukavu would know the historic square. It carried the spirits and bones of people who died in the Zaire Republic during the revolutionary march of 24 November 1965; their names were engraved on the monument erected in their honour. It was a junction between many important roads. It united the North and South Kivu, and joined the four Zones of Bukavu: Kadutu, Bagira, Ibanda and Kabare.

To avoid arousing suspicion, Risto gave a fake smile.

'Yes, I know it. Sorry, I was a bit distracted.'

'My daughter wants her medicines. Here they are, take them to her.' It was the same voice that Risto had heard a few minutes earlier. Risto stood at the Place du 24, terrified, wondering where he could run. There were other taxi drivers shouting, calling for customers who were going to Kadutu.

Chapter 11

Risto closed his eyes, but left the lights in his room on. Darkness scared him, and nights were getting worse and worse. He left his lights on all the time. Although people spent more time in darkness because of power-shedding, he had as a result told everyone they were never to switch off the lights in his room.

He listened carefully to the noise of children playing outside; it was getting late. They spoke about their plans for the next day, what their mothers were cooking, their schoolmates, and so on. He could hear them wishing each other goodnight.

Sleep would not come yet; it was still too early, only 6 or 6:30pm. His fear was greater than ever before. How would he feel when midnight approached? He didn't know what to do or how to protect himself. He waited for the voices to appear again; these voices without bodies wrenched Risto's bones and killed any hope of a better tomorrow.

He didn't know whose voice would strike at him next. Maybe the spirit of the Mai-Mai soldier he had shot would come for him. Maybe he would hear the cries of the woman and her daughter he saw being raped in the village of Birava. During his entire time in the jungle, he hadn't touched a woman, neither beaten nor raped one, but he had watched the others do these things. Now he was haunted by people without flesh, by awful voices that followed him wherever he went. He didn't know whose voice would be next, or what would follow. Maybe the people he had stolen from, maybe the people he had beaten and tortured, maybe ... there were a lot of possibilities. Worst of all, he might hear Benny's voice reproaching him. Maybe all of the people he had hurt or killed would appear at once in his room and attack him, striking with one voice. But he would be dead before they touched him. Their voices would be stronger and more powerful than he could bear.

Sleep still would not land in his eyes. It was quiet, very quiet outside. The children were already in their homes by now. He could hear his mother and father speaking; they were asking about him. But he didn't move; he knew if he left his room and spoke to them, the questions would be hot. They would ask about his visit to his uncle, and if he told them about the strange voices he had heard the whole day, they would think he was mad. And then they would never trust or believe his words again. All he ever said would be taken as the ramblings of a mad boy. They would think he belonged at the Heri-Kwetu, a well-known church centre for people who had mental and other handicaps.

But even worse, they would understand that he had killed people in the forest, and that their blood was now following him. They would believe that the spirits of his victims were now hunting him. His own family would no longer consider him a human being, but a devil, one that had killed and raped innocent people. Society would reject him; he would die of loneliness and depression. No, he couldn't risk telling those stories to anyone, not even Landu. Better to suffer alone, and if one day these tormenting spirits decided to take him with them, then he would go, but he would plead his innocence to their chiefs. He had never intended to kill or hurt anyone. He had done what he needed to in order to survive.

He heard someone knock at the door of the house. The voice was familiar; it was the mother of Néné, Mama Néné, as they called her. He didn't want to see her. Every time she visited, she asked about her daughter, and Risto knew she had come for that again. She awakened the dead for him, making him weep, and leaving him in dreadful fear of the night. He pitied her, but what could he do? He didn't have any news from the forest. He hated it when she looked at him as if she was waiting for him to do something, to somehow free her daughter. She continued asking questions about the health of her daughter, and her life in the Kahuzi-Biega National Park, like someone who didn't know what the militias did to women and girls. And after she finally left, he would remember life in the forest, the tortures, the killings, the looting and the fighting, and would go almost mad. She had come again to make him cry, so he pretended to be asleep when he was called.

Later, Risto came out of his room at the time for evening prayer, also a time for family counselling. Zaina told him that Mama Néné had come to see him, and he pretended to be sorry to have missed her.

His father looked at him across the table that separated them.

'So, Risto, what do you want to do with your life now that you are home safe?'

Risto had been waiting for this question; he was still unsure of his answer.

'I am still thinking about it …'

His father's eyes narrowed.

'I am thinking of going back to school … becoming a mechanic.'

His father smiled. Studies meant everything to Risto's father. He would be happy to starve as long as he could pay school fees for his children.

'Studies should be the first plan of a man of this century. A man who didn't go to school is worth nothing these days,' Mahuno told his son.

He was not angry about Risto's choice, but it surprised him nevertheless. Mechanics didn't make a lot of money. Nobody in their family had ever practiced that profession. Why not just go back to a normal school? his father wondered.

'I just want to acquire some professional skills.'

'Then you should start as soon as possible.'

His father didn't ask much more, but he wanted to take swift action. He knew this was the only way to redeem his son, to give him a fresh image and take away the bad reputation that people had painted on him.

Mahuno now revealed a truth that Risto had not known. He had paid a large sum of money to the commander of the army controlling the town of Bukavu so that the rebel movement would allow his son to live in peace. He had taken the money from his savings, and Papa François had also contributed. Without this ransom, Risto would have been targeted. The rebel movement wanted new soldiers, but no one in town wanted to join. So whoever was suspected of having worked with the militias or the national army, or was thought to be a deserter, was forced to join the rebel army or beaten to death. Risto's father had paid for his son's peace and freedom with almost all his savings.

But this did not mean Risto was free forever; he could easily be taken again if the current commander was replaced, so he had to make a move that would disguise him from the rebel movement, and so far, studies were the best way. Mahuno further advised his son to choose his friends carefully. If he was seen with someone who had a bad reputation, his history would come out, and he would be taken as someone who was a danger to society. In any armed robbery, he would be considered a suspect, as he was the only boy in their street who was known to have been a soldier. Studies were the only thing that could redeem Risto's position in society, said his father.

Risto kept his eyes turned down. His father promised to go with him to register at the school the next day.

The school was named CFP, which stood for Centre de Formation Professionnelle. It was an old building with many coats of faded paint. If people had competed to guess the name of the colour of the building, none of them would have won. It was located among dozens of state buildings that had been rented to private businesses. The local authority was almost non-existent; everyone who had a little power did what he wanted in order to get a bit of money, and many took over the state buildings.

CFP was run by a well-known mechanic, Donas Bafwa. He rented the building and taught at the school as well. He owned a couple of car repair shops in Bukavu. His reputation was growing, even in the neighbouring countries of Rwanda and Burundi. Donas was a rich man who drove an old car whose carcass was almost at the end of its life. He hadn't bought that car. Someone had come to him with two old and broken cars. These cars had toured all the repair shops in Bukavu, and no one had been able to get them back on the road. Then they reached the hands of Donas Bafwa. He made a deal: if he could get one of the cars working again, then he would take the other one to settle the bill. He worked without rest for a week, and got both cars running again. He never bought another car; he loved his old renovated car. He was also known for renovating a big boat with his own hands and the help of his students. He had taken the engine of a car and put it into the battered old boat, which could be seen down at Lake Kivu.

Bukavu was a place where stories moved faster than the wind. In less than a week, the whole centre sang the chorus about the militia boy who had enrolled at CFP to become a mechanic. Curious people came into Risto's class; they would stare at him for a couple of minutes before leaving. In every corner they spoke about the boy who had been a soldier, the one who had been with the foreign militia in the Kahuzi-Biega National Park for eight months. They told stories that Risto didn't understand or recognise. Someone even testified that he had ended up in hospital after a battle. He was headline news.

The same story was being told on the streets. As Risto passed by, people peeped through their windows, then spoke behind his back. Little children looked at him, then whispered in each other's ears; sometimes they even ran away. He was an alien in his own society.

He lived in daily fear of an eyewitness from Birava village coming to town and recognising him. Surely he would tell everyone what tortures Risto had carried out there. How would Risto be considered then? Without a doubt, his neighbours would wait for him in the street with sticks and stones. They would forget the honour and respect they gave to his parents and family; they would come to his home at night and drag him out; they would tell him to confess all the criminal acts he had committed. He would plead innocent, but they would burn tyres, chant songs, and in the end, they would beat him or stone him to death.

He had already spent two months in Bukavu, and those two months had turned his face into that of an alien zombie in a human society. After two weeks at CFP, it was worse than ever. He hated to see people gazing at him, knowing that as he passed, they were talking about him. If he had escaped death in the jungle, why wouldn't they give him peace in their streets? He had hoped that people would grow bored with gossiping about it, but each day the news spread further; new people would hurry to see the militia boy with their own eyes.

During the day, he was unwelcome among his own people, and during the dark of the night, he was hunted by the spirits of those he had hurt. Smiles were scarce on his face, and when he did smile, it was just to please his family, while inside his heart ached. He wished there was a hole where he could hide.

He found one place of peace. A place restricted to only a few people, a place that took people who had a rough history, a place that the society hated. This was the Ambassade house near the Major Vangu monument, in Essence Street. It was well known for noise, fighting and overcrowding. It was a brick house with small rooms where people smoked cannabis. The house was supposed to be a shop; a few basic things were sold from one big window facing the street. The rooms inside were for the smokers and no one else. The people here called cannabis 'aspirin'. A newcomer had to be accompanied by someone known to the house and had to use the word 'aspirin'.

After a long day of smoking, Risto used to leave the Ambassade for the Ruzizi River, where he would sit on the banks, his legs floating in the water. Sometimes he went to the lake and stayed there till late. He would come home with a packet of weed, which he smoked to help him fall asleep, to chase away all the evil spirits that hunted him. This was the advice of others at the Ambassade. They said that spirits were afraid of the smell of cannabis, so whoever smoked it had some protection.

Risto hated the Ambassade; he hated the men who hung around in its dark rooms, swearing as they smoked and praised the drug. Many of them were people with bad reputations: troublemakers, street kids, even gang members and criminals. Many of them had dropped out of school, and rejected their families. He smoked with them, but he was not one of them. They knew this and were afraid of him, the militia boy who had fought in the jungle.

Risto belonged nowhere. He could not even go back to Bugobe; the peace of the village had been destroyed for him. How could he face his grandparents and other members of Benny's family? How could he answer their questions, see their tears? He was sure that people in the village knew of his presence in the town. What must they think of him, he, the beloved grandchild and cousin, who could not even come to report on his cousin? How ungrateful they must think him. He felt guilty of cowardice and betrayal, and this tormented him. Worse, what if one day they came to see him, to ask him about Benny, to request a detailed account of their journey in the jungle? This idea terrified him.

The world map lay on his bed, along with a few magazines and newspapers. He unfolded the map of Africa, looking at the neighbouring countries. Rwanda was the nearest to where he lived; he could even get there on foot. It wasn't safe, though, because of the political turmoil, and there were no refugee camps in Rwanda. Burundi was the next closest, but it was yet another country in turmoil. Every day people were killed there by militias and armed groups. Uganda was a bit far; to reach it, he would have to pass through the North Kivu province and its main town Goma and then take a dangerous road where militias looted, raped and killed almost at will. Sudan was very far and had been at war so many times. Central Africa, Congo-Brazzaville and Angola were also very far away. He could go to Zambia, but the journey would need a lot of money. It was a long way to the Kasumbalesa border post, and they spoke English there, a language he didn't know.

He chose Tanzania instead. Tanzania, yes; it was peaceful and it had refugee camps. They spoke Swahili there, even though it was a bit different from his. The way to Tanzania seemed easier. He could take a bus from Essence bus stop, near the monument, to Uvira in the south. From Uvira he would have to take a boat or a ferry to Tanzania, and from there he could get to a refugee camp. There were other Congolese refugees in Tanzania; he would find a place to stay. Risto had made up his mind. He asked his father for the full school fees for the term, saying that they were obliged to pay before the end of the week. Then he waited. Risto woke at 4am after a long and almost sleepless night. As usual, his lights were on. He sat on the small chair in his room and leaned on the table with a pen in his hands. He scratched on a piece of paper.

Dear Papa and Mama,

I am leaving the country; please don't look for me.

I know how this will wrench your hearts, but it is all beyond our control; I am a lifeless soul with broken dreams, dying slowly from the pain of the wounds inside me. You loved me, dear parents, and did everything that you could to give me a better life, a better future; I appreciate it.

But you couldn't touch my heart or my soul, where my wounds lie; nobody can help me. I have been damaged to a point that no psychiatrist or medical doctor can heal. I can't bear it anymore.

Please do understand, dear parents, I am going to try to find the peace and dignity that I have lost. I know you will wonder why I didn't talk to you, or tell you I was going. Please understand that the damage done to me in the Kahuzi-Biega National Park is enormous, morally as well as physically. Papa and Mama, these wounds need to be cured, and that is what I am going to look for.

I am sorry for breaking your hearts.

My destination is unknown; I pray to God to prepare a place where I will land.

I will miss you (I miss you already), I will miss your love, I will miss my brother Landu and my sisters, I will miss home. I am going, but one day I will come back. Tell my sisters and my brother that I have left my heart in them.

Love,
Your son,
Risto Mahuno

He cried like a child as he wrote. He covered his mouth with his hands whenever his voice mounted. The pages before him were wet with tears. He was sad, and his sadness intensified as the day broke. He was leaving that same day; he was leaving behind his home, his family, love and heart. He was going naked; without father or mother, brother or sister, he was going into the unknown.

· Chapter 12 ·

Risto had 200 American dollars hidden in his underwear. He bought a bus ticket to Uvira, in South Kivu, which lay next to the borders with Tanzania and Burundi. He decided to travel the road that passed through Rwanda, and then come back to the Congo through Kamaniola. The roads in the Kivu were not safe, especially the direct one from Bukavu to Uvira. People lost their lives there on a daily basis in hijackings, lootings, robberies or in crossfire between different militia gangs. He had bought a loaf of bread in a plastic bag, his only luggage. He didn't want to look like someone who was travelling. He carried only his student card from the CFP. He didn't want to talk, and decided to act like someone who was sleepy. The bus began to move.

Sleep smashed him away, and he slept like a rock. He only opened his eyes three times. The first time, it was on the Rwandan border. He was not yet in a deep sleep, and woke with his student card in his hands. His heart pounded; he was afraid that they might find out that he had been a soldier. Although there were soldiers in uniform holding their firearms and roaming up and down, no one knew him there. The driver went to talk to them inside their office. After a few minutes, he came back, they set off, and Risto fell asleep again.

Later, the woman next to him woke him up; it was their second stop, on the border between Rwanda and Congo. There again he held out his student card. They crossed the Rwandan border back into Congo. Now they were at the border post of Kamaniola, which was controlled by Congolese soldiers from the rebel movement. These soldiers checked all the passengers' documents.

Two people were detained: a man in his forties and a young woman. The man was arrested because his picture was not clear on his ID. He explained that his document was too old, that it was out of date; there were no new IDs being printed. His explanation was correct; the IDs that people used dated from the seventies. Even if you applied for an ID, there were none to be had. The printing of IDs stopped in the eighties when the Zairian economy collapsed. To get an ID now required private cooperation with the authorities. Sometimes this type of cooperation meant that a young man turning eighteen would be given a very old ID. Sometimes a man of fifty would get a brand-new ID. The young woman didn't know the reason for her arrest. She asked several times without getting any response. One soldier finally said she had not shown respect for the commander when he had asked her where she was going. The driver left the car and went into a small house of mud and straw with the commander. When he came back, he asked the man and the young woman to give him $5 each. They did so, and were released.

By the time the bus stopped for the third and final time in Uvira, most of the passengers had left. Only two people remained in the bus, Risto and an old lady, who had begged the driver to go past the bus stop and let her off near the marketplace, where her children were waiting to help her. The bus stopped; the woman's children were outside. Risto didn't know whether he should get off the bus; the driver kept staring at him and asking where he was getting off. He decided to step off and look around. The land looked strange. It was already late afternoon.

He wandered near an ice-cream vendor and bought two cones. The vendor looked at him and smiled. 'Are you coming from Bukavu?' he asked.

'Yes. Why?'

'I can see that from your clothes. Uvira is always hot; it will take you time to get used to this heat.'

Uvira was different to Bukavu, with its own style. The traffic was not heavy. There were moto-taxis, but not as many as in Bukavu.

There were bicycle-taxis instead, and it seemed as though everyone had a bicycle.

The ice-cream vendor owned another small stand where he sold soap, toothbrushes, sweets, pens and so on. Fifty metres away there was another vendor with almost the same products. These two men, like a few others Risto saw selling goods, didn't look like people from the town, but rather from villages. They spoke Swahili quite well, but it sounded different from the version spoken in Bukvau. Their version included more English and pure Swahili words, whereas in Bukavu the Swahili was full of French words and words from other local languages.

The vendor had gone to visit his neighbour and returned. He found Risto still by his stand. The ice-cream man didn't speak, but opened his stand, which he had covered with a dozen thick plastic bags. The sun shone over the mountain in the west.

Risto offered to share his loaf of bread with the vendor.

'I am Risto.'

'I have two names: Jean-Marie is my Christian name and Abula is my family name. You can call me Abu.'

He took two ice-creams from the cooler-box and gave one to Risto.

'Where are you staying?' he asked Risto.

'Uhm ... you know I am from Bukavu.'

There was a moment of silence.

'I am from Bukavu, but I am here in Uvira for a while.'

Abu didn't seem to hear his last sentence; he was busy with a small child who was buying sweets.

'Have you ever been to Bukavu?' Risto asked.

'No, but I have family members there. I hear that it is a very nice place.'

'Not really! I love the layout of Uvira. No mountains, no mud, and I see the streets are well designed.'

Abu didn't seem to agree, and shook his head. 'But there is no money here, unlike in Bukavu. People there buy houses for $100 000 cash!'

'Yes ... but not everyone. Don't you see how poor I am?'

Abu looked at him with disbelieving eyes.

'You are not poor.' He laughed as he moved to serve a customer.

'If I wasn't poor, I wouldn't be in Uvira now.'

Abu looked at him, then at the giant mountain that was far in the west.

'So you came to look for money in Uvira?'

'You know, we are very hungry back home. Our uncle who lives in Tanzania told me to meet him here. He said he would give me something. That is why I am here; I don't have a family member or a person that I know here, except you – who I have just met. I don't even know where to sleep.'

Abu looked at him pityingly. He remained silent for a moment.

'So where will you sleep then?'

'I don't know, maybe God will send someone to help me, maybe I will sleep in the streets … I don't know.'

'Sleep in the streets? At this time? Are you crazy? Do you know how many street kids have disappeared here in Uvira? They are seen much later, far away, in military uniforms. When darkness falls, everyone has to be in their house. If you get caught at night you are gone; you will serve on the front line as a Kadogo Songambele.'

'I don't want to sleep in the streets, but if I don't get help …'

'Be careful, my friend. Do you know the Kadogo Songambele? Do you know how many of those children have died? They take them, put them on the front line on the battlefield. They don't even have the right to look behind, and terrible things are done to them if they try to escape. Do you want to take the risk of being in the street after dark?'

'Could you shelter me, please?'

'If you can fold yourself like a fish in a tin, then you will be fine. Just follow me after closing up.'

Abu put everything onto his bicycle and they pushed it together. As Abu had said, he didn't have much place for Risto. He shared a very tiny room with two other vendors. Their room was already full with three bicycles and two mattresses. Abu told him they could share the smaller mattress.

They walked past the small houses of Uvira and stopped to eat at a cafeteria. Abu refused to let Risto pay a cent. Risto was hungry, but too shy to eat, and he felt guilty about his lies. But that had been the only way he could have gained Abu's trust so quickly. They had fish and meat with foufou. Abu asked Risto to order more food, but Risto asked only for tea with soya powder, and requested that it be thick, like the typical tea of Bukavu.

Risto was the only strange face in the restaurant, he realised. Everyone who came in gave him an anxious look. All the rest were traders. Each person who arrived received greetings and was called by their nickname. Abu introduced him to his people. He said Risto was his good friend who had come for a visit. The talk moved from gossip to the politics of Uvira. The woman who owned the restaurant joined in the conversation. They complained about the greedy commander, who was asking for more free things every day. He wanted five cigarettes every day, he wanted ice-creams for his bodyguards, he wanted his bodyguards to get soap for free. The conversation jumped to the Mai-Mai group that had refused to join the rebel movement, and had gone back to the mountains. It was a strong battalion, some said, a big loss for the rebel movement. A trader sitting in the far corner objected: 'It wasn't the strongest battalion!'

A fat man at the door shouted, 'You don't know Commander Ramos the Lion very well. That man is a real fighter. His Mai-Mai group has magic! Didn't you hear how they got bees to attack rebel soldiers in the forest of Fizi, and how four of his men killed a hundred rebels in a two-day fight?'

'Man, that was because of witchcraft,' replied Abu.

'But that's what makes a strong man!' said the fat man.

The story didn't end there. There came another one, a rumour that Ramos the Lion and his group planned to attack Uvira the following Tuesday.

'They want to free us from the rebels,' said the woman who owned the restaurant. The room grew quiet for a while. Abu then interrupted the silence.

'It won't be their first time … they come, fight for a few hours, then they flee. They never take Uvira for more than two hours!'

'This time around they have a big plan,' said the woman.

Risto enjoyed the talking, but he was afraid of the darkness outside. Abu had warned him about the danger of walking around at night, but seemed to have forgotten his earlier words.

'Abu, it seems very dark outside, you told me about the soldiers …'

'The commander knows me; if anyone takes me, I will end up in his hands. I have the full right to move around the whole of Uvira at any time. Don't worry.' He forgot about Risto again as he carried on chatting. Risto had finished his food and tea; there was nothing to do anymore, and the stories were those of people who spent their time in the streets. They listened to anyone who passed by, whether they were mad, dull, drunk or normal, and repeated all those stories as worthy of being related. Finally, Abu was ready to leave.

· Chapter 13 ·

After a few days in Uvira, Risto was getting used to the town, but the sun still felt like a blaze. He drank the town's warm water almost every two hours. He would slip into a cafeteria for a glass of thick, cold milk and then carry on with his business. He had toured around Uvira on bicycle-taxis and knew the prices of each route. He knew where the black market for exchanging money was; he had been to the port; he knew where to get onto the boats and ferries. He became familiar with the hot and cool corners of the little town.

He jumped onto a torn bit of mattress laid on the rear seat of a bicycle-taxi. The driver dropped him at the place where money was exchanged on the black market. He quickly bought shilingi with his dollars; then he hopped onto another bicycle going to the port. There were no humps on the road, so the bicycle ran really fast. Risto had heard that travelling by ferry would not be the safest option for him. It was better to travel by boat – these were small, and the crews did not check documents. He had been told he should not trust anyone, and to be especially careful with policemen. The Tanzanian police arrested anyone they found without valid travel documents, and regardless of whether they were refugees or not, everyone spent six months in jail.

The harbour was empty and as silent as a cemetery; there were no boats or merchandise to be seen. A man sat under an umbrella, staring at Lake Tanganyika, outside a small brick house, newly painted. Risto wanted to stop there, but his bicycle driver shouted that they should carry on, the guy who worked there was a crook. The driver took him straight to the shore of the lake, where a young man drowsing on the rocks greeted Risto with a friendly smile. Risto went to sit on a rock some distance away, looking at the horizon, at what he thought must be Tanzania.

Silence ruled the harbour like the chilly breeze on the shores of the lake. Finally the man on the rocks introduced himself as Derrick, and asked where Risto was going. Was he waiting for someone? Risto knew it was not wise to share a secret with a stranger. A quick lie would surely satisfy Derrick's curiosity. So he told him he was waiting for an uncle who would come from Tanzania.

A few minutes passed, and Derrick smiled and nodded as he ruminated over Risto's lie. He wanted to know what person had told Risto that there would be a boat coming from Tanzania. His cousin lived in Tanzania, said Risto. Did he own a boat? Since when had he been travelling on the Tanganyika? The man carried on asking questions. He told Risto he had a boat and was leaving for Tanzania at 4pm that afternoon. Risto's ears opened wide, his mouth couldn't close, and he had many questions about Tanzania. Derrick was Tanzanian, as his Swahili testified, even if he had picked up a few Congolese slang expressions. He knew Tanzania very well. He told Risto about the refugee camps. They were synonyms for suffering, hunger and misery. He had been trafficking people over Lake Tanganyika for quite a long time.

As the day passed, boats appeared along the shores and crowds gathered around them. Derrick seemed to be a good person and slowly wore away Risto's suspicion. They shared fruit for lunch. Risto finally opened up and gave away his secret. He told Derrick he was running away from Congo, and wanted to go to Lugufu refugee camp in Tanzania. He had suffered terribly in the endless wars of Congo, now he wanted a quiet and peaceful place to rest, he said. Derrick promised to help him.

At 4:30pm, they left the shores of Uvira along with two other boats. People on board the boats waved to their families on shore, some promised to bring gifts, others called out farewells. Risto had no one to wave to, so he waved to his country, while he shed tears. It was then that he realised that he was leaving his beloved country behind: the country for which a charismatic leader like Patrice Lumumba had died; a country that many believed would become one of Africa's superpowers, a dream all Congolese had been waiting for since the dawn of their independence in 1960.

The boat moved like a rocking chair, but it didn't give any pleasure. Risto was afraid of the deep, cold lake underneath it. Heri, Derrick's co-captain, who was also Tanzanian, had the tales of Lake Tanganyika in his bones. He grew up on the lake, he said. He was nurtured by the Tanganyika and got everything that he needed from its blessed waters. He ate food from it and drank its waters and made money from it. In return, the lake had asked him for his most precious thing: his father.

His father was one of the masters of the lake. One night, he was fishing on the Tanganyika when a wave rose from nowhere. His boat sank and he never returned home. Now everyone believed that the spirit of Heri's father patrolled the waters, fighting for the fishermen when waves grew high. Heri became sad as he reached the climax of his story, but when he spoke about the spirit of his father being alive, he was proud; he spoke with a strong voice. Even though he could not touch his father, he believed his father was with him, protecting him whenever he crossed the lake. His father's spirit was in the whispering winds, in the soothing melodies of the water; his was the power that kept boats safe on the lake. Heri recounted more stories of his home country, stories of its lakes and rivers, stories that always ended up with his father as the hero of his people; his father who died for the good of all fishermen and boatmen. To him, his father was like a flag of victory for everyone travelling on Lake Tanganyika.

The midnight breeze struck the boat and the human bodies on the deck. Some people had set up tents, but Risto had no shelter from the cold breeze, which was turning his body into a solid ice cube. He shivered until a woman took pity on him and gave him one of her cloths. The lake murmured as the cold breeze passed over its surface. It was completely dark. In front of Heri's boat, another boat rocked its passengers; it was the only light that Risto could see.

An hour in the boat felt like a whole day. Heri sang to make his passengers forget about the boredom of the crossing. It usually took half a day to reach the shores of Tanzania. But something was happening to the lake; it seemed to be rising, growing. Heri said that maybe it had rained on the Tanzanian side. The breeze had changed into a wind; it became stronger and carried drops of water from the sky.

Within half an hour, things changed completely. Children were crying and women praying. The lake had grown restless and the wind stronger, as the boat moved like a wounded man walking on very sharp stones. It was now jumping on mountains of water. Heri prayed for the spirit of his father to come to the rescue. Next he threw the Nanga, the big rock used to stabilise the boat, into the lake, but nothing changed. There was already water in the boat. Risto took a bucket and helped the other crew members who were throwing water out of the boat. His shoes and clothes were soaked, but he didn't care, even though they were the only ones he had. He only tried to protect his money.

It was so easy to die on the Tanganyika. They were in the middle of the deepest lake in Africa, far from the shore. There was no rescue team; it was just a question of whether the boat would be swallowed by the water. Heri's eyes seemed to suggest that they were in really big trouble. He kept moving around in the small boat like a fly caught in the web of a spider, but there was no solution. The waves struck harder than before. A woman was screaming for her child, swept away by the swift waves, and a crew member jumped into the wildly undulating water to save the child; another lady's loincloth was already brandishing in the dancing water, she was half naked. Risto held onto his trousers tightly; life without his money was death.

It wasn't long before the plank boat started coming apart; Risto held firmly onto one plank and screamed as loudly as he could. There was a disarray of voices, shouts and screams blending with the angry sounds of wind and rain. A light approached, a torch shone upon him. He moved and screamed. The light drifted, the slow-moving boat changed direction, a few men jumped into the lake to save others, but they forgot him. His shoes fought with the water, he held tightly onto the waist of his pants, and his mouth called the names of unknown crew men, all the Tanzanian names he knew. The boats were pulling women and children from the water; then a hand touched Risto's head, and he stretched out his hands. It was all like a dream or a movie. They pulled him into another boat. People were counted, and by some miracle, no one was missing. Women and their children sat sobbing. Three passengers were vomiting water. A crew member said they were safe now; the boat was strong enough to resist the waves. Risto questioned his credibility, as the boat was still jumping hills of waves, and water was still washing in and out. The wind was the captain that night.

Later that night they stopped off the Burundian coast, seeking safety. Heri and Derrick had been talking for more than half an hour. They kept on looking ahead as they spoke. The boat moved like a tortoise. At last, Derrick announced that they were approaching the shores of Kigoma in Tanzania. One woman stood up and praised the Lord. Heri advised that they should rather pray to God not to be caught by the police. The woman replied in dismay that they were refugees in quest of safety. Heri's answer shocked her even more; he said that whether a refugee or not, any person on Tanzanian land or waters without a valid document would be arrested. Refugee status did not count; that person would go to jail, and it could take a long time to decide his or her fate. They could be placed in a refugee camp, but a frightening alternative was human trafficking.

Getting the passengers onto land was a simple game that Heri had played many times before. Everyone hid behind containers on the boat, while the captain moved swiftly towards the port, then made a sharp U-turn towards the shore to elude soldiers and local people. The game involved dropping off their smuggled goods and passengers before returning quickly to the port. On a hill near the coast, a tiny village of maybe forty small houses emerged from behind the shade of coconut trees. Derrick shouted a few names and a couple of young guys appeared from nowhere. They ran to offload the illegal goods – pagnes from Congo, which were very expensive and prized in Tanzania – and the passengers, who were taken inside a small house and told not to go outside, no matter what happened.

A bus arrived at dawn to collect the goods and the refugees; it came early to avoid contact with policemen. It already had a few people inside; most of them seemed foreign. All the pagnes were packed onto the bus, and then the women rushed to get on, but the driver explained that things were not going well in the camps. Tanzania had started a campaign to return refugees back to Congo. People on the bus confirmed that the camps had been closed, with new arrivals being deported back to their countries. They confirmed that the first group of Congolese refugees had already been returned home; it was just the beginning of the operation. The story of a peaceful Democratic Republic of Congo had travelled all around the world after pictures of a truce between rebel movements and the national government and news of a possible power-sharing deal had been published in newspapers everywhere. The world now believed that peace was being rebuilt in Congo, even while the Congolese people continued to live in terrible and chaotic times.

Risto could not believe this news, and his insistence made a man stand up. He confirmed that he was in the next group to be returned to Congo. But the women were tired of staying in that small room; they believed that it was for the police to listen to their story and sympathise with their pain, not passengers in a bus.

The bus driver advised Risto not to take any chances; as a young man alone, with no luggage, Tanzanian police would have no mercy for him. They would take him for a rebellious teenage boy, even a criminal; they might not even open their ears to listen to his story. Heri agreed; he advised Risto to stay with him and plan something else.

It seemed that Tanzania had its angels and its devils; death and happiness could easily come in the same package. Risto was ready for both. At around four in the afternoon, Heri came to Risto's small room with a plate of fish and rice. They ate slowly. Heri stared at Risto as if wondering who this young boy really was. Finally he broke the silence with many questions. Heri wanted to know all about him; which part of the Congo he was from; why he was in Tanzania; and where he was going exactly. Risto stopped eating and looked Heri in the eyes.

'You know, Heri,' he said, 'I know you see a young man leaving his country for a foreign one, with no documents, but yet you haven't understood the reason that would push someone to do this. I am from Bukavu; that is where I lived and grew up. I am running away from the war in my country.'

'Does it mean that all we used to hear about Congo is true?' Heri kept asking.

'Most of the things that you hear about Congo are true. Of course some of them might not reflect the full truth, but "there is no smoke without fire". People are being killed in Congo.' Risto didn't want to reveal that he had been a child soldier, forced to commit atrocities by foreign rebels, but he went on to tell him the stories of young girls like Mina, the young mother he had met at Panzi hospital, caring for a small child of a militia she hated, whose dreams had been stolen by wars.

'Listen, Heri,' he said finally. 'When you hear that people were buried alive in Congo by the rebels or a militia movement, know that it has happened. If you hear that an entire village was killed, it means that men, women and children were massacred. If a few managed to escape, then it would be just by the grace of God. How often do you listen to the radio or watch TV or read a newspaper?' he asked.

Heri laughed, 'There is no such thing on the lake.'

Risto tried to explain how his country, Congo, one of the richest countries on the planet, was a victim. The wealth of his country had awakened demons of greed within superpower countries and global corporations. He gave him the example of coltan, the mineral used to make vital parts of cell phones, computers, and so on. Of all places, it could only be found in Congo. The search for coltan had become a trail of blood, and the mines where it was found had become the graves of many men and their dreams. Congo was a victim of wars it had never wished for. He saw that Heri's sentiments about Congo had changed; his compassion towards Risto was visible.

'And where are you going then?' asked Heri.

'I don't know where I am going, but I am looking for a place where I can feel safe. A place where I can sleep without fear of raids at night, sleep without nightmares of unknown spirits trying to strangle me. A place where the noise of guns or stories of rebels won't exist; just a place that will allow me to dream again.'

They took a small canoe and paddled close to the coast towards Kigoma, as if they were local fishermen, so that soldiers would not suspect anything. The skies were clear as they reached Kigoma. They landed and walked slowly without talking to each other. As they walked through the town, an unknown voice behind them called 'Uncle' in French. The voice kept calling, and a French-speaking person in Tanzania meant a brother to Risto, so he turned round. It was a policeman, who gestured to him to stand still. Heri was a few steps ahead, and didn't hear Risto calling him.

The police had a lot of questions. First they wanted to see his passport; he had none. Second, they asked for his visa; he wondered if they thought his visa would have been stamped on his hands. He was a refugee from the Democratic Republic of Congo looking for a refugee camp in Tanzania. This didn't matter to the police; he was arrested for entering Tanzania illegally, which meant six months in jail with a fine of thousands of shilingi. Worst of all, he risked deportation to Congo after serving his sentence.

Risto could see Heri looking at him from afar. Risto's hands and feet were free; so far, it was an arrest in words only. He waited for the right moment to make the biggest decision of his journey, praying for his feet to be strong. He was standing between two policemen; they chatted in Swahili, one patting his palm with his baton. It was time. Risto jumped like a mad cow escaping from an abattoir and ran. The policemen chased behind him. Risto had the legs of an Olympic medallist; he couldn't believe his strength.

He yelled Heri's name as he passed him on the corner, and raced into the open square of a nearby mosque, running into the prayer room. Here he stood like a lost goat in an unknown house. A man came forward and rebuked the policemen, who were trying to enter. With his angry voice and wise beard, he told them to go away, the mosque was a holy place and open to everyone; the police couldn't come to look for people in a mosque. He told them to wait outside in the street and not in the holy place.

This man's name was Omar; he was a friend of Heri's. Heri had followed Risto into the mosque, and was pleased to see his old friend. Omar offered them shelter for a few hours, until the police got bored and left. In the meantime, he listened to Risto's story. He suggested that he should rather try to get to the refugee camps in neighbouring Mozambique.

The following afternoon, Risto hugged Heri and Omar at the train station in Kigoma. His seat was number 175, right next to the window. His neighbour was a woman in her late forties. She had a small boy, no more than ten years old, sitting next to her. After almost twenty minutes of shunting, the long, old train was on its way. It was packed, with many people standing. Their voices were like the clamour of singing parrots. Within a few minutes, a dispute broke out. A woman was said to have bought a stolen ticket, and now the owner was there with his friends, not to collect the ticket, but to demand the price of an emergency ticket in cash – twice the price of the ticket to Dar-es-Salaam. The owner of the ticket, a man in his early twenties, wanted reimbursement. It was a difficult dispute to resolve. The woman had bought the ticket from a young man outside the train station early that morning. There were no more tickets available from the cashier; she had no other choice. But in fact, Omar had advised Risto to be careful not to buy tickets from anyone except the cashier. There was a scam where someone would buy a large number of tickets on the first day of sale. Later, when the tickets were sold out, that person would open a private stand outside the train station with higher prices than normal. The salesmen would sell these tickets and then follow the customers onto the train, accusing them of stealing their tickets. This was exactly what Risto witnessed now. The ticket had a mark on it to prove that the robbers were the owners. This was a regular Kigoma business, and it happened because there were no police on the trains, leaving people vulnerable.

So the dispute carried on until the security guard came to handle it. The woman was told to pay only 15 000 shilingi, the price of a normal ticket. But strangely enough, at the following train station, the owner of the ticket and his two friends got off the train and didn't return. They had probably gone to another coach to extort a new victim.

The journey continued. Each train station became the set of a dramatic movie. The tired and sleepy bodies of the passengers would become electrified at the magical sight of the open markets at the stations: craft vendors, people frying chicken, singing and dancing boys and girls with half-naked bodies wishing travellers a peaceful journey. Passengers had to beware: sweet talkative Tanzanian youths sneaked onto coaches empty-handed and got off at the next station with heavy bags. It was most unfortunate for anyone who was a foreigner, as some of the youths had police IDs. Questions would be followed by a heavy fine if the traveller had no papers. To avoid being spotted, Risto pretended to be sleepy and sick, and swallowed without a word the pain caused by a fat lady who had imposed herself between his legs. He only breathed at the stations. When the train moved on, the crowd stood singing like friends saying farewell to a bride.

The sunrise didn't bring joy to Risto; instead, it came with thorns in its rays. His eyes were about to explode in his head. He couldn't see properly; all he wished was to soak his entire head in icy cold water. Many of his shilingi had gone into bottles of water that he had poured over his head, but in vain. The uneven movement of the old Tanzanian train worsened his torment. By 10am, he thought he needed to write a will for his remaining money; death was close by. He was unsure if it was him who was lost in a dizzy dance, or whether he was feeling the shaking movement of the train. He asked his neighbour to be his keeper; if the worst happened, she should take him to her place. If he died, he begged her to bury him and tell his family in Bukavu. The gracious woman handed him an aspirin. The pill called death closer; his head became a burning stove.

Morning gleams confused the public lights of Morogoro. Risto realised he had lost an entire day. Through the window, he watched a seemingly confused boy of almost his age drifting around; he looked like a child lost in the jungle. He had a Congolese face, a Congolese hairstyle, and his clothes said it all. With his blazing head, Risto got off the train and approached the boy, who moved away. A greeting in the Congolese Swahili slang couldn't buy him; Risto continued in French.

'I am your Congolese brother; I need help, I am sick. Don't be afraid. Please help me. My name is Risto. I am from Bukavu.'

'My name is Merci. I am coming from Uvira.'

'Do you stay here in Tanzania? I mean, where are you going?'

Merci stared at Risto and kept quiet.

'I am going to Dar-es-Salaam,' Risto said.

'Yes, I am going there too,' replied Merci.

It wasn't easy to win a stranger's trust just because one spoke his language.

'Merci, I think it is God who wanted us to meet. You know, you are my only brother here; no one else knows me. I am very sick. I have got nerve problems and my head is about to explode. I will take the bus with you, but please don't leave me if things get worse. You are my only brother in this strange country,' Risto's words came softly.

Merci nodded, then looked Risto in the eyes: 'Since when have you been sick?'

'Yesterday early morning.'

'Don't worry,' his new friend assured Risto.

The bus left a little later that morning, with both boys on it.

· Chapter 14 ·

Risto and Merci arrived in Dar-es-Salaam at around 11am. Neither of them had spoken a word on the bus. Omar's deep voice echoed in Risto's boiling head. Trust was the word he had repeated several times: 'Never seek help from a young boy; do not trust anyone, even drivers who seem to be very friendly and helpful. Some policemen are robbers in uniforms; do not trust them either.' This was a very difficult and strange journey, one that needed a lot of prayers and wisdom. Dar-es-Salaam was like hell if one didn't have valid documents. The eyes didn't want to see shilingi.

In Dar-es-Salaam, known by its inhabitants as Dar, the buildings confirmed the supremacy of this city as opposed to other Tanzanian towns. The traffic was intense and the vigilance of the police was tight. Risto needed some rest with a dish of pills, or maybe a quick injection, and then to carry on the journey the following day. Merci had another idea; he wanted to head south and approach the Malawian border as fast as he could. He thought he could find refuge in Malawi. He took a bus to Kariako market in Dar, leaving Risto behind, still on the main road where the bus had dropped them that morning.

Risto waited for the angel's call; his head was on the verge of exploding – in fact, he was certain he could feel it disintegrating. Merci was his only chance of rescue, and he had gone. His only fellow countryman had left him half-dead in a foreign country. The first eye that would see him would be the early bird to take the food, the few shilingi he had on him. He crawled to a corner where an abandoned house stood, went inside the broken-down walls and lay in a corner. He took out the three remaining pills the lady in the train had given him, and gathered spit in his mouth to swallow the bitter pills. His eyes closed. His head had no room for thoughts; it shut down, waiting for death to come.

Death didn't knock on his door that day. In his dreams, though, he saw a policeman holding out his hand, demanding a visa. Risto jumped; it was still daylight, he realised. He was back in the real world. Cars passed along the road. His head hadn't blown away; it hurt, but to his surprise, it was slightly better. Standing over him was a silhouette against the late afternoon sunshine; it revealed the figure of a young man. It was none other than Merci. He had become confused; he lost his map of Tanzania, and he didn't dare ask anyone in the Kariako market for directions in case he suddenly became a policeman. Any resistance would mean a visit to a police station. Policemen in uniforms were patrolling the market like the keepers of beehives.

The night in the abandoned structure seemed short, and their eyes soon found the daylight in the belly of dawn. They had learned there was a bus leaving town at 5am for Mutuara, a Tanzanian town close to the border with Mozambique. The journey took all day, and they reached Mutuara late that night.

While other travellers enjoyed the majestic beauty of the Tanzanian savannah, Risto and his friend observed silence throughout the journey, pretending to be either sick or asleep. Their great worry was how to rent a hotel room without documents. The driver, Mahamar, helped them to enter the small town and arranged a hotel room for them. They did not trust him, but they had no choice. Along the way, he had stopped for no reason and two fake policemen had entered the bus. They had checked only Risto and Merci's documents. Ten thousand shilingi ended the mysterious police crackdown. It was Mahamar's plan, they knew it.

The hotel receptionist wanted their passports. They put their student cards on her desk. She could not speak French, and the Mutuara accent of mixed Arabic and pure Swahili meant that any exchange could get the two boys in trouble. So they needed Mahamar's help to exchange money and make transport arrangements to get out of Mutuara. They sent him to get some supper, and after eating, it was time for Risto's soul-piercing sermon, his effort to move Mahamar. His heart wasn't made of stone; Risto's words touched him.

At dawn the next day, they were headed for the border in a pick-up truck arranged by Mahamar, after his share of ten per cent had been confirmed. They passed some men in a confusing uniform – no one could tell if they were police or soldiers, but they had firearms and scrutinised each movement in the little Muslim town. Mahamar had tipped the truck driver, so that when they reached the Ruvua River that separated Tanzania and Mozambique, he would help them cross in secret. He organised two bicycle drivers to help the boys cross the river with its majestic crocodiles, which were feared by even the bravest fishermen from the nearby villages.

Hussein was Risto's driver, while Bengera agreed to take Merci. Hussein called his customers 'Uncle'. 'Uncles, you are in the right hands,' he said.

They walked between little huts, avoiding the dirt road that led to the border post. A giant man, his skin covered with hundreds of marks, tried to start a conversation with Hussein; a few minutes later he cycled past them, heading towards the bush. The journey began once 5 000 shilingi got into the pockets of each bicycle driver. Within seconds, the jungle became a highway, as the bike drivers raced at top speed. The route led to some farms where a few women were working; the drivers stopped, and greetings followed. Then came a ten-minute walk.

At a stand of dense bush, a group of five young men loitered, as if waiting for them. The tattooed giant that had spoken to Hussein stood among them. He could have eaten a whole goat alone. An argument broke out between the youths and the bicycle drivers; the words, in mixed Swahili and Portuguese, seemed vicious. Eventually, with a regretful voice, Hussein handed Risto and Merci over to the group of five.

'These guys will help you.' Those were his last words before he and Bengera returned the way they had come.

Something swung on the hip of the giant, a sharp edge that scared Risto. He coughed to clear his throat: 'Thanks for your kindness, but we have to return to Mutuara; we have forgotten something there.'

The giant gave him an intimidating look. He scratched his head and ground his teeth. Risto was not going to wait for death on his knees, but before he could utter his words, the huge man had lifted him over his shoulder and held him fast.

'Please, let me walk alone,' screamed Risto.

'You are tired; I am helping you,' said the man, beginning to run.

After thirty minutes of being carried, the boys were thrown to the ground. The river winked only metres away; a little hill separated them from it. The gang of men were looking for money, Risto knew. He could read his fate in the anger of the overflowing Ruvua; it was craving his blood. The men would take their money, butcher them, and throw their bodies in the Ruvua. Crocodiles would celebrate and thank God for giving them a free and tasty meal. They would never know it was the meat of two innocent boys running away from war in their country, looking for a place where their minds and bodies could find peace, a place where their dreams could be born and breathe once again.

This was the end of their story. No one would ever know that two innocent boys had been killed on the Tanzanian boarder of Mozambique by thugs and robbers. Risto's mother would suffer eternal pain; she would no longer sleep nor eat, thinking that her beloved son had gone wild, left home and vanished in a soulless world. His Christian mother would fast and pray for months, arguing with God for what he had done to her. She would ask God, if her son had died, to show her his body or tomb; and if he was still alive, to tell her where he would be. But by then Risto would be part of the crocodile, and his spirit would be dwelling forever on the Ruvua River.

The mammoth took out his knife. He ground his teeth again; the other four men surrounded the boys. Risto and Merci were trapped.

'Hand over whatever you have on you,' hammered the giant.

'But … we thought you were helping! The two other guys took away everything we had; I am telling you, we don't have any more money,' said Merci, his tears dropping.

'I won't repeat it again. Give the money you are hiding. Take off your clothes, boys.'

Risto's and Merci's bodies vibrated.

The giant cut a small branch and started shaping the edge of it with his knife. It looked half a metre long; the edges of the blade could lighten the night. He stared at Merci, who quickly stripped off his trousers. This was not enough; he was told to take off his shorts and even his underpants. Merci did this, sobbing. Then it was Risto's turn. He took off his shoes, his trousers, then his shorts and underpants. The thieves took each piece of clothing and searched every part, carefully checking any suspicious areas.

'Congolese have gold, diamonds and American dollars,' the thugs murmured in Swahili. They took each cent they found; Merci was hiding some extra American dollars in pockets especially sewn in his trousers. Their underpants looked light, so the men did not waste their time in searching these. The giant man with the scars and tattoos gave two of his friends 10 000 shilingi each, threw the clothes to the two others, and walked away. Only their underpants remained on the ground. Risto hurried to put his back on, but Merci burst into tears.

'Please, chief, please, show us a little pity. How can you leave us naked? Please, we are refugees running away from the war in Congo. Please give us our clothes and even a small amount of money for food,' cried Merci as he followed the giant.

'Congolese people have got diamonds, gold, dollars ... you will get more, don't worry,' the mammoth responded.

Risto was gazing at the overflowing Ruvua River while Merci walked behind the giant man, pleading with him. He simply brandished his long, blazing knife, then yelled at him to go back, or crocodiles would breakfast on his body.

Risto's underpants carried his last hope, a hundred dollars, hidden as if he had predicted this tragedy. He had sewed the money into the thick front spot of his underpants. As soon as they were alone in the forest, Risto inspected his underpants; his money was safe and intact. Merci's eyes widened, wondering how that money could have escaped the scrutiny of those thugs. He took a deep breath and dried his tears.

Almost naked, the two boys walked nervously down the valley, crossing dried-out sandy streams. There were three small huts between a sandbar and the Ruvua. Risto wondered if the people who lived there were Mozambicans or Tanzanians, or whether that was their own tiny piece of country. The first person to see them was an old lady; she quickly stood up from her reed mat and went straight into her hut, ignoring their calls for help. A man who seemed to be in his late thirties came out. The boys did not understand that the old lady was avoiding them as a sign of respect. As a woman, she was not the one to deal with naked men; another man should be the one to speak to them.

The man spoke Swahili with a Portuguese accent, and showed great pity when they explained to him why they were naked, and described their ordeal. Risto went on to add his speech about why they had left their country, what it was like living in a war-torn country, and why they needed to reach Mozambique. The man's compassion was palpable. His name was Manuel, and despite the poverty in which he lived, he was able to help them with two pairs of shorts, old sandals and a shirt for each of them. In the hut, the old lady who had run away from them offered them water in green plastic cups that had gone blackish. The cups were dirtier than the yellowish water they drank. Merci refused to drink the ugly water.

Manuel volunteered to take them across the Ruvua. He had called another young man from the neighbouring hut for assistance. The two men got a wooden canoe ready for the crossing. When the old lady heard that they were heading to Mozambique, she warned them that the river was overflowing; they should wait for it to go down rather than risk a painful death in crocodile jaws. Risto couldn't wait; after their experience with the thieves, he felt that each second brought death closer. Better to face it than wait for it.

They entered the river praying. Merci, who had refused to drink the water he was offered in the hut, cried with thirst while in the canoe. Manuel took a piece of coconut shell and scooped water from the yellowish river. Merci again refused to drink, but Risto drank two coconut shells of the stinking water. There was no other way to survive, better to die from disease than from thirst. Risto had survived harsher situations than these when he was a child soldier.

The river was overflowing, just as the old woman had said. The current pushed the wooden canoe in the wrong direction. It brought back memories of the boat on the Tanganyika, but Risto believed history wouldn't repeat itself. The heavy currents were not as frightening as the strange thing that moved up and down in the murky water close to the Mozambican shore. The strange creature entered the anger of the boiling current and approached the frail canoe. Risto's heart had left his quaking body. He had been close to death so many times and had escaped, but this terror was so real that he told everyone his home address and the name of his parents; whoever survived, he said, should send word of his death.

The crocodile was so frightening that Merci's screams brought a small crowd of villagers to the edge of the river. They began shouting and casting stones into the river. More shouting, more stones; the crocodile finally retreated. The fight with the river currents carried on until suddenly they were in the shallows, and to his amazement, Risto found himself on Mozambican soil.

Risto wanted to pay Manuel for his help, but the man refused. They were refugees, and it was his duty to help them, he told them. So Risto told him that he needed to change dollars into meticais. They walked past small straw houses as people followed them through the village. They stopped at one larger hut and entered it as Manuel and his friend chased away the curious crowd. Risto and Merci were introduced to the owner of the house, Eduardo, and his two friends. Manuel winked at Risto, and the local men all left for another room. When they returned, Eduardo sent one of his friends to fetch a man they called the 'businessman', as he placed a pot on the fire. A few minutes later, the friend came back with a man wearing plastic sunglasses; this was the 'businessman'. The money exchange began. A huge, bony tasteless fish, with brown cassava pap on a dirty grey plastic plate, was served to seal the business. Merci refused to drink the water; it was full of dirt. They brought him three cups of water, and he refused all of them. He refused the food as well, saying it looked strange. It was enough for Risto.

The money exchange didn't go smoothly. The exchange rate was reversed three times in favour of the man with the plastic sunglasses. There were also a few coins that he refused to give them. Risto could not argue, and took the money.

They were told that a large and risky forest, which linked Moçimboa da Praia with Palma, lay ahead, full of dangerous wild animals. One of the men wore Congolese-style shoes. They had been found on the body of a Congolese refugee who had been killed and eaten by a wild animal in the same forest. It was a warning sign; death was close by, said one man. He added that he wished he could pick up another two pairs of shoes, but when he scrutinised Risto and Merci, he reversed his words, saying that he doubted if these two were Congolese. 'Congolese wear brands, they have American dollars and always have gold and diamonds.'

The boys were in a need of a guide. Eduardo went and fetched Edmundo, a well-known bicycle driver; he would guide Risto and Merci as far as the little town of Palma. The forest was majestic; life and death were in its dark leaves, Edmundo told them. He said that he had walked the same forest his entire life; he was twenty-five years old now. He had come accross wild animals several times, but the power of his ancestors had fought for him. With his smile and the Swahili that fell from his lips in slow motion, his seemed to be the face of a good guy. He wore broken sandals and had a very old bike with ropes holding some parts of it together. He was paid the equivalent of 5 000 shilingi.

Along the way, his song was the same one: Congolese meant money and clothes, gold and diamonds. They were not the first people from Congo to come that way; many had passed through, and what the locals had heard and seen of them suggested that the stories were true: Congolese had nice clothes, they paid well and they had American dollars. Edmundo echoed all this, but he admitted that this pair looked poor. With their broken sandals and dirty, torn clothes, they portrayed misery. Maybe they didn't want to wear expensive clothes this time,' Edmundo said. Risto frowned, but he hid his anger.

Edmundo added that there were only two things he was still waiting for – gold and diamonds. He said Congolese didn't want to give away their diamonds and gold, but everyone knew very well that they had them hidden somewhere. As he was helping them, Edmundo expected some gold or a diamond, even just a little gold dust; it didn't matter which, he said. He just wanted enough money to marry his fiancée.

Merci looked at him like a ghost; his face showed his contempt for the man's words.

'We are very poor. If we had money, we would hire two bikes for our transport to Palma,' said Risto with bitterness.

Edmundo laughed at Risto, his eyes astonished. 'But you guys … you had money to travel. I know you even have gold and diamonds, but you don't want to give them to me.'

Risto thought Edmundo had lost his mind; his twenty-five years were not reflected in his words.

It would take them ten hours to reach Palma if they walked fast. Merci was in tears of exhaustion and thirst, suffering from the burning sun, his swelling legs and huge fear as they passed by what Edmundo said were rhinos. Risto's body had become a fountain of sweat, but showed no sign of fatigue or pain. Edmundo refused to allow them to rest, as this would delay the journey, and the forest was dangerous at night. To allow Merci to keep up, Edmundo decided to give him a ride on his bicycle that would take them ahead of Risto; then they would rest until he caught up with them. Risto didn't mind, even though it was eerie to be alone in the forest. Soon it became like a game – ride, stop, sit and wait for Risto; ride again and repeat the whole sequence over and over again.

At last, Edmundo drove so far ahead that Risto's eyes couldn't reach him; he only knew that they had stopped somewhere ahead to wait for him. After half an hour of walking alone in the frightening forest, he finally found Merci, who sat alone on the ground. Edmundo had lied, saying he was going back to find Risto; but he had run away and left them, having grown weary of waiting for a little piece of gold or a diamond which he believed the two boys didn't want to give him. He had his money already, and there was nothing more to get from Risto and Merci, so he decided to abandon them and go home.

The boys were alone in the forest. Soon the sun would disappear and darkness would fall; if they didn't reach people soon, they would end up in the bellies of some wild animals. Getting lost was another option that would lead straight to death. Merci did not take this news well; he held his head in his hands and sobbed for a few minutes, but Risto knew that crying wasn't a solution.

Merci had received a tip from Edmundo; the way to Palma was the larger path that looked like a muddy road. But every single movement of leaves made their bones shake to death; they knew that in each empty clearing lions and leopards were gazing, waiting for the right moment to strike. Their own footsteps frightened them; many times they hid behind shrubs until finally realising they were hiding from their own noise, their own shadows.

Everything happened as if in a dream. As darkness fell slowly, the two boys heard human voices. Merci thought it was monkey sounds; Risto thought they were mystical spirits. But when they saw the roofs of huts, they knew they had found a village. Help was close, they thought. Soon they met people, but help was far from being found. The people wanted money; they knew the same refrain about Congolese: American dollars, smart clothes, diamonds and gold. Of course, these Congolese boys looked poor, but surely they could pay a few dollars or some gold dust. The boys were told about crooked policemen on the main road leading to Palma; they targeted refugees, arresting them and seizing their money and belongings. If those policemen heard that the villagers had shown the way to the foreigners, they would be in real trouble.

Darkness was close to engulfing the gleaming lights of the sky. Risto and Merci could see that they were approaching the end of the little village; dense bush lay ahead of them. Should they seek a place to sleep, or carry on with their journey? For the first time, they argued. Merci wanted to ask for shelter, Risto wanted to carry on. Their argument intensified.

A man in his thirties, who stood behind a nearby kiosk, called to them. He led them to his small derelict hut, its walls full of holes, a little away from the main path. There was no sign of a wife or a child. His name was Mendes. He asked them questions about their country of origin, why they were running away. When Risto realised that the man apparently lived alone in an empty hut with only reed mats and two clay pots, his heart pounded. He regretted not having followed his instinct; he should have carried on with his journey. The man said he would help them get to Palma, but what was the reason for his kindness? Risto's heart wanted to trust him. The heart doesn't follow logic, said his mind; this was risky. But he could not leave Merci behind; they had become more than friends. He needed to stick with Merci, whatever the cost. And for that reason, he had to stick to the strange man too.

Risto again began his long soul-touching litany about how and why he was a refugee; he needed to win the guy's compassion. His voice carried honest tears; the word 'refugee' carried deep pain. Now their pain came because of the irony of people's beliefs; people who expected to find gold, diamonds and money in the empty pockets of refugees, in the begging hands of lost boys searching for peace.

Mendes listened with tears in eyes. He told Risto and Merci that they were not the first refugees he had helped. He had recognised them, and his heart had told him to help them. He went on to show his unannounced visitors a pair of shoes that he had gotten from a Congolese refugee as a gift after helping him. He gave the boys a coconut, and told them that this was not a good time for them to travel. The police down the main road would most probably have already received the news about the two foreigners on the way, and they would be waiting. It would be better to wait, and go late at night.

Mendes said that his parents wanted to see him that evening; he apologised, but it was important and urgent. His parents lived a few metres away, where smoke could be seen above the huts.

Merci was panicking; he felt they should run away, as he was afraid that Mendes had gone to gather a mob that would come to kill them. The story of the Congolese shoes made Risto think like Merci; maybe this was the way Mendes treated refugees. Maybe he kept them in his empty house, then came back at night with friends to finish them off, and take every cent from them. But his heart resisted this idea. They did not look rich in their torn clothes and old sandals. However, his mind pushed him to run away. He feared for the small amount of money that remained; with no money, their journey would end. He dug underneath the mat close to his head and hid the money inside the soil. Merci, by his side, took a stick and kept it close to him, just in case … they wouldn't die like cowards.

Two hours slipped by quickly in the wind of ugly thoughts. Suddenly Mendes was back, alone. It was time to go; it was around 9pm. Darkness would keep them safe from curious eyes and lurking police crooks. Mendes smoked his cannabis for protection; neither of the boys wanted to smoke. After an hour of walking, they reached the forest that separated the village from the main road going to Palma. The forest was very dangerous, Mendes confirmed. He cut branches from some wild tree and gave one to each of them to hold in their left hand. This was to chase away any fierce wild animals, just as the cannabis smoke was supposed to chase away the evil spirits.

Risto was still scared. The reason for the man's kindness was not convincing enough. Mendes must have guessed at the mistrust their hearts were carrying, because he revealed his heart to the two strangers. He lived the simple life of an honest and trustworthy man. He believed that life exists in reciprocity. It was a simple principle he had learned from his father.

'What we sow is what we reap. The more we give, the more we receive; curse and blessing go beyond bloodline and generations,' he quoted his father. His father was a good man; his good deeds favoured even homeless birds and stray dogs; his community praised him. During the fight for Mozambican independence, his father was shot twice, once in his chest and once in the left leg. He waited for scavengers to finish him off, but some unknown foreign people risked their lives to take him to a missionary clinic. It was the harvest of his good deeds. Since then, he taught all his children the same principles.

At around midnight, they reached another village. Risto's and Merci's feet were sore and swollen. In this village, people always walked in pairs at night, but as they were only three, they walked in a horizontal line to prove that they were not intruders. They quietly crossed the village to the main road where they waited the rest of the night for a pick-up truck. The police had not yet arrived when a loaded truck came by. Mendes refused any gift or payment; he waved to the boys as the truck raced away down the dusty road.

Later that morning, at around 10am, the driver dropped them at a parking place where they waited for a truck to Nampula. From there, the Nampula refugee camp was just a few miles, they were told. At this point there was no more Swahili; everybody was now speaking Portuguese. Any other language attracted curious eyes and the risk of police arrest.

Thirst and hunger made the world around Risto and Merci spin. A beautiful white painted house stood in between low brick walls at a street crossing; the two boys approached it. Risto gazed down at his filthy clothes and old sandals; Merci could smell that his clothes were stinking. It was as if they came from another world, that of dirty pigs. Right then, survival was crucial; water at least would keep them alive until the day of a proper meal, if they ever had one again. A beautiful girl with long black hair appeared after they knocked. She was brown and barefoot, with honey lips. She spoke words that immediately vanished from their heads; it quickly changed their perception that Portuguese was a half-brother of French. Risto gestured.

'Agua,' he said.

'Agua!' repeated the girl.

Her finger went straight, pointing to an open market. Risto gestured that he had no money. The truth was that they were afraid of meeting police. The boys sat at the entrance without speaking until the girl came back with a bottle of water and a pencil and paper. They clapped their hands.

Suddenly, a car stopped in the main road, running footsteps vibrated; a police car stood not far from them as a couple of men in uniforms chased some young men who looked like foreigners. Risto and Merci kept standing with the girl to avoid attracting suspicion from the police. With the other foreigners escaping, and the police car still standing there, they thought they would be the next target. Police meant death to Risto, so they begged their legs to be strong. The girl stood in shock with her mouth wide open, still holding the bottle in her hand, as the two boys ran away at top speed.

· Chapter 15 ·

The open market was a few metres away; ahead was what looked like an informal parking lot. According to the itinerary that Mendes had explained to Risto and Merci, this was the place where they would be able to get a truck or bus to Nampula. Nampula had the biggest refugee camp in Mozambique; it was also the only open refugee camp, meaning it was the only one that was still taking in new refugees. Risto and Merci believed that the camp was the only place their dreams could flourish – once they could breathe peace again.

A big bus stopped and people got off. Four young boys lurking round a corner glanced at the bus, and then went back to their corner. They were the same youths the police had been chasing earlier that morning. They looked foreign, as if they came from the horn of Africa – Somalia, Eritrea or Ethiopia. When Risto and Merci approached them, the boys ran away. Risto and Merci retreated back to the hiding place they had found behind an empty container. A few minutes later, a policeman on a bike drove around; it was known as a place where illegal immigrants hung around looking for transport.

Later that afternoon, a truck stopped, and all six refugee boys presented themselves in front of the driver, each with the same plea, while eyeing the others, hoping to frighten them away. Unbelievably, Risto heard one of the four talking to the driver in a language that sounded like Swahili. He squeezed himself into the conversation, but got cut off by one boy, who looked Somali. He fell silent when Risto approached, giving him a look like he was 'mixing in their business'.

Risto persisted. 'Hello!' he said in Swahili.

'Where are you from?' asked the driver.

Risto painted a fresh smile on his tired and hungry face.

'I am a refugee, Congolese,' he replied, seeking sympathy with the word 'refugee'.

'Are you with these guys, are they also refugees?' the man asked, pointing to the Somali group.

'No, I am with my brother over there,' said Risto, indicating Merci.

'I am not going to Nampula; but I can drop you in Namialo, and from there you can take a truck to Nampula.'

The metical exchange rate was still beyond Risto's understanding. He could only think in shilingi and American dollars. The transport fees the driver asked for took every cent he had except for about twenty dollars in meticais. In a country where the laws of the road were above the laws of the state, Risto's payment was barely enough for two people. All six boys jumped into the rear of the truck and lay under a tarpaulin cover.

The heat was awful. Within an hour, the air under the cover had turned from a hot bath into a boiling pot. Before long, they were sweating like athletes running the Olympics in the Kalahari Desert. The Somali group had some water in a two-litre bottle, but it had heated up in the burning conditions. Yet they treasured that hot water. Everyone got a sip just to soften their throats. That bottle of water brought the two groups together; for the first time, they began speaking to one another.

The boy who spoke Swahili was called Amidi. He confirmed that they were indeed all Somalis, and in search of a refugee camp. Risto told him that they were Congolese refugees, also looking for a refugee camp. Amidi showed great interest in Risto and Merci's journey and background.

'Where did you learn Swahili, then? I thought people speak French in Congo?'

'Yes, French is the official language, but Swahili is one of the national languages. Actually it is one of the most widely spoken languages in the country,' replied Risto.

'I never knew that. So ... Congo-Brazzaville or Congo-Kinshasa?'

'Kinshasa,' Risto answered, taking off his shirt because of the massive heat under the tarpaulin. 'I didn't think Swahili was spoken in Somalia. How did you learn it?'

'I've lived in Kenya. I was a refugee there for a few years.' Amidi carried on with his questioning: 'Is the situation in Congo as bad as it is in Mogadishu?'

'I don't know how it is in Mogadishu, but yes ... things are bad in Congo ... wars and stuff.' Risto didn't want to be specific; it might lead to more personal questions.

'So, guns all over, like in Somalia? Shooting, burning of houses, and so on?'

Risto didn't like the way Amidi asked questions, as if he was investigating something. He knew Amidi was just asking out of curiosity, but Risto found it uncomfortable. Nevertheless, they talked of their difficult journey to an unknown destination and the problems they had encountered. They even laughed at some of the funny things they had seen.

In Mozambique, a country still recovering from a long civil war, any unidentified person represented a threat to the young government. They could be rebels or spies. Roadblocks were everywhere; here the police scrutinised every passenger's identity documents and every single item being transported. But just as not every sheep listens to the voice of the good shepherd, some policemen had made their own laws, and these reigned over the state's laws. The amount of money held out in one's hand determined to what extent people would be checked.

The truck carrying the refugees passed through the first roadblock. The driver spoke to the policemen and the truck went unchecked. From roadblock to roadblock, the boys in the rear of the truck lay still, trying not to breathe. Between roadblocks, the driver drove fast. He didn't have any time to waste, he said. He even refused to stop when one of the Somalis, almost crying, asked for a toilet break.

The truck stopped at yet another roadblock. This time the driver spoke to the police for almost a quarter of an hour, but they would not let the truck go. In the back, the boys smelled trouble, and indeed there was real trouble coming. The policemen climbed onto the truck, stepped on the passengers' heads and toes under the tarpaulin, trying to trap them into moving. When they lay still, the police repeated their stepping game, as if it was funny. The uneven shapes of their bodies betrayed the boys, and they were taken out from under the cover and lined up on the ground. No one had a passport or a valid ID.

The police asked questions about their mission in Mozambique. Through the mouth of the driver, the only translator, they explained that they were refugees looking for camps. Now came the time to be thoroughly frisked. The police went through their clothing pocket by pocket, then their shoes, one by one, even their underpants; all got searched thoroughly. Any note or coin found was taken. The Somalis cried out to the policemen in strange tongues; they replied with a strange form of Portuguese, difficult to understand.

Merci and Risto's clothes were torn and stinking. When one policeman gathered up the great courage to search Merci's smelly shorts and found that all the pockets were torn, he didn't bother to check Risto. When they were told to get back into their truck, Risto celebrated silently for still having a few notes. He knew he had been lucky. The police saw no point in arresting the refugees while they were looking for a camp, especially as they were not found with any contraband. Their presence in the country was illegal, but it wasn't the job of the police to deport them.

It was dark when the refugees were dropped off at the Namialo business centre; the wait for sunrise felt like a whole month. Risto changed his sleeping position on the pavement outside a shop hundreds of times. At first the dirty ground felt cold and bumpy; later it was as warm as a bed, and for short periods, he slept deeply. They no longer feared the police, as there was no more money to lose, no belongings to be taken away. In fact, Risto thought that an arrest would be a good thing, as it would save them from hunger and thirst. No one wanted to think about how they would get to Nampula or Maputo; they waited for the advice of the morning breeze.

The trip had become a pilgrimage; it had changed their hearts and strengthened friendships. Among the boys, there was neither Somali nor Congolese anymore. They had become one in the fight for survival; they had the same prayer, one that sought a common answer. Despite the torment of the journey, sharing their fears and believing that they would find peace had kept each of them strong.

Amidi had spoken of his previous journey from Sudan to Kenya. He explained how, in the absence of food and water, he had ended up eating leaves from unknown trees and even drinking his own urine. Even with no money, Amidi remained optimistic about the trip, and the chance of reaching a refugee camp. They were not in a desert or jungle, he said, and where there are people, there is always help.

Amidi thought about going ahead on foot; surely Nampula was not so far. But Risto and Merci had learned the hard lessons of going on foot in an unknown place. They had walked for more than fifteen hours in the forests of Mozambique at great risk of death from thirst, starvation and wild animals. They did not want to repeat such an adventure, and they refused to walk, better for the police to capture them than to walk hundreds of kilometres on a journey that would end in tears.

Risto, who was able to draw the entire political map of Africa and locate every capital city, was unable to point to Namialo or Nampula on the map; he had never heard of these towns before this journey, and could not say how far it was to Nampula. No one could decide what their greatest priority should be: searching for water and food, or seeking transport.

In the awakening town, a few cars were starting to move about, and two young men approached them. Maybe this unusual gathering of youths in the early morning had captured their attention. The refugees' hands waved, asking for water, but the men had none. Amidi showed them his shoes, then asked for money. The two men walked a few steps away and then came back. Amidi engaged them in vigorous discussion of price with his body language; he had an idea of the worth of the metical, at least. Finally, the two men gave him money and the broken shoes belonging to one of the Mozambicans in exchange for his shoes. Another Somali joined in the trading. Eventually, five Mozambicans were buying shoes, trousers and shirts from the unusual travellers. Two Somalis were left barefoot and dressed only in shorts, having sold everything. Merci wanted to sell his torn clothes too, but those to whom he showed his rags left laughing.

Risto yelled 'Nampula?' in the ears of the Mozambicans; at first they ignored him. He pulled at one man's shirt and gestured 'Where is Nampula?', then screamed 'Refugiado!' Their eyes widened and they looked at each other in amazement. One of them answered in Portuguese, then wrote on the ground with a stick: '+100 km'. Risto asked 'Maputo?' Everyone laughed, then a fearful silence hung in the air. The faces of the youths went soft. One of them wrote '++++1000 km', and then suddenly they all left without looking back.

The refugees rushed to the first pick-up truck of the day.

'Nampula!' they called.

'No, no,' said the old driver.

The second pick-up truck driver yelled a few angry words in Portuguese until they fell back.

The boys wandered around until they reached a petrol station where a huge truck stood. The driver was distracted, deep in conversation with a beautiful girl. The back doors of the truck were held together by a wire, and the boys managed to open it and climb in. The truck soon drove off, past villages and farms and patches of bush. They looked through a tiny window in the back, wishing to see Nampula written somewhere, and soon Amidi announced that he had seen a sign that read: Nampula 80 km. He and his fellow refugees all rejoiced, believing that soon they would be at peace; hope was stirring in their hearts. Freedom was in the air; there were no roadblocks, no men in uniform to search the truck. Their hearts nearly stopped beating when they saw a passing police car, but the truck didn't slow down.

Within the darkness of the truck, hunger and thirst became unbearable as the truck drove for hours. Risto slowly went deaf and mute as his body weakened. He believed that one more hour in the truck would mean death. The Somalis were very quiet too. They were saving their energy, they said; the more they talked or cried, the more energy their bodies would lose and the closer to death they would be.

When the truck stopped, the boys couldn't wait; they rushed to pull the wire on the doors. Both Risto's body and his universe were spinning, hunger and thirst made him too weak for a quick jump. The driver had stopped for refreshment at a sugar-cane farm. The four Somalis and Merci rushed to the other side of the farm in search of food. Risto wanted to follow, but he did not have the strength to move. So he lay where he was in the back of the truck.

Before his friends could make their way back, the driver jumped back in and raced off again. Risto was now half-conscious, alone in a truck speeding towards an unknown destination. He could not jump from a moving vehicle; in his weakened state, this might have been deadly. But he could not close the banging door at the back of the truck either. He heard humming in his head and felt the world spinning. Even moving felt like an impossible task. His body was so heavy that in the end he let himself drift.

The driver eventually realised something was wrong with his truck doors and stopped to look. He was stunned when he found a boy sleeping inside; his endless complaints in Portuguese did not change a thing. He dragged Risto into the cab of the truck and shouted at him, his rage visible in his wrinkles. He smelled so strongly of beer that he almost made Risto drunk.

'Nampula,' Risto shouted back at the man. 'Refugiado, refugee,' he kept repeating, hoping it meant something to the driver with the long beard. The driver kept asking for money. When he saw how weak Risto was, he searched his pockets. But they were empty, and the boy had nothing valuable on him.

'Money, money, money, money …' the driver screamed, his veins awakening in his skin. Risto held his head in his hands quietly; he could hardly hear the driver. The screaming seemed to be coming from a faraway mountain. The voice was deformed by distance and came in vibrating echoes in his ears.

Eventually the screaming stopped and Risto felt the truck moving again. When he woke, he saw a scene like a play with the driver as the main character. He was standing in front of his truck, holding a bottle of beer like the stick of an angry soldier. On either side of him were two smart men in their mid-thirties, surrounded by an amazed crowd that cheered each word and movement of the driver.

'My money … right now!' screamed the driver, almost beating the head of the man on the right with his beer bottle. The crowd shouted with excitement.

'I've brought you this poor thing … now pay back my petrol, food and water, or else!' He swung his bottle at the man on the right, missed, and fell on the ground.

At this time, two boys, almost Risto's age, came to open the truck cab and take him out. Fortunately, the drunkard driver had forgotten his key in the ignition. Risto was carried to a tent nearby and quickly given water and porridge. Later that day, he heard that the driver had wanted money for bringing Risto to the refugee camp. According to his account, he had found Risto dying by the road and decided to bring him to the Marathan refugee camp outside Nampula. He asked to be paid back what he had spent along the way to keep Risto alive: water and food, as well as money for petrol. The United Nations officials agreed to give him a reasonable amount to cover his expenses. Strangely, however, the man wanted ten times what they had given him, and that was what had caused the trouble and fighting.

But the story ended with the driver falling over. He was in such a state of drunkenness that he was unable to walk, so the people he was quarrelling with ended up watching over him. They sheltered him until late that afternoon. Once he had regained his strength and was sober, he asked for no more money, and drove off to Nampula in a hurry.

Later that evening Risto found himself placed with a host family in the camp. It was a cacophony of four-to-six-metre bungalows spread across a big flat open area, probably one kilometre square. Far away from Nampula town, it had no scenery to please the eyes, only tall indigenous fruitless trees.

At first glimpse, the refugee camp was a study in despair that a great painter would have rendered as a masterpiece canvas of misery. The houses were so small that a well-built, healthy and full-stomached woman would not be able to fit through the doors, that a tall man walking in his sleep would have touched the roof with his head.

Criss-crossing between the miserable muddy bungalows, Risto and his new hosts were followed by potbellied children with yellowish hair, who hoped that he might have something to give to them. He passed a few pitiful and over-exploited vegetable gardens and a tap surrounded by dozens of children with buckets and pots. Risto helped a little girl struggling to lift her five-litre container. He was surprised to hear that she was twelve years old; she looked eight or nine at most. She had lived in the camp for four years, and the yellowish hair said it all; she was suffering from malnutrition.

A boy who could not be older than twelve ran past them, breathing heavily; he was being chased by a woman carrying a child on her back. A little crowd behind them cheered with excitement. When Risto asked what was happening, a girl said that the boy had broken into the house of the lady and stolen her cooked food. Apparently, the boy, who was an obedient and respectful child, could no longer stand his hunger, so stealing the woman's food was his only remaining option.

They came across many men hanging around, some in groups, some with their ears against a radio, listening and commenting on politics, while others played different games to keep themselves busy. It frightened Risto when he pictured himself seated under a huge fruitless tree talking politics or playing games to kill time; there wouldn't be anything else to do.

· Chapter 16 ·

Everyone in the camp was speaking about the boy who, after two weeks there, was still waiting for the outcome of his asylum-seeker application. Some people said he might be deported; others said a second interview had been scheduled. But the mystery of his story had everyone talking. He had come with the recent flow of refugees who had entered the camp; during his interview, he went dumb when he was asked his reason for leaving his country.

In the camp, Bi Maimuna was the lady who could tell what a dead man had forgotten to tell before dying, or if an unborn child really would look like his father. She was known in the camp as Mama RFI, the acronym for the International French Radio, because each morning she had fresh breaking news. She was a famous hair braider in the camp, although her popularity was the result of her unique news broadcasts rather than her professional expertise. It was said that the gossiping spirits of the camp whispered daily news in her dreams. Each morning she woke with a swollen mouth and swollen eyes that she had to unburden by delivering precious news to her clients. Next she went to the little open markets where news grew and travelled across the camp.

Because of her brownish skin with red spots burned on her face by antiseptic, people believed that each year she manufactured a new skin for her face so she could look young and beautiful. Even her name, Bi Maimuna, was a way of refusing to grow older and accept the custom of local names. Normally a mother would be called 'Mama' plus the name of her oldest child. As Mama RFI had no child, she should have been called Maimuna, as that was her name, but she had kept the prefix 'Bi', meaning 'youthful', to prove that she was still young and fashionable.

Women cried whenever their husbands familiarised themselves with Bi Maimuna. First they ended up in her bed, and then the entire camp would hear her review of these men. She would expose their weaknesses to the entire camp, and would criticise them to justify why she wouldn't live with such a man.

Bi Maimuna always wanted to get to the bottom of any undying rumour, so she was very interested in the case of the boy who would not speak. She hurried to see him with a comb in her long braided hair, looking very busy, as if she had important work that she had abandoned for this emergency.

'Boy,' she addressed Risto, who sat at the edge of the yard under a tree. 'Where are the people of this house?'

'They went to the camp office; there is food distribution today.'

'Why didn't you go?'

Risto wondered why she hadn't gone either.

'I received mine two weeks ago.'

'Yes … yes, you are from the group that arrived in the camp recently.'

Bi Maimuna wasn't going anywhere; she moved closer to Risto, her eyes examining his body from head to toe.

'You are Risto, right?'

'Yes.'

'From which part of Congo?'

'Bukavu.'

'Is your family in this camp or …'

Bi Maimuna asked a question to which she already knew the answer.

'Still in Bukavu.'

'Your mother must be very worried, without her fifteen-year-old son …'

'Sixteen,' Risto interrupted.

'I heard that your interview was tough; why couldn't you talk? There is a risk of you being deported from the country. Do you know that? What went wrong?'

Bi Maimuna's ears were wide open, her eyes unblinking. She was craving Risto's long story. 'We have all gone through many things, and we manage to talk about them; talking about those tough moments brings peace; it heals one's heart.'

Risto ignored her last sentence.

'Are you hiding something? Don't you trust me, boy?' Bi Maimuna painted a fake smile on her face. Risto was busy drawing in the sand. She looked closely at his face; he had some scars from his beatings at the hands of the militia, and a birthmark on his chin. His hands bore scars too. Bi Maimuna peered, trying to guess where those marks had come from, wondering what was in the brain of the boy. Her eagerness to peep into Risto's soul was huge. Yet she went away disappointed, with little to share with the camp.

In a camp where people could easily guess what was hidden in the depths of their neighbour's mind, where people could sing the secrets of others in loud voices, Risto's story was still a mystery. How did such a young boy cross so many countries, all alone, ending up in a camp without any close relative? Not even the scrutiny of the United Nations interviewers could reveal his secrets. He puzzled them all; the curious Bi Maimuna, whose stinging mouth could easily break a clay calabash; the flea market vendors; Balaba, the feared witchdoctor whose intricate bones revealed to him the secrets of souls – none of them could figure Risto out.

The only person Risto spoke to was his friend Merci, who had arrived at the camp a few days after him; a farmer had taken pity on him and had given him a ride most of the way, and he had walked the rest. The family that had first hosted them had allocated them a tiny piece of land where they had built a mud hut.

Unusual things happened in the little house, according to the stories. A snake was found sleeping behind Risto's back, but it did not bite him. A whirlwind nearly blew him away when he was walking in the marketplace. All of these things were omens to say that the boy was hiding something that might hurt him. He should come clean, people whispered. Because Risto lived without disclosing the answers to the many questions about his hidden life, Balaba, the master of enchantments, told him the ancestors were not happy with his hidden secrets.

But Risto took all these experiences as part of his pilgrimage on earth. He enjoyed looking at things that didn't have any human explanation. It was through these that he drew his wisdom; he followed the movement of the evening birds, the giant spaces of the skies, the whispers of the wind at dawn, the invisible fire of the hot Mozambican winds, the murmurs of the standing rocks that stared at the camp from afar. All of these talked to him. Their words soothed his soul; they brought the peace and quiet he needed, free from fear of bullets and omnipresent shadows watching him from behind. In these he found the wisdom to overcome the madness of the camp, which had taken away the wisdom of even the oldest and most respected people.

As food was there in theory, but not in practice, even the most respected ones lost their principles and learned how to steal from their friends' gardens. At night, they would crawl into the vegetable gardens to take sweet potatoes and tomatoes to share with their families. To survive, they ended up stealing even the food of their own children, expecting them to have eaten from their friends' gardens in turn. It was tormenting to see a woman close to the end of her pregnancy standing in the long queues, begging for sugar and maize powder, a few tea bags and a pinch of beans. Food distribution in the refugee camp was a contradiction. A family of five would receive so little food that it wouldn't even make a full and balanced breakfast for them. Yet they were forced to make do with that ration until the following month's food distribution.

Yet Marathan slowly came closer to Risto's heart. It seemed to offer him the inner peace he was searching for, and there seemed to be a bit of acceptance from the people in the camp. Some loved his halting Portuguese spoken with a melodious French accent. Some women loved the shining black-brownish colour of his skin, and many enjoyed his optimistic spirit.

In this peaceful new world, Risto became a tomato cultivator. He worked on a little plot offered to him by a church. Merci followed in his steps. The camp, which looked like a desert, had little water for tomatoes, but the boys did not believe in impossibility, and were determined to cultivate tomatoes in the sandy soil of Marathan. They would wake up at around 4am to draw water from the communal tap. Then they carried watering cans to sprinkle their field. This was a daily exercise that could have been used for bodybuilding, as the tap was one kilometre away from their plot.

Their first harvest was moderate, but gave them a few meticais. Despite deciding to invest most of their money in seeds and more watering cans, they had enough to live on. Risto was able to phone home for the first time. There was no phone box in the camp, but a few big, old and battered cell phones lay on a three-legged table in a large mud house. The owner wore a huge white kanzu, and spoke polished Burundian Swahili. Risto picked up the phone as the owner concentrated on his large plastic watch to count the minutes.

'Allo?'

'Allo, Mama. It is Risto.'

He could hear her weeping with joy.

'How are you and where are you?'

'I am fine, Mama, I am calling from Mozambique.'

His mother couldn't believe her ears. How had he reached Mozambique, by airplane, train, bus, ship? Who had hosted him? Her questions and worries were endless. She wanted to pray over the phone to thank God for this miracle. She had missed him so much she had become sick after he left, she confessed as she cried, and Risto cried as well.

Risto had phoned for two reasons: first to say that he was alive and well; second, to apologise for having left home without saying goodbye. He told his mother that he would have gone mad had he not left Bukavu. He was sick of the country, sick of the situation in town and in the villages; each corner and street, each house and path, each story and voice of Bukavu held phantoms that tortured him until he could stand it no longer. He promised to send letters that same month. He gave her the cell number and the postal address of the Cellphone Man, as they called the man with the phones. He could be reached after making an appointment for a call.

A month later, letters from Bukavu arrived. Although Risto phoned home regularly and spoke to the whole Mahuno family, their letters were more meaningful to him than the phone calls. Yes, their voices came with the moisture of their heart's breath, but the letters brought them closer to him. He could feel them; he smelled them through their ink, through their writing. He could picture their faces through their handwriting; he felt their pain and touched it through the teardrops stamped on the paper. He could see how his mother sat on the chair, left hand on her chin, drafting her worries onto a piece of paper, asking what he had eaten the day before, and what he would eat the next. She sat wondering if there were other mothers who could look after her son, give him proper food, help him wash his clothes, speak to him softly when he got angry, tell him stories of her youth and so on … She sat wondering whether there was a mother there to hold her son in her arms and tell him that she loved him, that she would always be there for him. But she knew as she sat that there were none with her heart, none to give her son the love that he missed – her warm hands, her close heartbeat – and this feeling devastated her so that her tears dropped onto her letter. She couldn't tell the story of her weakness to her son, but Risto knew …

These letters were the spirit of his family. He could see his father with his dictionary looking for the right word; he would check, then call Landu to verify if the word was the right one. They would discuss the word for a few minutes before his father wrote it down. He could see him listening to the world news on his small radio, paying more attention to Mozambican news than to Congo's. He could see Nampula as a dot in the world atlas, but Marathan was invisible, so he would wonder if Marathan was an island in lost waters, or a land in forgotten forests. He wanted his son to have a bright future, a secure future with a degree at a recognised and respected university. While his son was in that faraway place, he was unable to provide him with that education. He thought he had failed; he couldn't provide his son with what he had promised him, and this haunted him. He sometimes blamed himself for the situation of his son; but Risto told him never to think that way. Nobody was to blame; history and time had made things happen the way they had.

Landu's letter focused on Risto's ghosts. His wish to contribute to the rebuilding of Risto's life was still in his mind, and he wanted to understand the reasons for Risto's departure. So he had gone into his background, and had learned of Risto's love for Néné. Landu had met a boy, Jeanvier, who had been part of Risto's group in the forest; he had escaped from the militia in the Kahuzi-Biega National Park. Jeanvier had confirmed Risto's account of Benny's death; he also told him it appeared that Néné was pregnant, and the situation in the forest was still the same: abuse and killing. These stories turned Risto's eyes into water fountains.

They say that meditation heals bruised hearts and deep wounds in the inner being. Maybe hard work in a forgotten and solitary land and in the blowing desolation of a place like Marathan glues and repairs torn-up souls. It was healing the wounds of two fragile hearts, Merci, with his rebellious scars, and Risto, with his invisible earthquakes and haunting past. Merci had never thought he would become a refugee, but his journey was triggered by his anger against his parents. His father, an ex-senior manager at the Sucrerie de Kiliba, one of the biggest sugar-producing companies of the former Zaire, became unemployed when the company went bankrupt. Merci had been used to luxury, a flashy lifestyle, expensive clothes and pocket money. Things went upside down; first his family was unable to buy him a bus ticket to school; then the school fees became a problem. This didn't bother Merci as much as not being able to buy fashionable shoes, or snacks at lunch breaks.

He grew angrier, believing his parents hadn't done enough to protect their good life. Soon he was rarely seen at home. He absented himself from his family's meagre lunches and dinners. During the fragile so-called peace in Uvira, he spent his days hanging around the markets babbling with street kids and vendors. It was during this time that he narrowly escaped two kidnappings, one by the rebel movement and another by the Mai-Mai, who were forcing children to join their army. He soon realised his life was at risk.

This was when Merci stole money from his father and headed off on the journey that had led him to the refugee camp, searching for gold in the sands of Mozambique. He now cultivated tomatoes in the desert. The journey had given him wisdom, and Risto had helped him to reconcile with his parents and family. Sometimes he would break the sacred silence that reigned in their little field and ask, 'Who taught you so much about life?' Risto had no answer. He did not believe he knew a lot about life; he was eager instead to learn about life.

But Risto felt the unfairness; he had heard Merci's story, but he had not shared with his friend the secrets of his own journey to Mozambique. Whenever he wanted to start telling him, his mouth went dumb and his heart sobbed.

'My past has starving ghosts who wait for me to turn back so that they can swallow me,' he told Merci.

'But how can you go back in history?' asked Merci, puzzled.

'Not literally ... but I have seen bad things, and talking about them will take me back to the horrors of that time. That is why I cannot speak about my past.'

'Take it easy, brother ... our friendship is strong, maybe it is not the right time. This will pass, believe me,' Mercy would say, trying to comfort him.

Risto enjoyed the early Sunday church services in the camp. These took place under a giant fruitless tree of unknown name whose branches created a double ceiling for the people in the straw and mud church. The church was packed with songbird women with magical tones and velvet-voiced men with trombone tunes. There was no pain on the faces of these forgotten people buried in a land of hopeless dreams, in a forgotten pocket of time; their singing was pure happiness and joy. It carried him back home, as if he was rocking on the majestic and sleeping Lake Kivu among brave fishermen as they performed their morning chanting. He saw again the colourful waving loincloths of women as they danced and sang for beloved friends soon to be wed in Bugobe village. He saw all these images as he dreamed of Congo and experienced the reality of the Sunday service in the Marathan refugee camp.

The voices of these women and men were more coordinated than in an opera. Each one knew the power of his or her voice, its mysterious effects on the souls of those waiting for heavenly whispers. Each one knew his or her time, when and where to lead and when to hand over to the next person. Their feet were like drumsticks tapping over the wooden floor. They stepped strongly and rhythmically, clapping their hands as their heads moved in cadence. Their souls melted in spiritual enchantment, their bodies breathed in joyful vapours. A woman, travelling in time and spirit above the universe and heaven, with eyes closed, banged two metal rods together. A stinging and piercing sound arose, adding its noise to the mass choir.

The church, which had no sophisticated electronic instruments, used African handmade instruments to invite the holy fire to cleanse people's souls. What happened next left Risto in wonder. Two women and one man came forward with tambourines made of goatskin hooked onto their hips. As the three tambourines were hit by six sweaty hands, a penetrating sound cut through the air, and the whole congregation sang hymns from a little book they had. Then the tambourines stopped and everyone burst into prayer. They prayed in unknown tongues that Risto had never heard before; some jumped up, others kneeled down as they clapped their hands; one would have thought that the holy fire had burned them.

When the prayers ended, the music became soft enough to change a rock into cream. It was a code indicating the need to remain quiet. Many people wiped away tears. Then the music stopped, and a man with a voice that was first velvet then harsh came forward with bible stories in different languages, Portuguese with French and Swahili translations. The crowd responded with hurrahs and hallelujahs. Risto thought that the Holy Spirit had descended to touch the heart of each person in the little church. The voice of the preacher whirled and the listeners followed like wind above a wave. But he was not preaching; he was giving a testimony, which left people in tears of joy this time; his entire life had been a miracle, he said.

While the man was still giving his testimony, a leader with a stinging but soft voice started a song and the whole congregation took over; the soulful dances went on. People were lost in soothing hymns, and sometimes it would be an old man with a thick deep voice who would start the singing. Everybody else would follow until the preacher would finally stand up in his beautiful suit to lead people through the stories from the bible.

Risto found the same scenes every Sunday. The pain and hardship that these people faced each new day were conquered by the celebration of faith, courage and love. Pain and suffering were ever-present in their lives. Many lived in tiny shacks, trading in any objects they could pick up, or working little fields for only a handful of vegetables. But these precious Sundays allowed them to conquer their hunger, their anger and grief at their lost inheritance, and to strengthen the dreams they carried within themselves.

· Chapter 17 ·

Risto arrived for his second interview. The curious were already lurking. In a camp where interviews took place in absolute privacy, it was a riddle to interviewers how the following day, women in the flea market would debate the outcomes. Many believed the nightly gossip spirits of the camp told everything to Bi Maimuna, Mama RFI. Rumours in the camp revealed what went on behind closed curtains; night-watchers reported that two of the men who sat at the interview table had each been spotted leaving her house early in the mornings.

Bi Maimuna was already in the office when Risto showed up; she greeted him in a rush as she passed. She said she had come to ask if any letters from the United States, a country that had agreed to take her for resettlement, had arrived. There were none. She left the office; Risto stayed in the little waiting-room scanning through magazines. Ten minutes hadn't gone by before she appeared again; this time she wanted to know if Risto's host family were at home. Yes, everyone was there. She left. A few minutes later, there she was again, itching to hear the mystery of the boy's history, but she had no questions left to ask.

She seemed puzzled by the four chairs and the small table that stood in the interview room, as if there should have been an extra chair for her. She smelled of an expensive floral perfume; her lips were honeyed; her loincloth was wrapped above tight trousers. She was in her seductive clothes, some people had whispered as she crossed the flea market.

'So, you know this is your last chance, eh Risto?' she said as she leaned closer to his ear.

Risto looked at her for a few seconds, and then went back to his magazine.

'Are you talking today? You should trust me; I can help you with this. What don't you want to say, what is it that your heart doesn't wish to share? I can help, if you will tell me.'

Risto ignored Mama RFI.

'We will know all, boy; don't think there is a secret in Marathan, this is our own small country,' she exclaimed, as she left, furious.

The interviewers started with their soft smiles, with easy questions, the news of the camp, and so on. Then they went on to ask about name, family, town and country of origin.

'The whole camp is talking about your last harvest of tomatoes,' said Mr Thomaso Dwanga, the only Mozambican at the interview table; he spoke a nice Swahili.

'You know this camp talks about anything, even a rain that the heavens have not yet thought about.'

The two refugees present, Mr Rashid and Mama Lemwalu, who represented the board on camp management, were astounded by the wisdom of the young boy; they had heard about it, but now they saw it for themselves.

'You know this is your second and last interview,' Mr Thomaso reminded Risto.

'Yes, Sir.'

'I believe you are ready to talk today,' added Mr Thomaso.

'Let me remind you, any lies will lead to rejection of your application for refugee status, and then deportation. We are here to help you formulate a good report for the United Nations. Ask questions when you don't understand well.' These were the wise words of Mama Lemwalu.

'This interview will determine whether you qualify for refugee status or not; so tell us now, your reasons for leaving your country, Congo.' It was Mr Thomaso speaking again, eyes flashing at Risto.

'Yes … um …'

Risto felt nervous; he didn't like it. He had come to tell all and get it done with.

'Could I have a glass of water, please?' he asked.

His throat was drying, talking was becoming difficult, he felt warmer. A glass rested in his hand, he coughed as he put it to his mouth, his shaking teeth were in danger of breaking the glass.

He needed to be strong, he told himself. But in the limpid water, he saw his life in slow motion: Risto with his parents; Risto with his siblings; Risto with Néné in a wedding gown, playing children's wedding games; Risto in military uniform in Kahuzi-Biega National Park; Risto with a machete butchering another child soldier who had disobeyed; Risto holding a smoking gun over a shaking, half-dead Mai-Mai soldier; Risto in Panzi hospital, his crutches by the bed, a crying girl with a baby; Risto running away from ghosts, voices; Risto in a broken boat on Lake Tanganyika. The pictures were so real, so vivid, they took him back, he was standing before a jury with eyes that judged, hearts that could not pardon, he was shaking without control.

There was so much hot hair stuck in his muscles, in his arteries, in his stomach, that his nostrils couldn't contain it. He swelled, he shook. The last picture in his head was of Néné putting the bracelet on his wrist. He wanted to touch that bracelet, but there was no more strength; he could hear voices calling his name, echoing from faraway mountains, the voices of Mr Thomaso and Mama Lemwalu, both calling together; he couldn't see them.

Mr Thomaso was the first to touch him, feeling for his heartbeat, racing, dying down. Mama Lemwalu had run to the phone. Mr Rashid had run for his car.

The car left dust and wind in the flea market as it went, leaving women guessing at all sorts of theories.

The clinic had no doctor, just a trainee nurse, who had nothing in mind but an injection for malaria. Mr Rashid refused; the poison in Risto's bloodstream was not malaria. By the time a man in a white lab coat arrived, Risto was begging to be left alone. He knew his illness, he said; he needed to be alone.

After this, Risto changed. He wanted to be away from any gathering. He enjoyed loneliness. Silence became his way of talking; people's eyes annoyed him, their stories bored him. He would spend an hour looking at the moving branch of a tree, or sitting on a remote rock where he listened to the wind whispering. Nothing seemed interesting to him any longer, and he would sometimes cry for unknown reasons. In the early hours in the tomato field, he would sit in the sand singing lamentations, staring at the sky, asking heaven impossible questions. He wished time could go back; he wished he could touch his past; he wept and refused Merci's consolation, and this in turn made Merci cry.

Risto's life story had become more important than Bi Maimuna's braiding job. Every day, a large crowd gathered at her place to listen to her analysis of the situation. There were rumours that the interviewers might be fired because they had caused the boy's collapse and withdrawal.

Mr Thomaso had argued that Risto should be resettled in the United States, as he had clearly suffered great trauma and danger. Many in the camp consulted the most powerful witchdoctors and made sacrifices so that their applications would be successful; others fasted and prayed for weeks, then celebrated for days and nights when they were approved.

But Risto's attitude worried everybody; he ignored Mr Thomaso and his proposal. Nobody could understand the strange boy, or read his face, or guess what was in his mind, and Bi Maimuna had no fresh news, merely speculations. But an anonymous reporter was the only one with breaking news. She had seen Risto talking to himself as he held a bracelet against his chest, crying and saying strange words with no meaning.

The entire camp expected something unprecedented, something that would leave a mark in the history of Marathan: if not a thunderstorm, death; if not death, madness. The majority agreed upon thunder and death; they read it in the eyeball of the sky; they said these two things followed the boy with the mysterious history. Some said what had happened to the boy was the result of a curse. Others believed that his ancestors were very upset. So they concluded that the boy had seen a warning sign; a storm was coming, death would follow.

Christmas arrived in the camp, but it was invisible. Risto wanted to see Christmas lights, hear the voices of children singing Christmas carols, but there were none. There were no flowers on doors, no Christmas trees in houses; all was dull and sad. He thought that if he could speak to his family, maybe their voices would heal his wounds. But when he was told that the Cellphone Man had been relocated to Canada, he whirled in such a bizarre mood that he no longer understood who he was anymore. He wondered what his family were doing on this special day. He kept wishing there was a payphone nearby, but it was a sterile wish. He was stuck in a dull maddened camp, angry and hungry, missing his family.

Christmas was a sacred time at home. A week before, the bells of the Catholic church rang each night with a special melody, and their lights and decorations could be seen from afar. At the same time, everyone sang carols, children shouted and called 'Noël' everywhere. There were decorations on the doors and gates of every home, and each child looked for flowers and a banana tree for the house. At home, Risto had been in charge of his family's flower garden; his sisters needed his permission to cut even one flower, but at Christmas they were allowed to cut whatever they needed, and even to give flowers to friends. He cut a banana tree in the garden to make the Christmas tree; his father bought Christmas lights, and his sisters did the decorating with his mother.

On Christmas Eve, his mother did not sleep; she would be busy baking and watching big boiling pots until midnight, when the streets sang that Jesus was born. At 4am, the whole family walked to church en masse. Christmas morning was the beginning of the party; the new clothes, the precious gifts that each child longed for. The nativity scene was performed at churches, followed by much singing and sweets for each child. The party mood brought children from different faiths to the churches, mostly to those with sweeties to give away.

In Marathan, Christmas existed on the calendar, but not in people's lives; they were busy scratching for things at the flea market, searching for fuel, looking for basic things that could keep them alive. There was no gathering of family or friends in the camp. Risto realised how much precious family time he had missed, how much he had not celebrated. And this day hurt terribly; it took him back to rivers of memories he had seen and could no longer touch; he understood now that the simplest things gave his life the most meaning. The healthy noise of children in the streets, the soothing Christmas carols, the smiles on the faces of the parents: these precious memories had injured his fragile soul; he could no longer hide within them when his soul craved happiness.

That night was very different to all his previous nights in the camp; he had hoped for Christmas dreams, but he didn't know which way he should bend his body or position his head on his small mattress. He even used his shoes as a pillow and put a rock beneath them to raise his head a bit higher, but breathing was still difficult. Finally he sat on his bed, pushing hard to breathe. It didn't change a thing, and the sweat was coming too.

Merci sat beside him, watching his friend closely. 'Talk when you feel like it, we all have a dark corner in our heart. Even though Congo has made us strangers to ourselves, it is sometimes good to release ourselves by opening our hearts. After all, we are all human,' he added softly.

He had many concerns about Risto's health; he had often found him crying for unknown reasons, holding a bracelet to his heart; he feared that things might be going seriously wrong. Now Risto began mumbling strings of unstable stories, names that meant nothing to Merci, but which left Risto devastated, begging forgiveness from a Néné whom he had betrayed. He spoke of an Amani that he would kill to free Néné, he called out to Benny, he argued that he had never wanted to harm anyone, he was forced, he had to follow orders or die. But the name of Néné kept coming back: 'Néné, I have betrayed you, Néné, I will come to save you, Néné, I am coming to tell you how much I love you,' he said until Merci hushed him to sleep.

By morning Risto was half-dead. He hardly breathed; sweat had left marks on the white T-shirt he wore, his chest made a whistling noise when the forced breath pierced the thick block that had built within. With the help of two men, Merci rushed Risto to the camp clinic that he himself had come to hate when he heard that the attendants, whom the poor people trusted and believed in, had no university degrees. Syringes penetrated Risto's body, a drip with endless drops brought no change. Merci was very worried that he might lose his only friend, a boy who had become a brother to him.

Risto was transferred to a hospital in Nampula, the third biggest city of Mozambique. It boasted old Portuguese construction, police on each street corner, and well-trained doctors with fairly modern medical tools. But their expertise could not help because they were unsure of what they were treating. The boy went into another world and came back as a drowning swimmer looking in vain for rescue. He kept screaming about Néné and Benny and Kahuzi-Biega. The sweating kept coming, and it was a struggle to keep him breathing. But a hospital was too expensive for the tiny pockets of Merci and Risto. Merci sought help from the United Nations, who insisted that they had invested in a clinic in Marathan; the boy could get free treatment there.

There was never such disappointment as when Merci brought his friend back to die in their hut. Risto's state seemed to infect many people in the camp; wherever they went and whatever they did, his fate was always the topic. They waited for the breaking news of his death and the end of his curse. Some became energetic; there was a potential business opportunity in the death of a boy who had emerged as the most successful tomato farmer in the camp; the coffee-seller used his string-knotted calculator to count the number of mourners who would be at the funeral, while rival grave-diggers gathered in bunches with their tools to show how ready and serious they were.

Mama RFI was no longer an authority on his state; fewer and fewer people asked her about the dying boy, so she decided to take action. She visited the boys' hut and cursed Merci for having taken Risto to powerless doctors with none of nature's wisdom, nurses who used Western syrup and aspirin instead of seeking the messages of the gods and ancestors.

She dragged Risto to see the feared witchdoctor Balaba, who was known for watching the world in his magical calabash. Balaba enclosed Risto's body in his secret chamber, away from everyone's gaze, then rushed to the marketplace, frightening people, as he was almost naked except for tiger-skin shorts and many necklaces with rare feathers and scales, bones and horns. He shouted warning words to rivals who might try to block his path as he travelled in his magical calabash to far countries, far continents. Even though the sun was still at a bitter strength, a sudden shower followed, and two thunderclaps were heard. In this part of the world, witchcraft spoke through thunder, and now it signified Balaba's journey to places where only chosen spirits could go, communicating with ancestors who handed him the power of healing. But Balaba was unable to get any answers to explain Risto's illness, or to drive it away. He too was defeated.

Finally the church tried its hand at healing the boy, believing that his miraculous deliverance would come from God. Everyone was ready with their strongest faith, and some had fasted for several days. First songs started with a few stretching hand movements, then the best vocalists followed one another with their most spirit-compelling songs. There were strings of incantations. Songs shook the roof straw of the mud house, poems were recited, drums and flutes called, the tam-tam answered. The pastor's voice silenced the sweating dancing women, waves of rhyming words and incantations followed, casting out spells and evil spirits. Then the vivid melodies of flutes and djembe drums and guitars blended with the pastor's voice. The healing, the returning, the claiming, the awakening of a soul never came; Risto never woke. He was doomed to death.

Chapter 18

The news of Risto's arrival back in Bukavu travelled faster than the plane; people seemed to know the time of the plane's landing better than the pilot himself. Risto did not feel the warm welcome of his family and friends upon his arrival at Kavumu airport; he was quickly rushed to an ambulance his family had organised and straightaway transported to Panzi hospital.

Here family members waited impatiently for the words of the senior doctor. It wasn't until three days later that the doctor allowed Risto's parents to visit him. No talking was allowed; they just took a brief look at where their son lay between strings of drips and ticking machines. His eyes were open, but he was unaware of what was happening. His mother broke the absolute silence by greeting her son; she received no reply.

'So how do you see the boy?' asked Papa François, who had been greatly affected by Risto's sickness. He seemed to be the only one with a bit of strength for questions.

'He is responding well,' said the doctor.

This answer attracted the attention of the entire family, and they flocked closer to the doctor.

'He is in a stable condition,' he added. Those were his only words; he patted Risto's mother on the shoulder and walked away down the corridor.

On his fourth day in the hospital, Risto spoke his first words. They troubled his doctor as they had no meaning, and the language was a strange one. It was mere mumbling that led to an injection to make him sleep. Doctors consulted other doctors, and it was declared that Risto's illness might be cerebral malaria.

In this section of the hospital, no family guard was allowed. While limited family visits were permitted, a doctor supervised the ward constantly while a nurse looked after the patients. Fear rose in the family when after a week, the doctor called Risto's father to discuss the progress of his son.

'The boy is doing well,' he whispered.

'Okay ...'

'But ... I'd like to tell you that it might be more than cerebral malaria.'

Mahuno rested his head in the palm of his right hand.

'It is not really bad ... he responded positively to our medications at the beginning. But he has not stopped mumbling. He wakes from sleeping and speaks endlessly until we inject him with something to calm him.'

'You are the doctor ...' said Risto's father helplessly.

'Well ... we are suggesting a psychiatrist.' The doctor's eyes were fixed on Mahuno, watching each slight movement his body made.

'Do you think that ...'

'Not madness, but you know ... well, we all work together; sometimes we need the advice of others. If the mumbling doesn't stop in two days, we will advise you to take him to Heri-Kwetu centre to see Dr Zongo. But let's see what happens in the meantime.'

The doctor could see Mahuno's confusion; with his right palm covering half of his mouth and his eyes fixed in a corner of the doctor's office, there was no need of words to describe his pain.

Picturing Risto among mentally ill patients was an agonising thing for his father. It hurt him so much that whenever he thought about it, tears fell uncontrollably. He knew the prejudices associated with mental illness in his society; he knew it was easy to be admitted to a mental hospital, but difficult to get out of it. Sometimes those who went in came out tremendously damaged. He feared for his son.

He avoided sharing this bad news with his wife. Papa François advised him to wait for an ideal moment to tell her. But this ideal time never came, as Risto's mother suffered more each day. She spoke less and ate less. She could not find consolation in the beauty of a bouquet of flowers, or the personal letters friends sent to her; even their physical presence did not bring her solace. Instead, she infected each person who came to console her; they would come with an encouraging message, but would leave in tears.

The two days went by with no positive change in Risto's health. The doctor concluded that Dr Zongo was the only hope. Risto continued to mumble about the Kahuzi-Biega forest and Amani, a man he hated and needed to kill. The news of Risto's transfer to the Heri-Kwetu centre destroyed his mother; she intensified her cries and went without food all day.

The Heri-Kwetu centre was housed in a pleasant building at the foot of Bugabo Hill in the Kadutu zone. It was owned by the Catholic Church and administered by nuns. The rules were as strict as in a monastery. There was a time to wake up, a time to brush teeth, a time to have breakfast, a time to sleep, and even a time to talk and listen to other people's stories. It was hard for anyone who enjoyed their independence. Nevertheless, when the people were let out of their small rooms to sit on the well-trimmed green lawn, the beauty of the garden eased their minds and they obeyed the rules with no objections. Those whose strength was uncontrollable would get a shot from a syringe to keep them quiet and make them sleep for a few hours. And if patients became very violent, a chain would be put on them to hold their spirit and body still.

Risto was considered a dangerous individual. All the housekeepers and sentinels had been warned. Upon his arrival, he had objected to too many things: his clothes being stripped off, the strict sleeping schedule, the injections and pills. The report from the hospital said that he was angry and wanted to kill a certain Amani; no visitors were allowed until they had watched him for a few days.

Three days of medication did not cure the mumbling and the

strangeness. Risto would walk in his sleep at night; he would speak endlessly about Amani and how he was going to kill him. He even threatened to break down the door of his room.

Risto's roommate was an endlessly smiling man in his early thirties, with a razor-bald head. His name was Bingwa Maurice, and he was not afraid of Risto, so he said he would stay with the dangerous boy during the day to see how he would react to other people, how he would manage his anger.

'What is your name?' Bingwa asked the first morning.

'Risto, and you?'

'Bingwa Maurice, son of Maurice Makwaba and Angela Maurice, born and raised in Bukavu.' A hysterical laugh followed.

'Risto, why are you here, are you mad as well?'

'No, are you?'

'No, but you are not mad either.'

Bingwa told Risto a story he wouldn't wish a fly to hear. He criticised the centre's management for forcing him to mix with mad people. Two days earlier, they had called together those who could differentiate colours, those who knew their own names and the names of their relatives, those who could differentiate between a man kneeling down and a shrub. All these were simple tests for Bingwa. Then the psychiatrist had drawn a nice swimming pool on the lawn with white paint. He told all the mad patients to go for a swim. All of them jumped into the drawing except for Bingwa.

'So why didn't you jump?' asked Risto.

'Would you if it were you?' Bingwa sounded very serious.

'But it wasn't me. Why didn't you swim?'

'After ten other people had jumped in the swimming pool? Even if it was a river, just think about it, Risto! I am not racist or tribalist or any of those things, right. But the water was dirty; I couldn't wash in the dirt of ten people, no, no, no!'

Risto felt free in the daily company of Bingwa because he knew his listener would forget everything he told him after a few minutes. So he would speak openly of his deepest secrets of unfulfilled love. He told

Bingwa the reason for his unstoppable tears, the story of the bracelet and the vow of love, as well as the haunting betrayal of that love. He wished only one thing, he confessed. To get out of that centre and travel to the Kahuzi-Biega National Park, whether with a gun or empty-handed, to free Néné. He would face the evil Amani and would leave him dead. He had only one thing to tell Néné, how he loved and continued to love her. But it was always a difficult story to tell; it reopened old wounds and usually left Bingwa in tears too.

'Love is the most precious thing in life, isn't it so?' Risto asked Bingwa, who had no answer, and only nodded his head.

'It is a mystery that every human being wants to learn about; but when it came to me, even though my heart craved it, my eyes were closed; my mouth was too shy to welcome it. Now I cry because I let go of the one thing the human spirit would die for – love.'

As the friendship between Risto and Bingwa became tighter, Risto started seeing more gaps in Bingwa's brain. There were times when he screamed, and when Risto asked the reason, Bingwa ignored him. Times came when Bingwa wanted to know Risto's name as if it was his first time meeting him. Then a day came when they fought in their small room, and that led to their separation.

Dr Zongo was a fine psychiatrist. He was renowned for the number of troubled souls that he had managed to rehabilitate. His reputation had gone beyond the borders of South Kivu and brought him a number of patients from the eastern Congo and neighbouring countries. It was believed that his eyes could see inside an individual soul, that he was able to tell the causes of trouble at first glance. He could easily tell if the trouble was genetic, a brain defect or injury, prenatal damage, trauma, a dysfunctional family life, anxiety, substance abuse or other specific factors. And for each cause or factor, he seemed to have some therapy.

But Risto was a new challenge. Even after his third interview, Dr Zongo was still unable to diagnose Risto's mental illness. The boy had responded correctly to all the necessary questions, and was very much aware of the little traps the doctor used to understand his mental acuity. Some of his patients, even though appearing clever, got caught in those traps.

Risto was different. He knew the names of all his family members and their exact dates of birth; he knew why he was at the centre, and what people thought about him. His only symptoms were his mumbling and the sense of confusion in his mind. He would sometimes sit, lost in thought, tears dropping down his face. At these times he looked vulnerable and in unimaginable agony. At other times, he would seem angry, fierce and dangerous as he shouted words that no one understood. He always ended up trembling and sometimes breaking down in tears.

Because Dr Zongo could not diagnose any mental illness in Risto, he could not prescribe any treatment. He wished he could get into the brain of the boy to see, to hear what tormented him. But there was always a barrier; the boy never let him get into his head. So Risto became a puzzle that he tried to solve by constantly observing him, until he even forgot his other duties. He observed him as he slept, and heard him mumbling and rumbling in his dreams. He observed him as he ate, and as he cried. But none of this brought him any answers.

One morning, Landu protested against the strict rules of Dr Zongo, and insisted on speaking to Risto.

'He is not yet okay,' said Dr Zongo.

'I know. I'd love to see him though.'

'You see ... I can't predict his reactions. He might be dangerous.'

'Maybe he might need somebody to talk to?'

'He had a roommate to talk to, you know that. It didn't go well. Remember?'

'Doctor, I've got some gifts for him.'

'Let me see them.'

Landu opened his school bag. He pulled out a game of Scrabble and two photos. In one photo, ten-year-old Risto was holding a white rabbit, with a big smile on his face. The other picture showed Risto among a group of boys in soccer uniforms in a school stadium. Dr Zongo looked at each item with great interest. What captured him the most were the pictures showing a healthy Risto, a happy Risto with a world of opportunities in front of him.

Landu found Risto at a vulnerable moment; he was mumbling quietly in a corner of the garden. He cleared his tears as Landu greeted him, and greeted him back. But then he carried on mumbling as if in a trance, lost in an unknown world.

'I've got gifts for you, Risto.'

There was no response.

'Your favourite pictures, I took them from your bedroom wall. Look …'

Still there was no word; Risto was focused on a passing flock of birds. The Scrabble board didn't move him either.

'Néné was looking for you,' said Landu as he stood up to leave. As he turned, he realised that Risto was staring at him with wide-open eyes.

'Yes … Néné … she was looking for you. She wanted to know about you.'

'Néné?' asked Risto, his eyes shining.

'Yes, Néné,' Landu replied.

Risto stood up and ran to the building. Landu followed him. He reached Risto coming out of his room, holding a bracelet in his right palm.

'I want to see her,' he said.

'Yes, sure, sure. But you are not allowed to go out yet.'

'Am I a prisoner in here?'

'No.'

'Then why can't I go where I please?'

'The doctor …'

Risto went back into the room, took off his slippers and put on a pair of shoes.

While Landu was excited to see Risto finally returning to the real world, he didn't know whether he was in a normal mood or a crazy one. He was also afraid of how he might react outside those walls.

'I need to give this bracelet to Néné, I don't think I deserve it.'

'Do you know where you are, Risto?'

Risto narrowed his eyes.

'Landu, I have to leave.'

Landu knew that the doctor would not allow Risto to go out, but he loved his cousin and wanted to help. He decided to smuggle him out.

Néné picked up the bottle underneath her bed. She carefully dipped a dry stick into it, and let a few drops fall on a little piece of cloth. When she scratched the little cloth, it burned. She breathed in and out with relief. This test proved that the street boy she had sent to buy sulphuric acid had not tricked her; it was indeed a strong acid, she concluded. But an expert's eye, looking at the light colour of the liquid and the tiny bubbles on top of it, would have recognised that the acid was greatly diluted. The street boy had done what he knew best, cheating by taking an innocent's money, buying very little acid and adding water.

Néné peeped through her bedroom window; judging by the weakness of the sun, it was late afternoon. Soon the sun will set, she thought; soon too, her soul would rest in peace. Soon the pain of her pregnancy would all be over. In her short life on earth, she had come to love the sunset in a way that she could never explain. Because she had this strong bond with the sunset, she believed it was the best time to take her life. It was a time when people's hearts were at peace with nature, when they took a moment to forget their daily pain and embraced the smile the heavens sent to them through orange lips.

Her pen and paper were lying on her table. She wished to write to two people before she terminated her life. She wanted to apologise to her mother for having been a burden and a source of sorrow. Her return to Bukavu had increased her mother's pain. People's judgmental eyes and gossiping mouths gave her family no peace. They looked at her as if she was an alien, whose swollen womb would bring forth a ghost to haunt them all. Some with spiteful tongues kept asking who the father of the baby was. They gave their pity to her mother when she was present, and debated the destiny of her daughter behind her back.

Néné could never understand where the love in their street had gone. A child belonged to the whole community, that's what their culture had taught them. But she could no longer see that spirit in her people. They could not feel pity for her pain, and the agonies of her experiences in the forest. When she thought about all this, she cursed the nurse who had led her to this heartless town; they should have left her to die in the jungle.

Everything had happened so fast. At the beginning of her pregnancy, Boneza, a militia woman who had become the midwife of the forest, had sensed trouble. But Amani had said she was bringing a curse to his wife by predicting trouble, and even laughed at Boneza when seven months passed without anything going wrong with Néné's pregnancy.

In the middle of the eighth month, something strange happened; Néné began to bleed. Boneza said it wasn't the usual menstrual bleeding. She had made a potion of wild herbs and mixed it with three roots, but it did not stop the bleeding. She gave Néné medicine from her mobile pharmacy, but this did not work either. Néné was getting weaker and weaker. When Boneza proposed sending Néné to a clinic in Birava, Amani opposed her. The man had no heart to see the pain Néné was going through. But when he woke up the next morning and realised that the girl could not speak, he was the first to call for help.

Néné was finally left in the hands of a senior nurse at Birava clinic. This woman could not stop the bleeding either, and feared the girl was dying, so she sent Néné to the hospital in Bukavu town. And so the girl finally came home, carrying shame in her womb.

Here people did not seem to see the pain she had endured, or the suffering her mother had experienced. They gossiped about them with hypocritical and scornful mouths, until she and her mother could stand it no longer; they decided to move out of their street into Bagira zone.

The second person Néné wished to leave a message for was Risto, although she did not know if it would reach him. She had heard that Risto was somewhere in Mozambique. She hoped that her letter would reach him someday. She didn't think about the pain it would cause Risto; she was too afraid of the incurable pain the child would bring Risto if she lived and allowed it to be born.

As the sun set, she opened her window and she gazed at it as if for the first time. The skies were smiling at her, she knew they were waiting for her. She was convinced that it was time to go. She was not sad, but rather felt at peace with herself and with the universe. She sang her last lullabies, then closed her window and double-checked that her bedroom door was locked. Then she lay down on her bed and drank the burning acid.

First there were soft knocks on the door. The knocks increased, and a voice whispered some names. The door did not open. The voice went high and the knocking intensified. The door stayed closed.

'Néné, it's your mother. Open, my darling.'

'Néné, Risto would like to talk to you.'

The door didn't open and no movement could be heard in the room.

'Néné, it's me, Risto. I need to talk to you. Please open.'

'She never does this. She is obedient,' her mother said with anxiety.

'What if we force the door open?' Landu asked.

'Can you?' asked Néné's mother with worried eyes.

It took a blow from a hammer for the door to swing open.

The body lay still on the bed, a container stood on the floor.

'Néné, Néné!' screamed her mother as she shook her daughter's body.

'Acid! ... Acid! She took acid!' Landu screamed as he grabbed the container and rushed to the mother.

That evening Néné lay in the intensive care unit of the hospital, surrounded by nervous doctors. Her mother was in the hands of other mothers, who had come from as far as Risto's street upon hearing the news. They came to give her sympathy, waiting to give her their condolences and weep with her when the bad news was confirmed. They were assuming that the girl would die, but a huge nurse kept coming to calm the weeping women.

'She is still breathing,' she would say. 'We are trying our best.'

But people were used to such words; these were the words that nurses and doctors used when they were still formulating a good way to tell a bad story. People knew that soon a senior doctor would come to announce the news of Néné's death. But the night went on and no senior doctor came; instead the big female nurse kept coming with her story.

'She will be fine,' she kept saying. 'We are trying our best,' she repeated.

At dawn, a senior doctor arrived, and everyone's ears turned to him.

'The girl is in a stable condition,' he said, as he cleared his throat and looked at his watch. 'She is lucky. The acid had not yet circulated through her system, and it was a very weak mix. In an hour she will be transferred to a room where you will have a chance to see her.'

Risto was among Néné's first visitors; she was surrounded by drips, and still too weak to speak, but after a few days of patience, they finally had a decent conversation. They had few words, though; they mostly spoke through silences and shy smiles. Then Néné's mood changed.

'I wanted to die in peace, Risto ... Why did you bring me here?' she cried. Risto held her hands in his.

'Peace is what we are all looking for, and your death would never bring it,' he answered, his voice breaking.

'Can't you see, Risto? My womb carries the poison of the evil Amani; I can't let it infect you and affect everybody around me ...' she wept.

Risto looked at the shining moon, which could be seen through the window.

'I just came here for one thing. I came to declare my love for you. If you die or live, I want you to know this truth,' he said, as he tried to stop his tears. 'I am sorry for having betrayed you. I left you in the hands of Amani, and I disappeared. I never wished to ... but it was beyond my control.' He sobbed, she sobbed too.

'And Néné, if you choose death, if you leave me alone in this heartless world, I want to give you back this bracelet.'

She held him tight as they both cried like babies. Then she dried her tears with Risto's shirt.

'I love you, Risto,' she said, and they held each other in silence.

· Chapter 19 ·

Risto's return brought a burning and holy silence to his street. The eyes of people spoke a stronger language than their mouths. Later, those mouths voiced amazing stories. Risto became a hero after Néné's letter was found in her room. It spoke of the love for Risto that she had kept inside her. She spoke of him as the only boy she had loved in her entire life, and the pain her departure might cause to him:

> 'You are the only one, the first and the last to hear this from me; and it is the first and the last time I say it because as I am writing it, my acid potion is waiting to be taken. I will die in a few minutes. Please don't cry … you will be hurt by this news, but try to stay strong. Better my death than the birth of this cursed child; think of the infinite pain it would have caused in our lives. Death is the only way to survive what I have been through; at least I will rest in peace.
>
> I have kept a lot of your secrets since childhood; I know you will keep mine too. Keep this as your own, as you are the only one who knows.'

People spoke about what they knew and could guess, but the extent of the love of a sixteen-year-old girl enchanted and bewildered them all. To those whose love was shrinking because of the thickness of their problems, this was a new story of love that came to bring them hope. It testified to the fact that love never dies, that love is mysterious, that love is the only magic that has always eluded the brave minds of scientists and philosophers. If after so much unbearable trauma and abuse, life could still shine in Néné's face, then love had magical healing power.

Risto's story seemed to have reached everyone: first his recovery from deadly injuries in the hospital, the sympathy he received from everyone, and then the suspicion and the fear when the rumour grew that he had been a child soldier. No child had escaped before from the evil of the militia. And few child soldiers who returned home managed to escape the seductive money that street gangsters offered those who could steal and kill with a gun. Risto was the first one. And now he came with this powerful story of love and healing. Many more unbelievable things would follow, people thought.

This story became a mirror for the street. People realised how unforgiving they had become, how they had forged their mouths into tools of gossip, how judgmental their eyes and hearts had become. They realised how the noise and smoke of war had turned their souls to steel. It was time for their souls to be healed. It was time to claim what war had stolen from them. Everyone renewed their vow that 'a child is a child of all'.

The child of Néné came to earth to heal the ancient wounds and bury the scars of the past. He came with a smile of heaven and the pure laughter of the gods. 'He will heal the world,' Risto's cheering heart whispered to the young mother's ears. They decided that the child should be called Risto Junior, because he did not have the spirit of his biological father, but that of his adoptive father. He would be a reminder of a persevering spirit; he would be a heroic soul sent by heaven to heal the memories of time and history. He would remind his mother of the happy days and future dreams yet to come. This news puzzled people, but it cleared the vapour of war that they breathed. It gave them another story to tell their grandchildren.

Risto officially became the father of the child, whom he privately called Benny, in honour of his best friend and cousin, lost in Kahuzi-Biega National Park. He went back to further his mechanical training at the Centre de Formation Professionnelle under the supervision of the famous mechanic, Donas Bafwa. He did this all for the future of his son and the rest of the family he dreamed of having one day with Néné.

Néné went back to school determined to become a teacher. Behind them, in their shadows and their dark and bright journeys, they could easily hear the great agony and pure laughter of the gods. And the child grew stronger day by day.

Acknowledgements

I owe many of my colleagues, friends and family members for their assistance, support and guidance. To my storyteller parents, who taught me how to pitch a story. To Elizabeth Mary Lanzi Mazzocchini for reading the first draft of this story and believing in it when I thought it was not worth telling, Prudence Papy N-Mubil for your invaluable help, Lauren Beukes for your guidance, Jenny Hobbs for your encouragement, Corinne Abel for your support and for giving me room to grow. Special thanks to Carol van der Rheede.

Thanks to Chris and Carol Cunningham-Moorat, Geraldine Do, and the wise Dorian Haarhoff.

Thanks to Les Amis BK (Friends of Bukavu Cape and Worldwide), Turudi Congo Youth Movement and its initiator Eric Casinga, members of Tagore's Grounding sessions (D'bi Young, Desiree Bailey, Erin Bosenberg) – you have been inspirational.

Patrick Zézéc Irenge, Paurtia Maumela, Kibareng Tsiana, Bill Morris, Maurice Mbikayi, Josué Bahati Chishugi, Freddy Muganza Munyololo, Alice Wamundiya, Lena Opfermann, Ricky Novis, Michael Tladi, Valerie Barossi Bacbar, Toni Giselle Stuart – true friends never part; your friendship has kept me going.

Lucie Pagé and family, Prof. John and Charlotte van Zyl, Carol Cunningham-Moorat – you have always been there for me.

Millan Padilla, Allison Horner, Pshasha Seakamela – I don't know how to thank my great friends.

Thanks to Karen Jennings for shaping my voice, to my editor and wonderful guide Helen Moffett for making me believe in my own voice – your patience amazes me. Thanks to Umuzi; to my publisher Frederik de Jager – thank you for believing so much in this project Fourie Botha, your dedication to this project kept me going; Carla Potgieter – thanks for believing in my voice.

I would never have finished this project without the support of Pamela Ikosa Musenga, Lezerine Mashaba, Viviane Ingha, Bongani Kheswa, Michael Mwila Mambwe and Francis Ziggy Konde.

My greatest gratitude to Pamela Musenga Ikosa for being there at the most difficult time of this book. I remain grateful for your invaluable support and great love. Many thanks to Matemba Seke Mathy and to the whole Lupasa Kisanga family.

The true heroes of this project are the Safari brothers and sisters and their extended families for being such a pillar to me: Dia Safari (our family owes you so much), Jacques Safari, Martinez Safari (there are too many Safaris ... next time I'll complete the list), Majirano Muderhwa, my brother-in-law Espoir Kalibanya and his wife Maombi, Papy Bashombana and his family.

'Therefore, whether you eat or drink, or whatever you do, do all to the glory of God.'
1 Corinthians 10:31.